J.P. Carter is the pseudonym of a bestselling author who has also written under the names Jaime and James Raven. Before becoming a full-time writer, he spent a year in journalism as a newspaper reporter and television producer. He was, for a number of years, director of a major UK news division and co-owned a TV production company. He now splits his time between homes in Hampshire and Spain with his wife.

IN SAFE HANDS

J. P. CARTER

avon.

Published by AVON
A division of HarperCollins*Publishers* Ltd
1 London Bridge Street
London SE1 9GF

www.harpercollins.co.uk

A Paperback Original 2019
5

First published in Great Britain by HarperCollins*Publishers* 2019

Copyright © J.P. Carter 2019

J.P. Carter asserts the moral right to be identified as the author of this work.

A catalogue copy of this book is available from the British Library.

ISBN: 978-0-00-831327-2

Typeset in Minion Pro by Palimpsest Book Production Ltd, Falkirk, Stirlingshire
Printed and bound in UK by CPI Group (UK) Ltd, Croydon CR0 4YY

MIX
Paper from
responsible sources
FSC
www.fsc.org
FSC™ C007454

This book is produced from independently certified FSC™ paper
to ensure responsible forest management.

For more information visit: www.harpercollins.co.uk/green

This one is for my loving wife Catherine

PROLOGUE

Tasha Norris loved her job as a nursery school teacher. Watching the children at play always filled her with a deep sense of wellbeing.

Today was no exception. There were only nine of the little mites in this morning, but their squeals and laughter had already lifted her spirits. They were so entertaining, so happy, and so excited to have been let loose in the nursery's bright and airy playroom.

Tasha's colleague, Paige, was trying to get them together so that they could listen to the first story of the day. But as usual, they weren't taking any notice.

Four-year-old Grace was lost in a world of her own as she pretended to cook a meal on the toy stove, concentrating hard as she boiled a wooden egg in a little saucepan. And five-year-old Sahib was too busy racing around the room on a red fire engine to pay the teacher any attention. Meanwhile, Daniel and Liam, both aged three, were fully focused on seeing who could build the highest tower using wooden bricks. Little Molly sat at a table next to them, seemingly oblivious to her surroundings as she worked on her latest masterpiece – a painting of her entire family, including mum, dad, brother and pet goldfish Flipper.

Just being here with them made Tasha realise yet again how much she wanted a child of her own. She and Steve had been married for less than a year, so she had to try and be patient. Aged twenty-three, Tasha knew she had plenty of time to keep trying, and in the meantime she would enjoy looking after other people's children. She couldn't imagine doing anything else for a living, and she was so grateful to Sarah Ramsay for taking her on seven months ago. Tasha had loved every minute of every working day. And she'd learned so much about toddlers, tantrums and those tearful confessions that challenge you to keep a straight face.

Paige was now clapping her hands to get the children's attention. But the only one who responded was four-year-old Simone, who rushed into the large plastic playhouse while shouting, 'You can't catch me, you can't catch me.'

As always, getting all the kids to stop what they were doing became a team effort. Emma, the other teacher on duty, tried to coax Sahib off the fire engine after he rammed it into one of the doors. And Tasha played her part by trying to convince Molly that her picture was finished and she should leave it to dry.

Sarah emerged from her office to help out. She was the owner of the Peabody Nursery chain and the most experienced at dealing with groups of pre-schoolers. To Tasha she was the perfect role model. She'd built up a successful business doing what she enjoyed and went to great lengths to make the staff as well as the children feel comfortable.

'It's time for a story, boys and girls,' she said aloud. 'Who wants to know what happens to the naughty monkey?'

Two of the children reacted by jumping up and down on the spot. Three others put their hands in the air but carried on with what they were doing. The rest ignored her.

'I see we're in for one of those mornings,' she said with a broad smile. 'It must be the warm weather.'

Before she could try again she was distracted by the sound of the front doorbell ringing.

'Do you want me to go and answer it?' Tasha asked, having persuaded Molly to stand up and step away from her paints.

Sarah shook her head. 'No, I'll get it. You carry on trying to round up the little munchkins.'

It didn't take long. As soon as a couple of them were sitting cross-legged in front of the storyteller's chair, the others followed suit. Tasha volunteered to be this morning's reader, and Emma handed her the book that had been chosen by one of the children.

But just as Tasha was about to begin reading, Sarah came back into the room with several visitors in tow. And from the look on her boss's face, Tasha sensed straight away that something was wrong.

Minutes later, the nightmare began.

CHAPTER ONE

Day one

It was a quiet morning so Detective Chief Inspector Anna Tate was taking the opportunity to get to grips with the pile of paperwork on her desk. There were witness statements, forensic reports, and dozens of crime scene photographs.

All the documents and pictures related to the eleven ongoing cases that were being dealt with by the Major Investigation Team based in Wandsworth, South London.

The team were making slow progress on most of them, partly because they had run out of leads and partly because resources were almost at breaking point. But it was the same story all across London, which had been hit by a perfect storm of soaring crime and police manpower cuts.

For Anna the quiet days were the hardest because she had too much time to dwell on the personal issues that made her life so difficult. This morning her thoughts kept switching between her troubled past and the argument she'd had the previous evening with Tom over their future together.

It was why she was finding it difficult to concentrate on

the file she was currently wading through. This one dealt with the murder of a teenage girl in Battersea. Her body had been found four months ago and they were still no nearer to finding her killer.

Anna sighed as she picked up a photograph of the girl's body lying in a narrow alley. She'd been badly beaten and sexually assaulted, and it had happened only three days before her sixteenth birthday.

Anna was still staring at the photo half a minute later when her office door was thrust open and Detective Inspector Max Walker came rushing in. His face was pinched and tense and his bald head was shiny with perspiration.

He held up a sheet of paper and said, 'We've got a live one, guv. Call just came in and it sounds pretty serious.'

Anna was at once alert. Even though he was still in his early thirties, Walker was one of the most experienced members of her team, and he was not prone to exaggeration.

'There's an ongoing incident at a nursery school in Peabody Street, Rotherhithe,' he said. 'Three men with guns entered the place and locked the all-female staff in a storeroom. There are four of them and one has been badly beaten.'

Anna jumped to her feet.

'Who called it in?'

'One of the women from inside the room. She used a phone the men didn't know they had.'

'Jesus. If it's a nursery then there must be children.'

Walker nodded. 'There are nine kids apparently, but the staff have no idea what's happening to them because they were put into another room.'

Anna felt her chest contract as the adrenalin fizzed through her veins.

'Have shots been fired?' she asked.

Walker shook his head. 'Not so far.'

'Thank God for that.' She grabbed her jacket from the back of her chair. 'We'd better get over there fast.'

Minutes later they were in an unmarked pool car that was among dozens of police vehicles from all over South London converging on the Peabody Nursery School in Rotherhithe. Walker was driving while Anna concentrated on the constant stream of updates over the radio.

She learned that an armed response team was being dispatched and that the three men who had descended on the nursery had posed as detectives from Rotherhithe CID.

She also took a call on her phone from her boss, Detective Chief Superintendent Bill Nash.

'I've just been told what's going down,' he said. 'I'm in a meeting at the Yard so I'll be monitoring the situation from here. Meanwhile, you're authorised to assume the role of senior investigating officer. Everyone will know by the time you get there.'

'Thank you, sir,' Anna said. 'I'll keep you posted.'

Information was continuing to come from the woman who had called it in. She'd identified herself as Sarah Ramsay, the owner and manager of the nursery. The emergency operator had kept her on the line so that she was effectively providing a running commentary. But what she had to say was useful only up to a point. She didn't know if the armed men were still on the premises or if the children were being held hostage.

Not knowing what to expect when they got there was causing Anna's stomach to twist with grim apprehension.

'We should be there in under ten minutes, guv,' Walker

said as he stamped on the accelerator, propelling them through a set of red lights with the siren blaring.

Anna did a Google search for the Peabody Nursery in Rotherhithe. She discovered that it was one of a chain of half a dozen Peabody Nurseries across London that catered for children between the ages of three and five. The one in Rotherhithe was the first, hence the name of the chain. There were exterior photos of the single-storey building and the bright and cheerful rooms inside.

It had its own website that described it as a school where parents could '*leave their little ones in the knowledge that they would always be safe and secure*'.

Anna reflected on the horrible irony of this statement as Walker steered them through the traffic at breakneck speed. She could no longer distinguish whether the pulsing in her ears and the hard pounding in her chest were caused by the shrill siren of the police car, or the sheer dread she felt as they got closer to Rotherhithe. Anna swallowed hard as she gripped the corner of her seat, concentrating on the road in front of her and pushing thoughts of what they might find when they reached their destination to the back of her mind.

CHAPTER TWO

They got to Peabody Street just minutes after the armed response team. Two squad cars had also just arrived and were being used to cordon off the road at both ends.

A uniformed officer waved them down and gestured for Walker to park against the kerb behind one of the ARVs.

Anna climbed out and flashed her warrant card, then hurried over to where the armed officers had gathered on the pavement in front of the nursery school. It was sandwiched between a three-storey block of flats and a church community centre. The small, red-brick building was set back behind a five-foot-high wall, and the front door stood half open. There were two cars parked on the forecourt, but no sign of life.

The armed officers – members of Scotland Yard's specialist firearms command – were waiting behind the wall for the signal to go in. All six were kitted out in black helmets, visors and Kevlar body armour. They carried assault rifles and Glock 17 pistols.

Anna approached the team leader and was pleased to

discover that they knew each other. Jason Fuller was a tall, middle-aged guy with craggy features and a strong jawline. Their paths had crossed more than a few times over the years.

'I heard you were on your way,' he said. 'And I'm guessing you know about as much as I do.'

Anna nodded. 'Four female staff members locked in a store-room by three men who turned up armed with guns. It happened about forty minutes ago. And there were nine children here at the time who were apparently put into another room.'

'And we don't know if the perps are still inside or if we're dealing with a hostage situation.'

'That about sums it up,' Anna said. 'But we can't afford to hang around waiting for something to happen. We have to go in.'

'I agree, but not before we're ready. There are no sounds coming from inside, and so far we haven't spotted movement at any of the windows. I've got my men checking the rear of the building and I want to see if we'll get a response through a megaphone appeal first.'

Anna knew that he was right to be cautious. If the three men were still inside then God only knew how they were going to react when they stormed the building. The counter-terrorism unit were also on standby, though the very thought of this being a terrorist attack caused the blood to stiffen in Anna's veins. Behind her, a police radio crackled and she heard a disembodied voice informing everyone that the women were still locked in the storeroom.

Walker was standing right behind her with several uniforms. She saw that two more squad cars and an ambulance had turned up. Neighbours had also started to gather beyond the cordons.

The scene was bathed in bright August sunshine and the temperature was rising. Anna's blouse was already sticking to her back beneath her jacket.

She'd been a copper for seventeen years and had never experienced a situation quite like this before, where nine infants were thought to be involved and at risk. Nine toddlers, presumed to be between the ages of three and five; completely helpless and vulnerable. Were they still in the building, locked up in a different room from that in which the staff were being held captive? And, if so, had they been harmed in any way? Or were they about to be?

Anna swallowed hard as an icy dread formed in her throat. There were too many unanswered questions at this stage. Too much they didn't know. It might have appeared to the onlookers that they had the situation under control but that was far from the truth.

'There's more info on the woman who's been beaten up,' Walker said, as he stepped up beside her while holding his phone against his ear. 'Her name's Tasha Norris and one of the gunman smashed her over the head with the butt of his pistol. She's unconscious and in a bad way apparently.'

All the more reason to go in, Anna thought. She turned back to Fuller and saw that he'd been handed a megaphone.

'I just heard from our guys around the back,' he told her. 'The garden's empty but the rear door is wide open. Nobody is visible, though.'

He raised the megaphone to his mouth and faced the nursery. As he spoke through it, his voice drowned out all other sound.

'This building is surrounded by armed police,' he said. 'I urge everyone inside to drop your weapons and leave through the front door with your arms in the air, otherwise we will be forced to enter the building.'

There was no response, and the silence that followed screamed in Anna's ears.

'We have no choice now but to go in,' she said after about twenty seconds.

That was Fuller's cue to mobilise his team. He waved his hand and gave instructions through his headset microphone.

His officers responded by rushing through the open gate and across the forecourt. Anna watched from beyond the wall. As always, she was impressed by their slick profession-alism and the fact that they were prepared to put their own lives on the line. The raw tension in the air was palpable and Anna found herself holding her breath as she waited for something to happen.

Thankfully the team encountered no resistance as they approached the building. They paused only briefly before stepping through the open door. The absence of gunfire prompted Anna to follow them, and Walker and several uniforms were close behind.

She heard shouting from inside as she got close to the entrance and assumed it was Fuller's men announcing their presence.

She stayed outside until the all-clear was given after less than a minute. Her internal dialogue was on prayer mode as she stepped inside: *Please, God, let the children be unharmed . . .*

Passing through the doorway, she noticed the security camera above it and the password-protected panel on the wall. She logged the information in her brain to consider later when it came to determining how the men had got into the building.

A short corridor led to a door giving access to a large, brightly coloured playroom. It was crammed with toys, miniature vehicles, a playhouse and several tables cluttered with crayons, drawing paper and books.

But Anna's attention was seized by loud cries coming from one of the four other rooms that led off the playroom.

'It must be the storeroom,' Fuller said, pointing to the closed door. 'We can't find the key so we're gonna have to break it open.'

One of his men was telling those inside to calm down and step away from the door. The same officer then used his boot to kick at it three times before it gave way.

There was a light on inside the storeroom and it revealed a sight that made every muscle in Anna's body go stiff.

A woman was lying on the floor with the back of her head resting in a small pool of her own blood. Two other women were kneeling beside her and a third was standing over them with a mobile phone in her hand.

'Tasha needs to get to a hospital,' one of them cried out. 'We can't wake her up.'

The distraught women all appeared to be in their twenties or early thirties and were casually dressed in matching blue T-shirts and jeans. Their eyes were cloudy with fear and their faces awash with tears.

'Stay calm and step out,' Anna said, keeping her voice low so as not to inflame an already stressful situation. 'We'll call the paramedics.'

The women quickly exited the room, and Anna half expected them to break down in floods of tears. But instead all three dashed across the playroom to one of the other doors that had a sign on it which read: *Quiet Room*.

The first to reach it peered inside and then let out an anguished cry that sent a bolt of ice down Anna's spine.

'Oh my God,' the woman screamed. 'They're gone.'

Anna stepped forward and looked into the room, which contained a sofa, a few chairs and a low table.

One of the other women turned to the nearest uniformed officer and said, 'Have you searched the rest of the building? Are the children here?'

The officer shook his head. 'I'm afraid not.'

The woman's hand flew to her mouth. 'Those men must have taken them,' she said, her voice cracking with emotion. 'They've been abducted.'

Anna closed her eyes, steadied her breathing. That word: *abducted*. As always, it stirred up painful memories and caused an ache to swell in her chest. She shook her head, swallowed hard, and realised that this case was going to be an emotional rollercoaster.

CHAPTER THREE

Ruth Brady checked her watch and saw that she had time for one more cup of coffee. She didn't have to be at the restaurant until midday and it would only take her roughly forty-five minutes to get there.

She put the kettle on and as it started to boil she decided to phone her husband to let him know about her change of plan.

She went back into the living room, fished her mobile from her handbag, and speed-dialled Ethan's number. While she waited for him to answer she stepped over to the window and looked out on a lovely bright morning. Their two-storey town house was in the heart of Bermondsey and overlooked a busy main road. But rush hour was over and the traffic was moving freely.

When Ethan didn't answer she assumed that he must be in a meeting, so she tapped out a short text message.

Had to drop Liam off at the nursery after all. Will explain why later. Will you be able to pick him up at 4pm if I'm not back in time? Xx

She hadn't planned on taking Liam to the nursery today. Ethan had bought them tickets for the Shrek Adventure attraction in central London. He'd had to pull out himself but had insisted that she should go and treat their son to a fun day out.

And she'd intended to do just that until she got the call from Howard Browning, the editor of a new London-based magazine. Browning had invited her to a meeting at a restaurant close to his office across the Thames in Wapping. He wanted to talk about some feature ideas Ruth had submitted. As a freelance journalist keen to increase the income from her work, it was too good an opportunity for her to pass up.

Ethan earned a good salary as a computer programmer, but living in London was expensive. There was the usual mortgage and bills, but council tax and parking fees were extortionate in comparison to other parts of the country. Plus there were the costs associated with Liam's condition, a condition that blighted his life and theirs.

She still turned cold whenever she thought back to how the hospital consultant broke the news to them shortly after their son was born three years ago.

'I'm sorry to have to tell you that Liam has cystic fibrosis,' he said, and when he saw the confusion on their faces, he added, 'It's a condition that can be treated but not cured. And life expectancy is in the mid-forties.'

In the weeks that followed they found out all they could about cystic fibrosis, or CF. While Ruth had become used to reeling off the same line as means of explanation: 'It causes mucus to clog vital arteries and the digestive system, making it difficult to breathe and digest food', she didn't think she would ever come to terms with the fact that Liam's life would be short and difficult, a journey he'd only just started.

Coping with it wasn't easy. Ruth hadn't been able to return to her full-time position as a staff journalist after maternity leave because looking after Liam was a job in itself, with frequent trips to the hospital for check-ups and physiotherapy sessions. They also had to administer regular doses of medication and do their best to ensure he didn't fall victim to infections.

And that was one of their concerns when they decided to enrol their son in the Peabody Nursery School. They wanted him to grow and develop and learn how to socialise with other children and adults, but they also wanted to make sure that he was in safe hands.

'We'll take good care of him, Mr and Mrs Brady,' the nursery owner, Sarah Ramsay, had assured them. 'We know how to respond to the needs of children with serious conditions who are nevertheless able to lead relatively normal lives.'

That had been seven months ago and not once had they had to call Ruth to say that he'd had any difficulties, or taken a turn for the worse.

Still, she couldn't help feeling guilty for not taking him to see Shrek today. And Ethan was surely going to be annoyed, having gone to the trouble of buying the tickets.

But Ruth was confident that Liam would be having just as much fun playing with his little friends, including his best pal Daniel, a little boy whose parents had moved from Ghana to the UK only a year ago. The pair were inseparable, and when she'd dropped Liam off this morning he had run straight over to Daniel who had surrounded himself with piles of colourful wooden bricks.

She'd noticed that there were relatively few children in – only nine as opposed to the usual twenty or so. Sarah Ramsay had explained that attendance always fell off once the holiday season got underway.

Ruth put her phone back in her bag and returned to the kitchen to pour her coffee, which she drank with a couple of digestive biscuits.

Before leaving the house she checked her reflection in the hall mirror, and contemplated the fact that the woman staring back at her looked older than twenty-nine. The last few years had taken their toll with the strain of looking after Liam.

Her long, ash-blonde hair was still in good shape, but there were bags beneath her eyes that seemed more pronounced through her wire-framed glasses. She'd also lost weight without meaning to, and she was sure that it made her look slightly emaciated.

Still, she'd never been one to fret about her appearance so she hadn't allowed any of that stuff to dent her self-confidence.

She always made an effort to look smart, and today she was hoping that the new trouser suit she was wearing would impress Howard Browning. She wanted to come across as a sharp and savvy journalist who could write interesting and original features for his new magazine.

It was approaching eleven o'clock when she left the house and went outside. Their car – a Peugeot 308 – was parked in a designated bay at the rear of the block. Because they lived in London it didn't get used much and there were still only seven thousand miles on the clock. Ethan travelled on the tube to work and when they went out as a family they used public transport.

Ruth was feeling upbeat and confident as she climbed in behind the wheel and started the engine. It helped that it was such a pleasant Monday morning. Up until the weekend August had been a washout and heavy showers had blasted London and the South East.

She switched on the radio and caught a top-of-the-hour news bulletin. There was a sense of real urgency in the announcer's voice as he told listeners about a breaking story in South London. Intrigued, Ruth paused before backing out of the bay.

'*Reports are coming in of a serious ongoing incident at a nursery school in Peabody Street, Rotherhithe. Armed police have been called there and the street has been cordoned off. It's understood the incident involves children and staff members. That's all we know at the moment, but we'll bring you further details as soon as we have them.*'

Ruth froze as she tried to process what she had just heard. She couldn't believe it. Or rather she didn't want to believe it. Surely it had to be a terrible mistake – or a cruel example of fake news.

Nevertheless the announcer's words sat cold inside her, and her heart started banging in her throat.

She took out her phone and her hand shook as she scrolled through her contacts for the Peabody Nursery number. But after tapping the call icon all she got was the engaged tone.

She knew what she had to do. The nursery was only about a mile away and she could be there in minutes, traffic permitting.

As she shoved the gearstick into reverse the fear and dread swelled up inside her. She started yelling at herself not to panic, that everything was going to be all right and that Liam was perfectly safe.

But there was a voice inside her head that said otherwise. It was telling her that something bad had happened to her precious little boy.

CHAPTER FOUR

The paramedics who attended to Tasha Norris confirmed that her condition was serious and that it was touch and go as to whether she'd survive.

She was the only one who'd been attacked and it was because she put up a fight when they were being forced into the storeroom.

She'd received two vicious blows to the head and one to the face. Her nose was shattered and there were two open wounds below her unruly mop of dark brown hair.

As Tasha was being stretchered out of the building, Anna was approached by Sarah Ramsay, who was understandably still shocked and confused after the ordeal.

'One of us should go with her to the hospital,' she said. 'We can't let her go by herself.'

'You and your colleagues need to stay here so that you can give me more details about what happened,' Anna said. 'But don't worry. She's in good hands and will be accompanied by one of my officers.'

'Then someone should call her husband,' Sarah said, as she took a mobile phone from her jeans pocket and held it up. 'This belongs to her. His number will be on it.'

'What's his name?'

'Steve. Steve Norris. They live in Salter Road.'

Anna took the phone from her and gave it to DI Walker, who was standing beside her.

'Make the call, Max,' she said. 'And then phone the office and get more bodies down here, fast. Tell them to drop everything else.'

Anna returned her attention to Sarah, who was still struggling to compose herself. She was a tall, sinewy woman of about thirty, with thick, lustrous black hair and a pale, flawless complexion. Black rivulets of mascara stained her cheeks.

Just thirty minutes had elapsed since she and the two teachers who worked for her had emerged from the cramped storeroom. So far they had given only a brief account of what had happened because of the state they were all in. Anna now needed them to flesh out their story; every detail could be pivotal to the investigation and to the search for the children.

'I'd like you to join your colleagues,' Anna said. 'I want to go through everything again from the moment the three men turned up.'

Sarah nodded. 'Of course, but I don't think there's much more I can tell you that would be helpful. It happened so quickly.'

'Let me be the judge of that, Miss Ramsay. I'll come and talk to you in just a minute. There are a few things I have to do first.'

Anna asked a PC to escort Sarah next door to the community centre, which had been commandeered because the nursery was now a crime scene and forensic officers would soon be all over it, looking for any evidence the men had left behind.

Sarah's two colleagues were already there, but Sarah hadn't yet joined them because she'd been asked to provide a list of the children who'd been taken. The list, complete with photographs, was now being circulated, and the parents were being informed as a matter of urgency.

There were four boys and five girls. Their innocence shone through in each photograph and Anna blinked away the tears that began filling her eyes as she stared at them, desperately trying to keep her mind on the next steps of the case to avoid thinking of what awful things might soon be happening to them.

She paused for a moment to take stock of the situation. She was still in the playroom, surrounded by detectives and uniformed officers who were waiting to be told what to do.

This was a high-impact crime that was going to appal the nation and present MIT with its toughest ever challenge. As the SIO, Anna would be under considerable pressure to resolve it quickly. But she knew already that it wasn't going to be easy. It was obvious that the gang had carefully planned the crime and had executed it with shocking precision.

She felt sure that it would have involved more than just three men. It was likely that they'd had at least one other person waiting outside while they went into the building. He or she might have been tasked with looking after whatever vehicle was used to take the children away.

Anna had already made it clear to everyone that she was

in charge and had called DCS Nash to update him. Now she began issuing instructions to those around her.

'Someone should check the security camera at the front entrance,' she said. 'It should have picked up the men when they arrived. I also want details of all CCTV cameras located within a half-mile radius of Peabody Street. And start questioning neighbours. I can't believe the kids weren't seen being led out of the building and into a large van or small coach. It would have taken time, especially if some of the children were upset and didn't want to go.'

She was told that a couple of the parents had got in touch before being contacted because the story had broken and was being carried on TV and radio bulletins.

'We should make preparations to talk to them in the community centre,' Anna said. 'My guess is they'll be desperate to come here and see for themselves what's going on. I know I would. It'll suit us because we can speak to them all together as well as individually and that'll save time.'

'I'll put the wheels in motion,' Walker said. 'Meanwhile, I just spoke to Tasha Norris's husband. He was at work but now he's on his way to the hospital.'

'Well, let's hope that the poor woman pulls through,' Anna said. 'If she doesn't then we could find ourselves dealing with a murder as well as a kidnapping.'

Anna left it at that for the time being and went outside. Two support vehicles were now parked on the community centre forecourt, and more people had joined the crowds at either end of the street. Some were holding mobile phones aloft to take photos of what was going on.

Anna was gagging for a cigarette but there was no time. She needed to have another conversation with Sarah Ramsay and the teachers, then bring a semblance of order to the investigation. Right now, things were a bit chaotic and too many questions remained unanswered.

As she walked towards the community centre she spotted a Sky News van with a large satellite dish perched on the roof. It never ceased to amaze her how quickly the media managed to turn up at crime scenes. She suspected that they were regularly monitoring police radio frequencies.

It suddenly occurred to her that the sooner they appealed for help from the public, the better. The Yard's media liaison team would probably tell her to hold fire until she had more information. But she saw no need to.

She made it known that she wanted to give the media a short statement and told uniform to allow the TV crew and any press people through the cordon.

It transpired that there were two newspaper reporters present as well as the Sky crew. Anna introduced herself and explained that she was only prepared to make a brief statement and was not in a position to answer lots of questions.

'The facts are these,' she said, making a point of not looking directly into the camera. 'Three men with pistols burst into the Peabody Nursery here in Rotherhithe just before nine this morning. There were nine children inside at the time and the men herded them into one of the side rooms. The men then forced the four members of staff, all female, into a separate room. One of the women is on her way to hospital to be treated for a serious head injury.

'The police were alerted at nine twenty-three a.m. from a mobile belonging to a member of staff. We arrived at the scene approximately fifteen minutes later to find that none of the children were present at the nursery. We are therefore treating this as a serious abduction and are appealing for anyone who might have information to come forward.

'The kidnappers would almost certainly have put the children into a small bus or large van. Hopefully we'll soon know more about that after we've examined CCTV footage. But in the meantime we'd like to hear from anyone who saw the children being led away or saw anything else that appeared suspicious this morning in Peabody Street.'

'Have you got descriptions of the men?' the Sky reporter asked as she thrust her microphone towards Anna.

'They were all white,' Anna said. 'Two of them looked to be in their late twenties or thirties and one was older, perhaps mid to late fifties. They were wearing suits and they were posing as detectives from a local police station, which is how they gained access to the building.'

'Is it possible this is a terrorist attack?' This from a young fresh-faced hack who identified himself as Luke Dennis from the *Evening Standard*.

Anna's expression remained neutral. 'At this stage we don't know who they are or what their motive is. But we'll be liaising with the Anti-Terrorism Command as well as the Met's Kidnap Unit. Currently the Major Investigation Team, of which I'm the senior officer, is leading the operation.'

The same reporter then asked a second question that completely threw Anna.

'Can you please confirm that you're the same detective whose own daughter was abducted ten years ago and who recently gave an interview to a Sunday magazine?'

Anna drew a sharp breath and felt an uncomfortable tightness in her chest.

She could see where the reporter was going with this and

she wasn't happy. It was a good human interest angle to the story, the sort of thing the papers loved, but Anna refused to let it be pursued.

'That has no relevance to the investigation,' she said brusquely.

The reporter raised his brow. 'Well, I beg to differ, DCI Tate. Surely you can see—'

She shook her head. 'All I can see is you trying to make something out of nothing, Mr Dennis. What happened to my own daughter has no bearing on this case whatsoever. And I'm not prepared to waste precious time talking about it.'

'But the families will want to know that—'

He didn't get to finish what he was saying because he was suddenly distracted by an ear-splitting scream.

Anna, along with everyone else, turned towards the sound and saw a woman struggling with a police officer in the road between two squad cars.

She knew instinctively that the woman would turn out to be the mother of one of the nine children – and that she had rushed here to confront what was her and every other parent's worst nightmare.

CHAPTER FIVE

Ruth screamed again, this time at the stupid fucking copper who was holding her back. He had her arm in a vice-like grip and was squeezing so hard it hurt.

'You need to calm down, madam,' he was saying. 'This area has been closed off to members of the public.'

'But I want to see my son,' she told him for the third time. 'I need to know that he's all right. He's in the nursery.'

The officer put his other arm around her shoulders and his voice softened.

'Look, let me sit you in one of the patrol cars while I go and find someone to help you.'

'You can help by letting me through,' she yelled at him. 'I need to know what's going on. Is Liam OK? Has he been hurt? Please let me go inside so that I can find out.'

'I'm sorry, but that's just not possible.'

She was suddenly aware that she was attracting a lot of attention. Other people were coming towards her, including a man who was holding what looked like a large video camera. It made her panic even more, and a wave of fear crashed over her like a wave.

'Will someone please tell me what is happening?' she cried. 'My name is Ruth Brady and my son Liam is here in the nursery. Why won't you let me see him? He's three years old for heaven's sake.'

She was hyperventilating now, unable to get her breathing under control. Tears of frustration blurred her vision, and her heart was pumping so fast it was making her dizzy.

The policeman released his grip on her arm and said something to her that she didn't understand.

Then she heard another voice. A woman's voice. It was calmer, clearer, friendlier.

'Just try to relax and take some deep breaths,' the woman was saying. 'You're going to be all right. I promise. My name is Anna. Detective Anna Tate. And I'm going to explain everything to you.'

Ruth gradually started to breathe normally again as she was taken under the wing of the detective with the strong but kindly voice.

The woman held onto her elbow and steered her away from the group of people who had gathered in the road. A couple of individuals tried to ask her questions but they were prevented from doing so by police officers who shouted at them to step back.

When Ruth realised that she wasn't being escorted into the nursery she stopped walking and turned to the detective.

'Where are you taking me?' she said, her voice high and shrill.

'Next door to the community centre,' the detective said.

'The people who manage it have made it available to us.'

Ruth shook her head. 'But I don't understand. Why are you stopping people from going into the nursery? Where are the children? Where's my son?'

Detective Tate sucked in a breath and cleared her throat. For some reason the woman seemed familiar to Ruth, though she was sure they had never met.

Ruth guessed that Tate was in her early forties. She had an attractive face, but the lines around her mouth and the sagging skin beneath her eyes told Ruth that Detective Tate hadn't had an easy life.

'The thing is, a serious crime has been committed here,' the detective said. 'I'm really sorry to have to tell you that your son and the other children who were here this morning have been abducted by three men who entered the nursery posing as police officers. The staff were locked in the store-room. We're going to do everything we can to get the children back safely.'

Ruth felt a tight spasm in her chest as the shock resonated through her. Her centre of gravity seemed to tilt, and she had to lean against Tate for support.

On the drive here, she had tried to brace herself for bad news, but this wasn't what she had expected to hear. This was simply beyond belief.

She attempted to speak, to ask another question, but all she managed to do was make a strange noise in the back of her throat.

'Let me get you into the centre,' Detective Tate said. 'You're in shock and you need to sit down.'

Ruth felt the detective's arm around her waist and then she was gently urged along the pavement to the community centre, a building she had seen many times but had never set foot in before.

She walked quickly, autopilot taking over, while at the same time her mind flooded with images of Liam. She saw him as he was this morning, dressed in his favourite Superman T-shirt and baggy denim jeans with the drawstring waistband.

She recalled how she had kissed him goodbye and told him that either mummy or daddy would pick him up later. And she remembered how excited he'd been as he rushed across the playroom to join his little pal Daniel.

But then Ruth remembered something else. She remembered that today she was supposed to have taken Liam to the Shrek Adventure on the South Bank. But she had decided not to because she'd elected to meet up with a magazine editor instead. A hot spike of guilt sliced through her chest.

CHAPTER SIX

Anna's heart ached for Ruth Brady. The poor mother's anguish brought it home to her just how traumatic this case was going to be.

Ruth was only the first of the frantic parents who would be turning up demanding answers. It was likely that they all lived within a short distance of Peabody Street and had enrolled their children in the nursery so that they could go to work or pursue other interests. They couldn't possibly have imagined that something like this would ever happen.

Ruth was clearly finding it hard to handle the news. Her breath was now ragged and distorted, her eyes dull with shock. It was as though she had fallen into an almost trance-like state.

But as they approached the entrance to the community centre her mobile phone rang and it jolted the woman out of herself. She stopped to rummage frantically through her leather handbag that hung on a long strap over her right shoulder.

When she found it she glanced at the caller ID and said,

'Oh God, it's my husband. I tried to phone him on the way here.'

She answered it and started to speak, but was obviously interrupted as she stopped mid-sentence to listen to what the person on the other end of the line had to say.

Anna could hear a raised voice but she couldn't make out the words. Ruth reacted by clenching her eyes shut and gritting her teeth.

After a moment her eyes snapped open and she yelled into the phone.

'Look, I know and I'm sorry, Ethan. But they've all been taken. Liam is gone. Our baby's gone, and I'm scared we'll never see him again.'

Her words gave way to uncontrollable sobs, and Anna reached out to grab the phone when it looked like it was going to slip through Ruth's fingers onto the ground.

She raised it to her own ear and said, 'I'm DCI Tate, Mr Brady. Your wife is with me and she'll be looked after. But I suggest you get over here as quickly as you can. We'll be in the community centre next door to the nursery.'

'I'm on my way,' Ethan Brady said. 'But can you please tell me what you know?'

'Not over the phone, Mr Brady. It will have to wait until you get here.'

Anna hung up and held onto the phone because Ruth was still crying, with her head now in her hands.

She pulled a hanky from her pocket and gave it to her, and then she tried to console her by gently rubbing her back.

It was several minutes before Ruth managed to stop crying and as soon as she did Anna handed her back her phone and ushered her into the community centre.

They entered a spacious reception area that was swarming with police officers, some in high-vis jackets.

There was a small cafeteria to the right and straight ahead an open door revealed a large hall with some rows of seating and a makeshift stage.

Anna led Ruth to the cafeteria and pulled out a chair for her at one of the tables. Then she looked around, spotted a WPC, and called her over.

'This is Mrs Ruth Brady,' Anna said to the officer. 'She's the mother of one of the children and I'd like you to stay with her for a while. Her husband will be here shortly.'

'Of course, ma'am. There's someone behind the counter making tea so shall I go and fetch her one?'

'That's a good idea. Thank you.'

Anna turned back to Ruth, who was drying her eyes with the hanky, and said, 'I'm expecting the other parents to start turning up now and I'm going to arrange for you all to move into a room where I can keep you up to date with progress and answer your questions. Would that be OK?'

Ruth looked up and nodded.

'If you're wondering why my husband was cross with me on the phone, it's because Liam wasn't meant to be coming here today,' she said. 'Ethan bought us tickets for the Shrek Adventure, but then shortly after he left for work this morning I got invited to a lunch meeting in connection with my work as a freelance journalist. I felt it was important so I agreed to go and brought Liam here.' Her eyes filled with tears once more. 'It's my fault that he's been taken. If only I hadn't been so selfish.'

'You shouldn't blame yourself, Mrs Brady,' Anna said. 'You weren't to know that this would happen.'

'Well, that's not going to stop me feeling responsible. I put myself before Liam and now I have no idea where he is and what's happening to him.'

'You need to remain positive,' Anna said. 'We'll be throwing all our resources into this investigation. Every police officer in London is on the lookout for the children and the men who took them.'

Ruth shook her head, clearly unconvinced.

'I have more reason than the other mothers to be concerned,' she said. 'My son is not well. He has cystic fibrosis. If he doesn't get his medication he'll become very ill, very fast.'

Anna tried to review in her head what she knew about cystic fibrosis. Her limited understanding of the disease came from reading magazines in which sufferers explained how it had affected their lives.

'A bag with his medication inside is kept in the nursery,' Ruth said. 'But I rather doubt that the kidnappers were told about it before they took him away.'

'I'll ask Sarah Ramsay about that,' Anna said. 'I'm going to speak to her now along with the two teachers who were here with her.'

Ruth frowned. 'Why only two teachers? There were three here when I dropped Liam off. Emma, Tasha and Paige.'

'Tasha is on her way to hospital.'

'Oh Jesus. Is she badly hurt?'

Anna nodded. 'She's suffered a serious head injury, but she's receiving the best possible care now.'

The WPC returned then with a steaming mug of tea which she placed on the table in front of Ruth.

'Get that down you,' Anna said. 'I'll be back in a few minutes. In the meantime, if there's anything you need, just ask the officer here.'

Anna turned to go but Ruth reached out and grabbed the bottom of her jacket.

'I've just remembered something,' Ruth said. 'It's something I saw when I dropped Liam off.'

Anna looked down at her. 'And what was that, Mrs Brady?'

'A minibus. I saw a minibus. It was parked at the kerb in front of the nursery when I arrived. I parked my own car right behind it.'

'Was it there when you left?'

Ruth thought about it and nodded. 'It was. Definitely.'

'Did you see if there was anyone inside?'

Ruth shook her head. 'No, I didn't. The windows were tinted. That struck me as unusual.'

'Had you seen the vehicle there before?'

'I don't know for certain. The nursery occasionally arranges for the children to go on short visits such as to the park, and they get taken in buses similar to that one.'

'And how big was it?'

'I would say big enough for about a dozen people.'

Anna experienced a surge of adrenalin. She was willing to bet that the minibus Ruth saw was the one used by the kidnappers, and that this was a significant lead.

She got Ruth to describe the vehicle in more detail and then phoned the information straight through to central control.

CHAPTER SEVEN

Anna spent the next ten minutes soliciting updates from members of her team, including DI Walker who had some bad news to impart.

'The recorder for the outside security camera has been removed along with the hard drive,' he said. 'It was kept in a cupboard in the office so it wouldn't have been difficult to find. All they had to do was unplug it.'

'Shit,' Anna said.

It was a serious blow but not a complete surprise. The gang would have spotted the camera at the entrance and taken steps to ensure the tape of them showing up did not get into the hands of the police.

Another detective told her that a mobile incident van had arrived and was being positioned outside on the forecourt. Once it was set up they'd be able to receive feeds from central control and monitor footage from CCTV cameras. It would enable them to carry out essential tasks without having to return to base.

Anna also learned that a police forensic artist was on his way over to produce computer-generated e-fits of the three kidnappers. She was keen to get these out to the media as soon as possible, along with the description of the minibus. Every minute that passed gave the bastards time to cover their tracks and go to ground.

Sarah Ramsay and the two teachers were waiting in one of the community centre's four meeting rooms when Anna eventually got back to them. They were sitting around a table along with an MIT detective named Bellingham who'd been eliciting information from them about the children who'd been taken.

The teachers' names were Emma Stevens and Paige Quinlan. Anna had to remind herself which one was which. Paige was the one with lank, shoulder-length brown hair and a porcelain complexion. She was wearing a wedding ring and what might be considered too much make-up for a day shift at a nursery. Emma was the smallest of the three women at about five two. She had compact features and short fair hair and wasn't wearing any jewellery. Anna had already ascertained that she was divorced, thirty years old, and living by herself.

It was Sarah who spoke first, asking if there was any news on Tasha Norris.

'All I know is that she arrived at the hospital and is in surgery,' Anna said. 'I'm told she has a depressed cranial fracture with internal bleeding. Her husband should be there by now.'

'We're all praying for her,' Emma said. 'It was horrible what that man did to her.'

Anna could tell from their faces how desperately concerned they were for their colleague. And they had good reason to be. By all accounts the twenty-three-year-old teacher was in a bad way and the surgeons were fighting to save her life.

Anna then took a seat and apologised for keeping them waiting.

'A lot's been happening,' she said, and went on to tell them that it was believed the children had been taken away in a grey minibus that had been parked on the road outside in front of the nursery.

'It was Mrs Ruth Brady who saw it when she dropped her son Liam off,' she said. 'She arrived here just a few minutes ago and told me that the bus had tinted windows so she couldn't see inside. But we're assuming it was the vehicle used by the kidnappers.' Anna looked at Sarah, adding, 'Mrs Brady said that you sometimes use minibuses to take the children out. Did you arrange for one to be here this morning? And does this particular vehicle sound familiar?'

Sarah shook her head. 'We didn't book a bus for today and we have an arrangement with a local firm called Cresta Transport. We use them exclusively and they only have dark blue buses.'

'Did any of you see the bus outside?' Anna asked.

The three women shook their heads in unison.

'We were all here by seven thirty,' Sarah said. 'There's a lot of preparation work we have to do before the morning session begins. I'm sure that if it had been outside we would have seen it.'

'My officers have already established that there are no traffic cameras in Peabody Street,' Anna said. 'But there are plenty in this area so I'm confident that we'll soon have footage of the grey minibus and hopefully be able to track its movements across London.'

'What about our own security camera?' Emma asked. 'Those men should be on tape.'

'Unfortunately they took the digital recorder that was in the office,' Anna said. 'For that reason I need you to provide us with more detailed descriptions. A computer artist will be here shortly and I'd appreciate it if you would help him work up e-fit images of the men. At the same time you'll need to provide us with fingerprint and DNA samples. Our forensic team will be examining every surface in the nursery in the hope that the men left traces of themselves behind.'

Anna could tell that Emma and Paige were struggling to hold it together. Their eyes were red and puffy and they were finding it hard to focus. Sarah, on the other hand, appeared to have recovered from the initial shock. She had wiped the trails of mascara from her cheeks and tidied up her hair. And it seemed like she was trying hard to keep a lid on her emotions.

'I'd like you to take me through again precisely what happened,' Anna said. 'But first tell me about the children. I know that Liam Brady has cystic fibrosis. But is he the only one of the nine with a serious condition?'

Sarah nodded. 'He is. And I'm sorry I didn't think to mention that earlier. I should have.'

'His mother told me about the bag with his medication inside. Where do you keep it?'

'In the first aid cupboard in the kitchen,' Sarah said.

'And I don't suppose the kidnappers would have known about it?'

Sarah shrugged. 'I don't see how. We never got the opportunity to tell them because we had no idea what was going to happen.'

Anna made a note on her pad and said, 'Now is it correct that there are usually more than nine children here?'

Sarah said it was, adding, 'It's the summer break so lots of families are away on holiday.'

'So if there had been more kids here today then just three men would presumably have struggled to take them away.'

'I suppose so,' Sarah answered. 'Even nine children can be quite a handful. Especially given that the boys and girls here this morning are little extroverts. And they were all in a playful mood, so as long as the men didn't shout at them or appear threatening they would probably have gone with them without a fuss.'

Anna was surprised. 'Really?'

Sarah nodded. 'Those men would only have had to say to the kids that they were going for a ride to somewhere special. They might even have given them sweets. That's all it would have taken to win their trust. After all, we're talking about children aged between three and five.'

Anna then repeated a question she had asked earlier – whether the women had recognised any of the men. The answer from all three was an emphatic no.

'So you're all sure that they had never been inside the nursery before?'

'We're positive,' Paige said. 'We'd remember.'

'You told me the men were white and wearing suits,' Anna said, as she consulted her notes. 'Two were in their twenties or thirties and one quite a bit older, perhaps in his fifties.'

'That's right,' Sarah said.

'OK, so now let's go through it again. You were all in the playroom and about to tell the children a story when the doorbell rang.'

'I went to answer it,' Sarah said. 'The men were standing outside. I could see them through the glass doors. I spoke to them through the intercom and asked them who they were and what they wanted. At that point all three held up identity cards and the older guy said he was Detective Inspector Roger Milton from Rotherhithe CID. He was the only one of them to speak and he had a South London accent. He introduced the others as DS Willis and DC Moore and said he needed to talk to the proprietor Sarah Ramsay about a private matter.'

'So he didn't know that was you,' Anna said.

'Apparently not. He said they wouldn't keep me long so, like a fool, I opened the doors. I know it was a stupid thing to do. I should have called the police station to confirm that they were who they said they were but I was caught off-guard and I didn't think. I was curious and I should have been suspicious.'

'So what happened then?'

'As soon as the doors were open all three of them burst in and at the same time produced pistols from under their jackets. They warned me that if I moved or screamed they would shoot me.'

Anna looked at her notes again.

'You told me earlier that this man Milton then asked you how many children and staff were in.'

'That's correct.'

'And then he told you to walk back into the playroom and to herd the children into one of the smaller rooms so that he could speak to you and the teachers.'

'They put their guns back under their jackets and made me act as though nothing was wrong,' Sarah said. 'I had to tell Emma, Paige and Tasha that they were police officers and wanted to talk to us without the children being present.'

'We thought it was strange,' Emma said. 'But the fact is they looked like policemen and so we thought we ought to comply. I ushered the kids into the Quiet Room and one of the younger men went inside with them.'

'That was when they whipped out their guns,' Paige said. 'It was terrifying. The one calling himself Milton said that if we didn't do as we were told he would shoot Sarah in the head and then start picking off the children. So we felt we had no choice.'

'So what did Tasha do?' Anna asked.

'She didn't do anything until we were inside the storeroom,' Sarah said. 'Milton took a plastic bag from his pocket and told us to put our mobile phones inside it. I did and so did Emma. Paige didn't have hers with her and as the guy was telling her to turn around Tasha leapt at him.

'But she wasn't fast enough. He managed to step back and hit her with the butt of his gun. Not once but three times. She collapsed on the floor and he backed out of the room and locked the door behind him. We were all screaming and shouting and trying to revive Tasha. After about ten minutes I realised she had her mobile phone in her jeans pocket so I used it to call the emergency service.'

Anna was satisfied that their story was consistent with the one they had told earlier. It was far more detailed now, though, and raised many more questions.

Were the guns the men used real or fake?

Had the children happily trooped out of the nursery and got on the bus believing they were in for a special treat?

Had one or more of the men visited the nursery before today to check the interior layout?

Or had they received information from someone who was

familiar with it – someone such as a parent or even a member of staff?

This last question was an uncomfortable one and filled Anna with a shuddering sense of unease.

CHAPTER EIGHT

Ruth had been joined by three other mothers and two fathers who had rushed straight to Peabody Street after being told what had happened to their children.

They were gathered in the community centre cafeteria where a bald detective inspector named Walker had told them that his boss, DCI Anna Tate, would soon provide them with an update. But this had done nothing to quell their distress and anger.

Daniel Neville's mum Belinda was so anxious that she'd vomited on the floor. And Grace Tenant's dad Kenneth had threatened to punch a uniformed officer who told him he couldn't go next door into the nursery.

Ruth was beside herself with worry and only half aware of what was going on around her. Her voice was hoarse from crying and there was a lead weight in her chest.

Every time she closed her eyes she saw Liam's face, and tears began to form, while at the same time various disturbing scenarios played out in her mind.

What if Liam and the others had been snatched by child sex traffickers who were going to smuggle them out of the country? Or maybe the three kidnappers were part of an abhorrent paedophile ring based in London that preyed on young, defenceless kids.

She also feared that Liam and his friends might be the latest victims of ruthless terrorists who planned to kill them in order to draw attention to their ghastly cause.

These days the news was full of so many despicable crimes that nothing could be ruled out. Only a month ago the papers were dominated by the story of a married couple in Leeds who had allowed men to have sex with their six-year-old daughter in return for cash. And about a year ago there was an armed siege at a nursery school in Paris where fifteen children were held hostage for eleven hours by a Somalian man with a rifle. He was eventually shot and killed by commandos who stormed the building and released the children. It turned out his aim had been to get back at the French government for refusing to grant him asylum.

Ruth was desperate to know why Liam had been taken. She could imagine that by now he'd be asking for his mummy. And if he got upset he would get into an awful state and struggle to breathe. His cystic fibrosis was a life-threatening curse. His daily regimen included tablets to loosen the mucus in his lungs and keep his airways clear. And then there were the enzyme supplements, which replaced those his pancreas failed to make.

Usually the drugs were administered by the nursery staff and Ruth ensured that the bag she left with them was replenished on a regular basis. But Liam wouldn't be able to tell his captors what he needed to keep him alive. And since he had never once had to do without his medication for a whole day, Ruth didn't know how quickly his condition would deteriorate. It was a frightening thought, and the sense of hopelessness she felt was paralysing.

By the time Ethan turned up, Ruth was smothered in a dark blanket of despair. She couldn't think straight, and her brain was starting to blur at the edges.

Her husband was escorted into the community centre along with two other sets of parents who had arrived at the same time.

He'd come straight from work but had discarded his suit jacket and tie, and his white shirt hung over his belt. His face was taut with tension and his skin sheened with perspiration.

As soon as he spotted Ruth he rushed straight to her and the relief she felt was overwhelming. He put his arms around her and pulled her close, and she sobbed into his shoulder.

'I got here as quickly as I could,' he said. 'Is there any more news?'

She continued to sob, and when she didn't respond to his question Ethan eased her gently away from him.

'You need to speak to me, Ruth,' he said, his voice clipped. 'Have the police found out where Liam is?'

Ruth swallowed hard and sucked air through her teeth. Her mind was turning somersaults and she could hear the blood thundering in her ears.

'No, they haven't,' she said eventually, wiping at her eyes. 'The officer in charge is going to update us soon. They've been waiting for more parents to get here.'

Ruth lifted her head to look at her husband's face. She didn't like what she saw. His jaw was tight and blood vessels bulged at his temples. He shifted his gaze away from her, as though unable to look her in the eyes.

'I'm so sorry,' she said. 'I know that Liam wasn't meant to be here today. And trust me, nothing you can say will make me feel any worse than I do right now.'

He turned back to her and spoke quietly, but not so quietly that those around them couldn't hear. 'So what was so important that you couldn't spend the day with our son?'

'I was invited to lunch with that magazine editor I told you about,' she said. 'I thought it would be an opportunity to secure some more work. I told Liam I'd take him to see Shrek another time.'

Ethan's nostrils flared and he ran a hand across his forehead.

'But now there might not be another time,' he said. 'Who knows what's going to happen to our boy?'

Tears welled up in his eyes then and his face suddenly crumpled like a paper bag. Ruth hadn't seen him cry since the doctor broke the news to them that Liam had cystic fibrosis. That was three years ago. Since then he had been a devoted father and had done everything possible to ensure that Liam enjoyed life despite his illness. He'd been overprotective for sure and had never given up searching for that elusive cure. He had even been talking recently about remortgaging the house to raise money for experimental treatment for CF that was being pioneered in the United States.

So Ruth could well appreciate how he felt now and she told herself that it was understandable that he would take it out on her. After all, she was to blame. If she hadn't agreed to meet Howard Browning then she would be having fun with Liam right now instead of standing in a room surrounded by police officers and other distraught parents.

Ethan's whole body was shaking as Ruth reached out and pulled him into an embrace.

'We both have to stay strong,' she said. 'The police are doing everything they can. And that Detective Tate seems to be on top of things.'

As if on cue, Anna Tate emerged from one of the side rooms. Trailing behind her were Sarah Ramsay and the two teachers, Emma and Paige.

The sight of the nursery owner sent a rush of heat through Ruth's body. She let go of Ethan and bolted across the room, her head filled with a fiery rage.

Sarah saw her coming and stopped walking. Ruth got to within a couple of feet of her and pointed an accusing finger.

'It's about bloody time you showed your face,' she screamed. 'We entrusted our children to your care. You were supposed to look after them. So why did you let those men walk in and take them away? If any harm comes to Liam I swear I will make sure you suffer.'

Ruth was about to lunge forward and strike Sarah when Detective Tate stepped between them, holding up her hands.

At the same time Ethan grabbed Ruth from behind and pulled her back.

'Please calm down, Mrs Brady,' the detective said. 'This won't help the situation.'

'But she needs to know how I feel,' Ruth shouted. 'How we all feel. That woman and her staff undertook to keep our kids safe and they failed.'

Paige Quinlan stepped out from behind Sarah. 'It wasn't our fault, Ruth,' she said. 'The men had guns. They threatened to shoot us.'

'That's no excuse,' Ruth responded. 'You should have protected our kids, no matter what.'

Detective Tate came forward and placed a hand on Ruth's shoulder.

'I can understand that you're angry and very worried, Mrs Brady,' she said. 'But this really isn't the time or place to start attributing blame. We all need to focus one hundred per cent on getting the children back.'

For the second time that morning, it was the detective who took the wind out of Ruth's sails. She felt her anger subside along with the pounding of her heart.

'Look, I'm going to organise a room for you and the other parents so that I can fill you all in on what we're doing,' Tate said. 'I also intend to assign a specific officer to each family. But you need to bear with me for a few more minutes.'

The detective then turned and motioned for Sarah and the teachers to follow her as she stepped away from the cafeteria.

Ruth felt Ethan's hand on her back and when he spoke he sounded resigned rather than angry.

'Come and sit down, Ruth. I want you to tell me everything you know about what happened.'

And so she sat on one of the chairs and told him what the detective had said to her earlier about the kidnapping. And as she spoke the other parents gathered round to listen.

But it all proved too much for Daniel's mother, Belinda. She threw up again, only this time it went all over the table.

CHAPTER NINE

Anna could have asked the members of her team to deal with the parents while she got on with the investigation. But she chose not to, and not just because she knew from personal experience the hell they were going through.

She wanted to engage with them so that she could suss them out. After all, she couldn't rule out the possibility that one or more of them was somehow involved in the abductions. It was unlikely but not impossible given that the kidnappers had seemed to know what to expect when they entered the nursery.

But first she had to make sure that Sarah, Emma and Paige were out of harm's way. Ruth Brady wouldn't be the only parent to point the finger of blame at them, and next time it might actually get physical.

DI Walker, her trusted wingman, was on hand to help her sort things out.

'I've already arranged for one of the other meeting rooms

to be made available,' he said. 'It's on the other side of the hall. I'll take them straight there and alert the techies.'

Anna thanked the three women for being so patient.

'We'll get your fingerprints and DNA samples and you can help us put together the e-fits,' she said. Then she took Sarah to one side and told her that she needed to stay on the premises so that they could have another conversation.

'There are questions I want to ask you about the nursery, Miss Ramsay,' she said. 'For instance, I'd like the names of everyone who has access to the building, including cleaners, workmen and other staff members not in today, plus former employees. Also, have you or any of the staff been threatened at any time? And is there anyone that you know of who has a grudge against you or the business? Perhaps you could start giving it some thought.'

Sarah didn't react other than to nod and blow out her cheeks.

'And don't let what just happened get to you,' Anna said. 'Ruth and the other parents are in a fearful state and they need to vent their anger and frustration. Unfortunately you're an easy target.'

'I'm sure I'd feel exactly the same if I were in their position,' Sarah said. Then she followed Walker and the others towards the hall.

Anna looked at her watch. It was approaching midday, which meant that almost three hours had passed since the children were taken. The kidnappers had had plenty of time to put distance between themselves and Peabody Street. Were they still in London? she wondered. Or had they fled the capital and driven to a pre-arranged secret location in the sticks?

She was pleased to see so many Met personnel on the scene. They were still arriving at the community centre – uniforms, civilian support staff, crime scene coordinators and computer technicians.

At the same time, things were happening outside. Several police helicopters had taken to the skies, ready to respond to a sighting or a tip-off from a member of the public. Beat coppers were on high alert and armed tactical teams were cruising the streets.

Meanwhile, counter-terrorism officers were searching for likely suspects on their watch lists, but the latest word from them was that they didn't think this was the work of extremists.

Having the community centre right next door to the nursery was a godsend and Anna made a mental note to seek out and thank the management for letting them set up camp here.

She decided to see what progress was being made before going back to talk to the parents. After slipping outside she resisted the urge to light up a cigarette and headed for the mobile incident van on the forecourt.

The sun was still shining proudly in a clear blue sky and the temperature was continuing to rise.

There were more people on the street now, too. The Sky News team had been joined by crews from the BBC and ITV. The kidnapping had sparked a media frenzy, and Anna knew that soon she would have to mount a press conference and answer a barrage of questions.

The mobile incident van – or command centre as it was also known – was already operational. It was more like a small lorry than a van, and inside there was a desk, some chairs and a computer station with three screens.

An officer sat in front of the screens operating a keyboard, and DC Megan Sweeny from MIT stood behind him. She was a new addition to Anna's team, having joined only a few months ago, but she had already made a big impression and seemed destined to rise swiftly through the ranks.

'So what have you got for me, Megan?' Anna asked her.

DC Sweeny grinned and pointed to one of the screens which showed a freeze-frame of a grey minibus.

'We're pretty sure that's the vehicle we're looking for, guv,' she said. 'It's the first hit we've had from traffic cameras in the area. This particular camera is located in Manor Road, which is just half a mile from here. We can't see inside the bus because of the tinted windows but we've managed to blow up and identify the registration. It turns out the bus was stolen a week ago from an industrial site in Greenwich.'

'Bingo,' Anna said. 'You need to keep at it, though. I want to know where the fuck it's going.'

'Will do, guv.'

'And I'm assuming this image is being circulated.'

'Of course. The alert went out as soon as we got it.'

'Well done, Megan. Let me know as soon as you get another hit.'

'I've got something else for you, guv,' she said, and picked up a sheet of paper from the desk. 'Sarah Ramsay provided us with a list of the nine children but we've added to it. So now it includes the names of their parents and their addresses.'

Anna glanced at the sheet which included head-and-shoulder shots of the children.

Daniel Neville, aged 3 (parents Belinda and Wesley)

Liam Brady, aged 3 (parents Ruth and Ethan)

Grace Tenant, aged 4 (parents Laura and Kenneth)

Simone Green, aged 4 (parents Wendy and Phil – divorced)

Toby Chandler, aged 4 (parents Rebecca and James)

Abdul Ahmed, aged 4 (mother Melek – father deceased)

Justine Brooks, aged 4 (parents Rachel and William)

Molly Wilson, aged 5 (parents Janet and Ben – divorced)

Sahib Hussein, aged 5 (parents Sabina and Rafi)

Below was a list of addresses, all of them within a couple of miles of the nursery.

'This is great, Megan,' Anna said. 'I want everyone involved in the case to have a copy. But don't release it to the media until I say so.'

Anna then went in search of the crime scene manager for an update on the forensic sweep of the nursery. But on the way she was collared by an anxious-looking PC. He was with a thin, grey-haired woman who must have been in her late sixties or early seventies.

'You need to speak to this lady, ma'am,' he said. 'Her name is Felicity Bradshaw and she lives on Peabody Street a few doors down from the nursery. She actually saw the children being taken away.'

Anna felt a jolt of anticipation as she introduced herself.

'Please tell me exactly what you saw, Mrs Bradshaw,' she said.

The woman spoke in a voice that was loud and clear, though charged with emotion.

'I was walking back from the shops,' she said. 'I saw the minibus parked outside the nursery. It hadn't been there when I walked past the spot earlier so I assumed it had only just arrived. And it struck me that it was a different colour to the buses that are usually parked outside. They're blue.

'Anyway, I was just approaching it when the children came marching out of the nursery so I stopped to watch them. As usual they were all wide-eyed and in a state of high excitement. They didn't look at all distressed. They were in a line and holding hands and three men in suits were with them. One of the men actually smiled at me and I smiled back.

'The children were talking and laughing as they were herded onto the bus and I enjoyed watching them. The men then got on with them, but I couldn't see them once they were inside because the windows were blacked out. As soon as the door closed the bus drove off and I assumed they were going on an outing.'

'Did you notice anything else?' Anna said. 'Anything at all?'

Mrs Bradshaw thought about it for a beat and said, 'Actually I forgot to mention the young woman who was there.'

'Woman?'

'That's right. She was standing just inside the door and it looked as though she was welcoming the kids on board the bus.'

'Can you describe her for me?'

'I didn't really pay her much attention, but I think she had short reddish hair and was wearing a yellow top and jeans. I suppose she must have been in her early twenties or perhaps even younger. But I do remember that she was greeting the kids with a big smile while handing out what looked like sweets from a bag.'

CHAPTER TEN

The parents had been moved from the cafeteria to the largest of the meeting rooms. It looked out on the forecourt so they could see all the activity through the slatted blinds. The room had been due to host a lunch for a group of local pensioners. The lunch had been cancelled and the chairs and tables rearranged so that the parents could sit facing Anna when she spoke to them.

By the time she got there twelve people had turned up – four married couples, two divorced wives without their ex-husbands and two husbands without their wives. That left five of the parents who were still absent. Anna was told that the police hadn't yet been able to contact the parents of four-year-old Toby Chandler or Phil Green, the father of Simone Green, who was also four. But the mother of Abdul Ahmed had been informed and was on her way to Peabody Street. Meanwhile, Molly Wilson's mother was stuck at home with two other children and a family liaison officer was with her.

Anna's plan was to provide them with an update and then later her team of detectives would interview them individually. She wanted to find out as much as possible about them and their children. She needed to know if any of them had their suspicions about who might be involved in the kidnapping. She wanted details of where they lived and worked, and access to their phone records. She also needed to check whether any of them were on the criminal records database.

Doing all that here rather than in their homes would speed up the process considerably. Time was a major factor now and it was already working against them. But at least they were beginning to make some progress. They had identified the minibus believed to have been used and were now tracking it across London.

And they had a witness who had seen the children boarding the vehicle. The same witness had also revealed that there was a fourth gang member – a young woman who'd been waiting on the bus to greet the children. No doubt her role had been to make them feel comfortable in the presence of so many strangers.

Anna felt ill-at-ease as she stood before her audience of desperate mothers and fathers, and she was aware that beads of sweat were gathering on her forehead.

She began by giving the parents the option of staying in the community centre for as long as they wanted or being taken home to wait for news there.

'You might find that being here together for a time will help you cope with the situation,' she said. 'Officers are available to answer your questions and we can be of assistance when it comes to talking to the media. They are likely to hound you for interviews, which we would advise you to decline for the time being. Just let it be known what you'd prefer to do.'

She then asked them to introduce themselves and the first to respond was Ethan Brady, who said, 'I'm Liam Brady's father. You've already met my wife so you know that our son has cystic fibrosis. If he doesn't get his medication he could die. So you need to do whatever you can to get him back quickly.'

Ethan Brady was much taller than his wife and came across as far more assertive. His narrow face sported designer stubble and his dark eyes had a piercing quality even from a distance.

He was about to say something else when one of the other fathers leapt to his feet and fixed Ethan with a hostile stare.

'That's typical of you, Brady,' the man shouted. 'But this time it's not all about your precious fucking son. The rest of us have as much reason to worry as you do.'

'I'm not saying you don't,' Ethan reacted. 'But you know how ill Liam is.'

'Sure we do, because you and your wife never stop telling us. I've told you before that I don't think a kid with cystic fibrosis should be allowed in the nursery anyway. It's too risky. And the staff ignore our kids because they spend too much time fretting over him.'

Anna was taken aback by the outburst and stepped in to stop things getting out of hand.

'Please would you not raise your voice or be disrespectful to others, sir,' she said. 'One of the reasons for bringing you together like this is so that you can offer support to each other.'

The man puffed out his chest and appeared keen to carry on his rant but his wife took hold of his arm and pulled him back onto his seat. Ethan glared at the back of the guy's head but remained silent, much to Anna's relief.

'OK, so let's now moderate the tone and can you please carry on telling me who you are,' she said.

Mr Angry turned out to be Kenneth Tenant, father of four-year-old Grace, the same man who had apparently threatened a PC when he was refused entry into the nursery earlier.

He was a rough-looking individual with stern features and a downturned mouth. His behaviour revealed what Anna took to be simmering tensions between him and the Brady couple. She just hoped the situation they were in did not make matters between them much worse. The last thing she needed was the parents turning on each other as the pressure on them mounted, as it surely would.

They got through the rest of the introductions quickly and with no more awkward moments. Anna then tried to inject an element of optimism into the proceedings by telling them that the minibus had been picked up on a traffic camera. She also told them what the neighbour, Mrs Bradshaw, had seen.

They were shocked to hear that a young woman had been involved. And all were adamant that they had no idea who the perps were.

'This is a very unusual case in that so many children were taken,' Anna said. 'We don't yet know what the motive is, but it's possible that we'll hear from the kidnappers soon if their intention is to demand a ransom.'

'And what if that's not what they want?' asked Simone Green's mother, Wendy, who had reverted to her maiden name of Ryan. 'What if they took the kids because they want to . . .' Her voice broke. 'What if they want to do bad things to them?'

'I think that's extremely unlikely,' Anna said, but stopped short of ruling it out altogether. 'And for what it's worth, we also think it's doubtful that the kidnappers are terrorists. I'm sure if they were we would have heard from them by now.'

She was then asked to explain how the children had been taken so she talked them through what she'd been told. There was sympathy expressed for Tasha Norris, but a good deal of vitriol was directed at all the staff, especially Sarah Ramsay.

The others echoed what Ruth Brady had said earlier and Toby Chandler's mother, Rebecca, revealed that she had raised the issue of security with Sarah Ramsay on several occasions.

'Before we moved here from Stratford we sent our daughter to a nursery that had much tougher procedures in place,' she said. 'It had a fingerprint entry system and a webcam so that we could watch our kids from home. I told Sarah that I didn't think her nursery was as secure as it should be. She disagreed and told me that it met government requirements and that she took safety seriously.'

'But that's total bollocks,' said Daniel Neville's dad, Wesley. 'At the end of the day she's a businesswoman who doesn't even have a kid of her own. With her it's all about money and what happened at her nursery in Lewisham last year cost her a small fortune. So the last thing she wants is to have to fork out on expensive security equipment.'

'Could you tell us what happened in Lewisham, Mr Neville?' Anna asked.

Wesley, a pot-bellied black man with sunglasses perched on his head, said, 'A little girl died after choking on a grape at the Peabody Nursery there. The inquest returned a verdict of accidental death and she had to pay a three-hundred-thousand-pound fine for gross negligence.'

Anna hadn't heard about the case and it annoyed her that nobody back at the station had made her aware of it. Surely officers researching the nurseries would have unearthed the information before now. She would have to ask Sarah about it when she next spoke to her. Right now, however, she couldn't see how it would have a bearing on what had happened this morning.

She checked her watch, saw that she had been with the parents for forty-five minutes, and decided it was time for her detectives to talk to them individually.

She finished off by telling them that she and her team were doing everything possible to find the children.

'Scores of officers are already involved in the search,' she said. 'We've set up a mobile command outside on the forecourt and for the time being we're using this community centre as a base for our operations. Officers all across London are on the lookout for the minibus and I've already issued a short television appeal for information.'

Kenneth Tenant shot to his feet again and this time he locked his angry gaze on Anna.

'I just watched the interview you gave on the telly earlier,' he said. 'One of the reporters asked you a question that you didn't answer because you got interrupted. So I'll ask it now. Is it true that your own kid was snatched ten years ago?'

Anna drew a deep, steadying breath and said, 'It is true that my daughter was taken from me, Mr Tenant, but as I made clear to that reporter it has absolutely no relevance to what's happening now.'

'Well, it's relevant as far as I'm concerned,' he said.

'And why is that, Mr Tenant?'

'Surely that's bloody obvious.'

She held his gaze and said, 'Not to me it isn't, Mr Tenant. So perhaps you could explain what you mean.'

His wife tried to say something to him but he gestured for her to be quiet.

Then his eyes narrowed and he said, 'If you've been searching for your own little girl for ten years and still haven't found her, then why should we trust that you're up to the job of finding our kids?'

She'd known where he was going with his accusation as soon as he began the sentence; each of his words felt like a blow to her stomach, but Anna knew she had to roll with the punches. The man was clearly distressed and aggression was obviously a coping mechanism that helped him avoid becoming outwardly emotional.

'I have been appointed as the senior officer on this case and I can assure you, as will the entire MIT that have chosen me to be the leader of this investigation, that I am up to the job, Mr Tenant,' she said, keeping her voice low and even. 'The circumstances surrounding my own daughter's abduction were entirely different to this. And for reasons that you may or may not be aware of, for most of the last ten years I've been the only person looking for her. But in the search for your children and the people who took them I have the support of every police officer in the country and access to an unlimited amount of resources. Plus, I hope you can take comfort from the fact that, because of what I've experienced, I can more fully appreciate exactly what you and the other parents are going through.'

Tenant's whole demeanour changed in an instant and blood coloured his cheeks. He ran a hand through his thin brown hair and blew out a long, slow breath.

Then he shook his head and said, 'I'm a fucking dickhead and I'm sorry. I shouldn't have had a go at you like that. I'm just worked up and my mind's all over the place.'

'No need to apologise, Mr Tenant,' Anna said. 'Just please understand that myself and my colleagues will not rest until we find your children.'

After telling the other detectives to stay with the parents until the family liaison officers arrived, she made a swift exit from the room.

She went straight outside and round to the side of the building where she rested her back against the wall and fired up a fag, her first of the day.

The blood was beating in her ears and adrenalin charging through her body. It wasn't that she was hurt by what Kenneth Tenant had said. It was that his words had made her realise just how hard it was going to be to head up this particular investigation.

She wasn't going to be able to squeeze the memories to one side like she usually did while working. It had started already. She was being reminded of how it had felt after her daughter had been taken from her. As each moment had passed, she'd known that she was less and less likely to see Chloe ever again. Anna had walked around in a fog for weeks, out of sync with her surroundings, and the pain was constant, crushing and unbearable.

She closed her eyes and dragged heavily on the cigarette, then let the smoke drift from her nostrils.

She tried to keep the memories at bay by focusing on the

nine children who were missing. But she couldn't. Her hands started to shake and the cigarette fell from her fingers as her back slid down the wall. When she hit the ground she put her head in her hands and her mind spiralled back through the years to when her life was changed forever.

CHAPTER ELEVEN

July 2009

It was the end of Anna's first week as a detective constable in the Met. She was feeling tired but upbeat as she left the station in Eltham and headed home at the height of the Friday evening rush hour.

She knew it might take her up to an hour to get to Vauxhall, but that was OK because she had the whole weekend to look forward to. She'd be able to relax and unwind while spending quality time with Chloe.

She still found it hard to believe that her daughter was two already, and would soon be three. The time had flown by; it seemed like only yesterday that she'd given birth to her little bundle of joy.

Back then everything was perfect. She and Matthew had just celebrated their third wedding anniversary, and the future had looked really bright.

But that was before he began to change. It started when he was overlooked for a promotion at work. It was a big blow to his ego and he didn't try to hide the fact that he was jealous of his wife's success as a copper.

He became argumentative and controlling. And then he embarked on an affair with a woman in his office which lasted for five months. When Anna found out, he was contrite and begged her to forgive him. But she couldn't because she knew she would never trust him again. She also knew that Matthew Dobson was no longer the man she had married.

At Anna's insistence, he moved out into a rented flat. And he wasn't happy when she applied for a divorce. Throughout the process he pleaded with her to take him back. But the voice of reason in her head convinced her not to.

The divorce was finalised six months ago but Matthew had not given up trying to win her back. When his widowed mother died two months later, leaving him and his sister a sizeable inheritance – over a quarter of a million pounds each – he actually believed it would make her change her mind. But, of course, it didn't and he was mortified.

They'd been granted joint custody of Chloe. Matthew had her every other weekend and occasionally, by mutual agreement, on weekdays. Chloe had actually spent the last two nights with him at his flat in Chiswick. He'd asked to have her so that he could take her to his sister Charlotte's birthday party.

But by now Chloe would be back home where Anna's mother would be taking care of her. Without her mother's help Anna would never have been able to hold down a full-time job, especially one that entailed such unsocial hours.

The drive home was slow and uneventful, and she was relieved when she pulled up outside her terraced house at just before seven. She couldn't wait to see Chloe, and was glad she'd told her mother to keep her up so that she could read her a bedtime story.

For that reason she expected to see her daughter in her mother's arms when the door flew open as she approached it. But her mother was alone and had a face like thunder.

'Why haven't you answered your bloody phone?' her mother said. 'I've called and sent you two messages.'

Anna felt her heart miss a beat. Her phone was in her handbag, but she knew without looking what had happened.

'Oh shit,' she said. 'I had a meeting just before I left the office and put it on silent. And because I was in such a hurry to get away I didn't think to check it.'

'Well, you should have.'

'Why mum? What's wrong? Where's Chloe?'

'That's just it,' her mother said. 'You told me that Matthew was supposed to bring her back at three but he hasn't shown up yet. I've tried ringing him but there's no answer. And quite frankly I'm worried. You know I don't trust that man.'

CHAPTER TWELVE

Anna's eyes snapped open to the roar of a helicopter over-head. The flashback to the worst day of her life was thankfully cut short, but Chloe's face was still there in her head. Her button nose and dimpled chin. The bright, cheeky smile that lit up the lives of all those who came into contact with her.

She would be twelve now, and in three months she'd become a teenager. And yet Anna had no idea where she was or if she was happy. All she had were memories and questions. Lots of questions.

What does she look like now?

Does she ever ask about her mother?

Does she even remember her mother?

Is she being taken care of?

Is she healthy?

Is she alive?

Anna had never given up hope of one day being reunited with her baby. Nine years ago she'd set up a website dedicated to finding her. She'd launched pages on Facebook and Twitter and they now had a combined following of fourteen thousand people.

A month ago she'd marked the tenth anniversary of Chloe's abduction with a fresh appeal through social media and she'd managed to get one of the popular Sunday supplements to run an interview with her. She'd even got them to publish an age-progression photo of Chloe and her shit of a father. But so far nothing had come of it except for dozens of sympathy messages and some cruel comments from internet trolls.

Anna remained undeterred, though. The search would go on, even though her lone efforts were time-consuming and soul-destroying. She could never imagine herself giving up.

And neither could she ever countenance forgiving her ex-husband. The bastard had shattered her life into a million pieces and changed her forever. She used to be an easy-going and tolerant individual with a positive attitude to life. Now she was short-tempered, impatient, and found it hard to trust people. It was as though losing Chloe had unleashed a darkness that had been lurking inside her.

She swallowed back the lump that had risen in her throat and started to pull her thoughts together. She owed it to the parents of those nine stolen children to stay fully focused. They were depending on her to stop their lives imploding, to save them from the kind of abject misery that she was all too familiar with. She was determined not to let them down.

She had allowed herself to be thrown off-track briefly by what Kenneth Tenant and that reporter had said. But she wasn't going to let it happen again, even if some other bright spark questioned her ability to lead this investigation.

She pushed herself away from the wall and walked back

around to the front of the community centre, where she almost bumped into none other than DI Walker.

'So there you are, guv,' he said. 'I've been looking for you, and it just occurred to me that you'd probably sneaked off for a quiet puff.'

'And you were right,' she said. 'Which just goes to show what a great detective you are.'

He smiled as he polished his glistening bald head with the palm of his hand.

'I heard what happened with the parents,' he said. 'Wish I'd been there to put that prick in his place.'

'It was no big deal, Max. The poor sod is all messed up. And to be fair to him he did apologise.'

'Not the point,' Walker said. 'There was no need to bring it up. He was out of order.'

Walker was one of only a handful of her colleagues who actually encouraged her to continue searching for Chloe. Unlike some of the others, he didn't regard it as a waste of time. It was probably because he had two daughters of his own aged six and eight and he'd told her that he could never imagine being separated from them.

'So why were you looking for me, Max?' Anna said, glancing at her watch. 'For the record, I slipped around the back only five minutes ago.'

Max pointed towards the mobile incident van. 'Which is why you weren't there to greet our esteemed leader when he arrived three minutes ago.'

DCS Nash was standing outside the van speaking to a couple of detectives. He didn't ordinarily turn up at crime scenes but understandably this one was an exception.

He was a tall, broad-shouldered man with a commanding

presence and a short beard that didn't quite suit him. He'd been Anna's boss for three years and they got on reasonably well. He was one of those officers who liked to delegate most of the hard work while at the same time taking credit for it.

'There you are, Anna,' he said as she approached him. 'I came straight from the Yard as soon as I realised how serious this is. For obvious reasons, the Commissioner himself is taking a personal interest in the case and I want to make sure that we're on top of things.'

'We're getting there, sir,' she said. 'It's a strange one, though, and as yet I'm not sure what to make of it.'

'Well, the world's media is camped out there on the road and we need to stage a formal press conference as soon as possible. In the meantime I've said I'll go and update them after I've spoken to you. So talk me through it, Anna. And do it while you show me the crime scene.'

This time they had to don hooded white paper suits and shoe covers to enter the nursery. The SOCOs were busy dusting for prints and searching for clues, but Anna doubted that the kidnappers had left many behind, if any at all. They were quite clearly professionals, who'd had this abduction intricately planned.

She explained to Nash how the men had gained access to the building and what had happened once they were inside. She showed him the storeroom and the Quiet Room. And while in the playroom she drew his attention to the dozens of pictures on the walls that had been drawn or painted by the children. Names were scrawled on the bottom of each one, and Anna spotted works of art by some of those who'd been taken, including Daniel, Liam, Simone, Molly and Grace.

And there were a few group photographs of the kids with

the staff. They were gathered in the garden on a sunny day, standing in front of a large Christmas tree and sitting around a table containing a birthday cake with four candles on it.

'I'm pretty sure that those men knew what to expect before they came in here,' Anna said to Nash. 'So the question is, had they been here before to look around? Or did someone provide them with all the information they needed?'

'So what's your impression of the owner?' Nash asked.

'I haven't yet formed one,' she said. 'But I intend to speak to her again before I get the troops together for a briefing. I want to ask her about an incident last year at one of the Peabody Nurseries. Apparently she was fined three hundred thousand pounds after a child choked to death on a grape.'

'I can vaguely recall that case,' he said. 'But I didn't realise the nursery involved received such a whopping fine.'

'Well it could mean that she's got serious money problems,' Anna said. 'So maybe she decided to arrange for the kids to be taken so that she can now hold them to ransom?'

Nash shrugged. 'It sounds a bit far-fetched to me, Anna.'

'Perhaps, but we shouldn't rule it out. After all, this wasn't a difficult crime to commit. All those blokes had to do was get inside the nursery and she made it bloody easy for them.'

Back at the community centre, Nash said he was satisfied that Anna had everything under control.

'I'll bring the Commissioner up to date and make sure you get everything you need,' he added. 'But before I go, I want to know that you're happy to remain at the helm of this one. I know the circumstances are close to your heart and I saw the news clip where the reporter put you on the spot earlier. It won't surprise me if the press continue to make a big thing of what happened to you. I can see the headlines now –

detective whose own daughter was kidnapped by her ex leads hunt for the nursery school kidnappers.'

'I can live with it, sir,' Anna said. 'And I guarantee that it won't be a distraction.'

Nash gave a stiff nod. 'And that's exactly what I intend to tell anyone who asks me if it's an issue, including those reporters out front. But if it does become one, then you need to tell me, Anna.'

'You'll be the first to know, sir, but please don't hold your breath.'

Nash grinned, showing white, even teeth. 'Just keep me updated,' he said. 'And rest assured that I've got your back.'

After Nash went off to speak to the media Anna went to find DI Walker. She told him to round up the team for a full briefing in the hall.

'I'll be along as soon as I've had another word with Sarah Ramsay,' she said.

CHAPTER THIRTEEN

Sarah Ramsay had opted to sit at one of the tables in the rear courtyard so that she could smoke. This suited Anna because it gave her the opportunity to have another one herself.

'I started smoking for the first time nine years ago when I was thirty-three,' Anna said as she took a seat opposite the nursery owner. 'It was a shame because I'd steered clear of them up until then, mainly because my dad died of lung cancer.'

'I began puffing on the buggers five years ago after my marriage ended,' Sarah said as smoke trailed languidly from her nostrils. 'Now I can't kick the habit no matter how hard I try. And days like this don't help.'

Anna took out her pack of Silk Cuts and plucked one from it. While lighting up, she studied the other woman. Sarah was sitting stiffly in the chair, her pert breasts thrust forward beneath her tight T-shirt. Anna now noticed that the words 'Peabody Nurseries' were printed just below the neckline of her polo shirt. It was the staff uniform, she realised, which was why the teachers were also wearing it.

The sun was still strong and bright but they were in the shade so it was bearable. Anna inhaled a lungful of smoke and said, 'So have you thought about those questions, Miss Ramsay? First I need to know the names of everyone who has access to the nursery, including part-time staff and cleaners.'

Sarah put her burning cigarette in the ashtray on the table and reached down to pick up a leather handbag that had been placed on the ground between her legs. From it she extracted a small notebook. She tore out a page and passed it to Anna.

'I've jotted down the names of all the staff here and at my other nurseries, both full- and part-timers,' she said. 'Only those staff based here can access this building. More details about them are in the office but I'm not able to get to them at the moment. I've also included the names of the local cleaning company we use and the firm that carries out maintenance work on all the buildings. Plus former staff going back six months. I'm not allowed to keep their details on file for any longer than that. I hope that's enough.'

'This is exactly what I wanted,' Anna said. 'In a moment I'll have someone accompany you back to your office to dig out the detailed paperwork.'

'A lot of it's on my computer so I'll have to print it off for you.'

'That won't be a problem. Now, we don't yet know what the motive is behind the abductions so I need to ask if it's possible that it was carried out by someone who wants to get back at you, or even the parents? Someone who holds a grudge for any reason or perhaps has made threats.'

Sarah picked her cigarette up, drew on it, and said, 'Well, there's only one person who fits that bill, inspector, and I've written his name and address below the others.'

Anna glanced at the sheet. The name 'JONAS PLATT' was written in capital letters and underlined.

'There was a tragic accident at my establishment in Lewisham early last year,' Sarah explained. 'Mr Platt's three-year-old daughter Kelly died after she choked on a grape. Mr Platt holds me personally responsible and ever since he's harassed me and even made threats. It got so bad that the court issued a restraining order against him and he's not allowed within two hundred yards of any of the nurseries.

'I'm not accusing him of being involved in what's happened today. He wasn't one of the three men. But he has been a source of great concern to me, my staff and the parents.'

'Has he made threats against them?'

She shook her head. 'He hasn't threatened them directly, but he has intimidated them. On five separate occasions he turned up at the Lewisham premises and stood outside with a placard accusing the staff of murdering his daughter. He also came here three times because it's where I'm based. He shouted at the parents and told them they were stupid to leave their children here. Plus, he went to the county council demanding that all my nurseries be closed down. The story was picked up by the local press and spread around on social media.'

'I gather you were given a hefty fine for gross negligence,' Anna said.

'That's right. It was totally unexpected and I felt that it was unfair because up until then our safety record had been impeccable. It was an unfortunate accident and we were all mortified. But I'm sure you'll agree that it's impossible to ensure that children don't ever get bits of food stuck in their throats.'

Sarah was shaking now and her breath was coming in

shallow gulps. At the same time, her eyes filmed over with tears and it seemed to Anna that the woman was on the verge of breaking down. It was the first time Anna had seen her lose her composure, but she managed to carry on speaking even though she struggled to form the words.

'So you can probably imagine how I feel right now,' she said. 'Everyone will blame me for what's happened.'

She started to sob then and Anna made sympathetic noises, but she had no intention of halting the interview. There were more questions she wanted to ask about Jonas Platt, the man who was now their one and only suspect.

'I'm sorry,' Sarah said after a time. 'This is all so terribly upsetting.'

'I can appreciate that, Miss Ramsay, so don't worry.'

Sarah blew her nose, wiped her eyes, pushed back her fringe.

'Please carry on, inspector,' she said. 'That won't happen again.'

Anna asked her to be more specific about the threats she'd received from Jonas Platt.

Sarah scrunched up her brow. 'A week after his daughter's funeral he waited outside the nursery here for me to close up. He then confronted me on the forecourt and I thought he was going to attack me. Instead, he poked a finger at me and said he would make me suffer for what had happened to Kelly. I was reminded of it earlier when Ruth had a go at me. I expect I'm now in for a lot more of that.'

'And what other threats were there?'

Sarah leaned forward, resting her arms on the table.

'Just after I got handed the fine he actually turned up at my home,' she said. 'It's within walking distance of here and

I didn't know if he'd followed me there. I opened the door without knowing it was him and he was verbally abusive. He called me a murdering slut. He was livid that the Peabody Nurseries weren't being forced to close and said that three hundred thousand pounds wasn't enough of a punishment. I slammed the door on him and phoned the police, but he was gone before they arrived.'

'Do you live alone, Miss Ramsay?'

'I do. I don't have family in London and there's been no man in my life for some time so I had to deal with it by myself and it really freaked me out.'

'Tell me about Mr Platt,' Anna said. 'What was he like before his daughter died?'

She shrugged. 'I never met the man because whenever I dropped in on Lewisham he wasn't there. I did meet his wife Angela a couple of times, though. She's a nice lady. But I gather they split up six months after Kelly's death. He's now living on his own in a flat in Kennington.'

'Any idea what he does for a living?'

'He used to be a builder, but the last I heard he was out of work having lost his job. I did hear that he has a criminal record. I don't know if it's true, though. One of the mothers whose son attended Lewisham mentioned it.'

Anna looked at her watch, anxious now to get the word out on Jonas Platt. They needed to find him pronto in order to determine whether or not he was implicated. On the face of it he was an extremely strong suspect. Not only did he have a motive for doing harm to Sarah and her business, but he also sounded pretty unstable. Was it therefore possible that he had managed to get a team together to carry out the kidnappings on his behalf?

'Look, you've been really helpful, Miss Ramsay,' Anna said. 'I do have more questions I'd like to ask you but they can wait. Right now I need to pass on the information you've given me. I'll find an officer to go with you to get the detailed paperwork on the staff, then we can arrange for you to be accompanied to your home. If you wouldn't mind staying there at least for the rest of the day I'd appreciate it.'

'Of course,' she said. 'I want to be as helpful as I can, inspector. If I'd been more careful this morning none of this would have happened. I don't think I will ever be able to forgive myself for all the pain I've caused. I just pray that those children are found safe and well.'

Anna didn't have a ready reply so she didn't try to come up with one. Instead, she got up and went back inside the community centre where she told a detective to go with Sarah to her office for the paperwork she'd mentioned.

CHAPTER FOURTEEN

The room was filled with tension and misery, and Ruth was aching to walk out. But if she did the only place to go would be home and that would be even worse.

The other parents were clearly just as restless and frustrated. Kenneth Tenant kept pacing the floor and telling everyone that he regretted putting his trust in Sarah Ramsay after what had happened to the Platt girl. The rest of them sat at the tables sobbing into their hands, speaking into their phones or sending and receiving messages on them. Ruth had received a text from Howard Browning asking why she'd stood him up. Her response was brief and to the point.

My son's been kidnapped.

Nothing had happened since Detective Tate had spoken to them, except that they'd been served teas and coffees and bottles of water. And a bunch of family liaison officers had come to sit with them, as if that would make the waiting more bearable.

But waiting was the only option open to them, and as the clock ticked a stream of tortured thoughts tore through Ruth's mind. She wanted to believe that the people who had taken Liam wouldn't hurt him. But she knew that it could well be their intention. Perhaps it had already begun and her baby was now being abused by one or more of the sick bastards.

She tried and failed to shut out the image of him crying for his mummy and it caused a sob to explode in her throat.

'Drink some more tea,' Ethan said, as he reached across the table to take her hand. 'And try to stay positive.'

That was exactly what Detective Tate had told her. And the FLOs were dishing out the same advice to the other parents. But it was a stupid thing to say because how the fuck could they stay positive when there was nothing to suggest that this day would end happily?

She was surprised that Ethan was managing to stay so calm. It was almost as if the reality of the situation hadn't yet hit him. After breaking down earlier he had managed to seize control of his emotions. His voice was laced with despair, but he was one of the few still able to speak without losing it.

He had asked one of the officers to go and check if the bag containing Liam's medicines was still in the kitchen. When he was told that it was he'd put his arms around Ruth and held her so tight that for several seconds she couldn't breathe.

Now he was sitting opposite her, his face washed out and pale. Whenever Kenneth Tenant walked past him he stiffened and Ruth knew that he was showing great restraint in not giving the man a piece of his mind.

What Tenant had said earlier about Liam had been uncalled for and it had made Ruth's blood boil. But it wasn't the first time he'd made it known that he wasn't happy that Liam was attending the nursery. He'd first aired his views a couple of months ago. Ethan had arrived at the nursery to pick Liam up, as he often did, and he noticed that Tenant's daughter Grace had a really bad cold and was coughing and sneezing and spreading germs like wildfire.

He had approached her parents, who were both there, and asked them politely not to let Grace return to the nursery until she was better so that Liam wouldn't catch what she had, which for him could be very serious. Tenant had blown a fuse and had told Ethan that Liam was the one who shouldn't be attending the nursery if he was so ill. He said Liam required too much attention and mistakenly claimed that cystic fibrosis was contagious and that the other kids were being put at risk.

Ethan had hit back, saying that Liam was well enough to be there and that the staff and parents simply needed to be mindful of his condition and take precautions. To her credit, Sarah Ramsay had made a point of telling Tenant that Liam was welcome at the Peabody Nursery, and that if he had a problem with it then he should take Grace elsewhere. But he'd decided not to.

Ethan's and Tenant's paths had crossed only twice since then and they had pointedly ignored each other on both occasions. But today Tenant had had to go and open his big, ugly mouth.

'Please just ignore the creep,' Ruth said when she saw that Tenant had spotted Ethan watching him. 'The last thing any of us wants is the two of you coming to blows.'

Ethan gave a barely perceptible nod and wrenched his eyes away from Tenant. He then looked through the window to see what was going on outside.

There were even more coppers in front of the community centre now, a mix of suits and uniforms and white forensic gear. From where Ruth was sitting she could see the nursery forecourt next door and that too was a hive of activity.

It didn't seem possible that only a few hours ago the place had been deserted. From talking to the others she'd learned that she'd been the last person to drop a child off. But she hadn't been alone in spotting the minibus outside. Both Belinda Neville and Laura Tenant had also seen the vehicle, but like Ruth they'd thought nothing of it.

Ruth was reassured by the fact that the police seemed to be fully mobilised and were throwing everything into the investigation. She'd been told that the detectives were now gathering in the hall where Anna Tate was going to tell them what needed to be done.

The DCI had made an impression on Ruth and she was confident that she would put her all into finding the children. She was also glad that the detective had faced down Kenneth Tenant. It was outrageous of him to call her leadership into question and to Ruth his pathetic apology had come across as hollow and insincere.

But when he'd brought up the woman's own tragic past Ruth had realised why the detective's face was familiar. She'd seen it before, most recently on the front page of the magazine that Ethan got with his Sunday paper.

In an interview spread across two inside pages, Tate had described how she'd never given up searching for the daughter who was abducted a decade ago by the ex-husband. It was a heart-breaking story and one that showed what a strong and tenacious woman Anna Tate was.

Ruth just hoped that the detective was now able to draw on that strength and tenacity in the search for Liam and his eight little friends.

And that this time her efforts would prove more successful.

CHAPTER FIFTEEN

Normally when Anna briefed her team there were about twenty officers in attendance. Today, there were twice that many, and included MIT detectives, support staff, uniforms, SOCOs and media liaison personnel from the Yard.

'OK, listen up everyone,' she said as she stood between the rows of seats and the makeshift stage at one end of the hall. 'I'm going to start by stating the bloody obvious – that this investigation now has priority over everything else. The lives of nine small children are at stake and the eyes of the world are on us. Therefore all leave is suspended and you'll be expected to work your socks off until the kids are found.'

There were no dissenting voices or shaking of heads, but Anna hadn't expected there to be.

'You all know by now what happened in the nursery next door earlier this morning,' she said. 'Three men turned up armed with pistols which we have to assume were real. They locked the four female staff in the storeroom and one of them, Tasha Norris, was attacked when she tried to fight back. She's now in a serious condition in hospital. The men then got the children to follow them outside and onto a minibus. A witness has told us that there was a fourth gang member, a young woman, waiting on the bus.

'I can confirm that the vehicle in question has now been picked up on two traffic cameras as it headed southwards from here.

'Meanwhile, I've spoken to most of the parents and they're all naturally very upset. But they need to be interviewed individually and in couples. We have to find out as much as we can about them and the children. I want their phone records checked and I want to know if any of them have form. But this must be done sensitively. These people are emotionally raw, but we've got to rule them out as suspects as fast as we can.

'We now have a list of everyone who has access to the nursery, including staff who weren't in today and cleaners. I've given it to DI Baines who will make arrangements for them all to be spoken to.'

Anna paused there to let it all sink in and to consult her notes. She then went on to say that e-fits of the three men were being prepared and would be circulated, and that the names they gave to the staff did not belong to anyone based at the CID office in Rotherhithe.

'My gut tells me that these blokes are not terrorists,' she said. 'But they're obviously ruthless and well organised. At this stage we can only speculate as to why they've done this.

'On the forensic side we're continuing to sweep the nursery in the hope that they touched something and left a mark. But, to be honest, I'm not holding out any hope of a breakthrough there.'

Anna then made a specific point of mentioning Liam Brady and explained that he had cystic fibrosis.

'This is a life-threatening condition,' she said. 'In order to stay alive the poor boy needs regular medication and physiotherapy. I've told the media office to put out an appeal in order to alert the kidnappers to this. We're pleading with them to drop Liam off at a hospital or pharmacy but it's probably too much to expect them to do so.'

Anna's phone buzzed then to indicate an incoming text message. She took it from her pocket and read it. Then she held it up and said, 'Before coming into the hall I asked DC Sweeny to check out a name for me. The name is Jonas Platt and he's now our first suspect. He's a person of interest because he's nursing a bitter grudge against Sarah Ramsay and her chain of nurseries.'

Anna told the team what happened to Platt's daughter and that he blamed Sarah Ramsay.

'He's made threats against her and a court issued a restraining order against him so he's not allowed near the nurseries,' she said. 'He wasn't one of the three men who took the children, but that doesn't mean he's not involved. DC Sweeny has just carried out a criminal records check and discovered that Mr Platt is known to us. Seven years ago he was banged up for fifteen months for assaulting a man in a pub. And before that he did a spell of community service for drug offences. So I want him brought in asap.'

Anna cast her eyes around the room and pointed to a young sallow-faced detective with spiky and quiffed brown hair.

'Get your skates on, Detective Prebble, and go and find the guy,' she said. 'Take Detective Crawford with you. Sweeny has got all his details, including his address.'

As Prebble and Crawford rushed out of the hall, Anna asked another detective, DI Bellingham, to dig up what he could on Sarah Ramsay.

'We should treat the nursery owner as a suspect as well as a victim,' she said. 'Miss Ramsay is the person who allowed the men onto the premises, which she now admits was a ghastly error of judgement. But perhaps it wasn't. It seems the gang knew what to expect when they entered the building, which means that a member of staff, or Miss Ramsay herself, might well have provided them with information.'

A uniformed officer who Anna didn't recognise raised his hand. 'But what possible motive would she have for abducting kids from her own nursery?' he asked.

'That's a very good question, officer,' she replied. 'But until we know why the children were taken I can't possibly answer it.'

For the next fifteen minutes they discussed possible motives – that the gang planned to sell the children to sex traffickers, that the kids were going to be farmed out to a network of paedophiles, or that they could be used to extract a very large ransom from the parents and the authorities. All three were unfortunately completely credible scenarios.

In this day and age crimes involving children, or groups of children, were all too common. According to the latest statistics that Anna had seen, well over two million children fell victim each year to sex traffickers across the globe.

'I'm actually surprised that it's taken so long for a crime like this to be committed in the UK,' she said. 'Nurseries are vulnerable places and therefore soft targets. They all have different levels of security but I guarantee that there are very few, if any, that could keep out a determined bunch of armed men.'

Earlier she had asked Jessica Moody, one of the support staff, to do some online research into previous attacks on nursery schools around the world. She now invited Moody to talk about what she'd found.

The woman read from her notes and what she had to say came as a surprise to most of the people in the hall, including Anna.

'In recent years there have been attacks on nursery schools in France, Luxembourg, Norway, Belgium, India, Tunisia and the US,' she said. 'Most involved children being taken hostage by men with shooters. In Luxembourg a lone gunman held twenty-eight children captive before he was shot by police. In India a five-year-old boy was snatched from a nursery and later beheaded by his kidnapper.

'And only last year our own intelligence services issued a warning that ISIS were planning imminent attacks on Jewish nurseries across Europe. As a point of interest there are over three thousand nursery schools in the UK.'

Moody finished reading from her notes and handed back to Anna. The briefing continued with updates from the crime scene manager, the media liaison people and those detectives with something to report.

The meeting was told that all but one of the parents of the nine children had now been contacted. The only one officers hadn't been able to track down was Simone Green's dad, Phil Green. His ex-wife Wendy was here in the community centre and she didn't know where he was.

'She says she's been trying to ring her ex to tell him what's happened but he hasn't answered his phone,' said the PC who'd been monitoring progress on that front. 'But she's not surprised because the couple only recently got divorced and were involved in an acrimonious custody battle relating to Simone. She got sole custody and he was furious, apparently.'

Anna's ears pricked up. How many times, she wondered, had bitter divorces and custody battles resulted in a husband or wife abducting their own child or children? Her own sad story was a case in point.

'This is something that needs to be followed up right away,' she said. 'Run down this Phil Green and talk to his wife again. Find out how bad things are between them and if she thinks it's conceivable he could have organised this to get back at her. And check with Sarah Ramsay and the teachers. I'm assuming he wasn't one of the three kidnappers, otherwise they would have said. Unless, of course, they've never met the man, in which case get a photo from his wife and show it to them.'

Anna acknowledged that they were clutching at straws and that Phil Green probably had nothing to do with the abductions.

'But at this stage every lead, however tenuous, needs to be pursued,' she said.

There followed further discussion and Anna handed out more assignments. She asked two detectives to trawl through the names on the various watch lists maintained by the Met and MI5.

'Whilst I don't believe terrorists are responsible, I want every person of interest checked out along with key members of organised gangs,' she said. 'And compare photos with the e-fits that have been put together with the help of the staff. It's a mammoth task, I know, so let's get cracking on it straight away.'

She then brought the briefing to an end by saying they

would use the community centre as their base of operations at least until tomorrow, so long as the management didn't have a problem with that.

'With luck the kids will be back with their parents by then anyway and we can wrap up and go back to Wandsworth,' she said.

As the team began to disperse she received another text message on her phone, which she was still holding. As she read it a glimmer of hope blossomed in her chest.

'Hold up everyone,' she called out. 'There's been a development. A guy just phoned in to say he drove past a grey minibus with tinted windows a short time ago. It was parked next to a field in Kent.'

CHAPTER SIXTEEN

Before leaving the community centre, Anna and Walker grabbed a takeaway sandwich and coffee from the cafeteria. As usual, Anna had skipped breakfast so by now she was starving.

Walker drove the pool car again with Anna in the front passenger seat. This time they headed south out of London as part of a fleet of speeding police vehicles.

It was the middle of the afternoon so traffic was relatively light. The minibus was apparently parked near the Kent village of Farningham. Or at least it had been two hours ago when it was spotted by the man who drove past it in his car. He hadn't realised the police were looking for it until after he got home and saw it on the news. But according to the emergency operator who took his call, he was a hundred per cent certain that it was the same vehicle.

Anna was still waiting for confirmation from Kent police who had dispatched a patrol to the scene and were expecting it to arrive there at any minute.

Farningham was about twenty miles from Rotherhithe, just outside the Greater London perimeter. The route could not have been more straightforward. The A20 road took them right there as it ran through outer London and past the towns of Sidcup and Swanley.

Anna knew Farningham well because for five years as a child she'd lived in the neighbouring village of Eynsford. That was before her grandmother had died, leaving her house in Tooting to her only son, Anna's dad. He had decided they should up sticks as a family and move there. It meant they could sell the bungalow in Eynsford and be mortgage-free.

So Anna had fond memories of Farningham, where her parents had sometimes taken her for pub lunches and to feed the ducks on the River Darent which ran through it.

After Chloe was born she and Matthew had actually discussed the possibility of perhaps moving there one day. They'd both agreed that it offered a better and safer environment in which to bring up a child. Anna had even gone to the trouble of perusing job vacancies at Kent police headquarters in nearby Maidstone.

But they never took it further because those first two years with Chloe at the house in Vauxhall flew by and there were so many other things to occupy their minds.

Anna had often wondered what would have happened if they had taken the plunge back then. Would Matthew have stayed faithful? Would she have been able to see her daughter grow from a toddler into a beautiful little girl?

She would never know, of course, and just thinking about it brought a hard lump to her throat.

*

Before they arrived at the scene they received word that it was indeed the minibus they'd been looking for. It was the same one picked up on CCTV earlier and the registration plates matched.

That was the good news. The bad news was that it had been abandoned and there was no sign of the children.

The spot was just half a mile south of the village along a little used lane. The minibus was parked on a large gravel layby a few yards back from a high hedge. A field lay beyond the hedge and there were woods across the road. No properties were visible in any direction.

There were already two patrol cars there so Walker pulled the pool car onto a grass verge opposite, which left just enough room for vehicles to move along the lane.

Anna's heartbeat quickened at the sight of the minibus and she was out of the car before Walker had switched off the engine.

She took out her warrant card and waved it at the two uniforms who were standing between their patrol cars and the bus. They'd been forewarned that MIT was on the way and instructed not to enter the bus if it was empty so as not to contaminate possible evidence.

'I'm DCI Anna Tate,' she told them. 'I'm with DI Max Walker. I see the door is open on the bus. Was it like that when you arrived?'

One of them shook his head and said, 'I opened it myself to check that there was nobody inside. But I used gloves and didn't go on board.'

'How long have you been here?'

'Twenty minutes or so. Two of our colleagues are having a look around. One went off across the field and the other into the woods. But so far they haven't seen any children or adults acting suspiciously.'

'And I very much doubt that they will,' Anna said. 'The kidnappers probably came here just so that they could transfer the kids to another vehicle.'

The officer nodded. 'And from here you can drive for miles without coming across a traffic camera. There are lots of minor roads that bypass all the villages and towns.'

'A forensic team will be here soon,' Anna said. 'So I'd like you to move your vehicles onto the road. They'll need to check every inch of this layby.'

Walker came up behind her and handed her a pair of latex gloves.

'We'd better have a look inside,' he said.

Anna snapped on the gloves, but before stepping onto the minibus she walked around it and Walker followed.

'I'm guessing they were moved onto another minibus or van,' she said. 'And it was either waiting here for a while beforehand or it arrived about the same time they did.'

'So if we're very, very lucky someone local will have spotted it,' Walker said. 'Just like the guy who noticed this one. On a quiet road like this any stationary vehicle is likely to stand out and attract attention.'

'We'll send some uniforms into the village,' Anna said. 'And we'll need to sound out those people who live in houses off the beaten track.'

They'd now arrived back at the minibus's sliding door. Anna stepped on board, and the first thing that struck her was how large the interior was. There were ten leather seats arranged in pairs along one side and singles along the other, plus a row of four across the back. It was plenty big enough to accommodate nine children and four adults.

The second thing that Anna spotted was a box of disposable gloves resting on the dashboard. It had been opened and some of the gloves had been removed.

'I think we can safely assume that the bastards won't have left any prints behind,' she said.

'But they did leave something,' Walker observed, pointing to a sheet of paper lying on the driver's seat.

They could see there was writing on it so Anna reached down and carefully picked it up between forefinger and thumb.

Seven words had been scribbled on it in black felt-tip pen and they sent a chill along Anna's spine.

THE KIDS HAVE NOT BEEN HARMED – YET

CHAPTER SEVENTEEN

Seventy-five minutes. That was how long it took for the flutter of hope to take flight.

The parents had been told that the minibus had been found just outside the village of Farningham in Kent. But now they were being informed that the children weren't on it. It was a bitter blow and it filled Ruth with a heart-stopping dread.

Detective Tate had rushed to the spot and had relayed the information back to her team in the community centre. She said she believed the children had been transferred to another minibus before being taken elsewhere.

So the nightmare wasn't over for the mothers and fathers who were now venting their shock and disappointment in different ways. Rebecca Chandler and Melek Ahmed were crying hysterically. Belinda Neville just sat in her chair shaking her head, her mouth open in a silent, anguished scream. And Kenneth Tenant was stomping around the room in a murderous rage, telling everyone that if he ever got his hands on the kidnappers he would slit their throats and cut out their tongues.

Ethan could not keep still either and he'd spent much of the past seventy-five minutes outside in the centre's courtyard speaking on the phone to his parents, his boss and several of his work colleagues who had rung to see what was going on.

He was now back at the table drumming his fingers nervously on the surface while tapping his shoes on the wooden floorboards.

The police, meanwhile, decided it was time the parents went home. They'd all been interviewed and had provided their personal details. Most had also emailed across photos and videos of their children from their phones. Detectives had said that the more images of the kids they had the better.

'We're not expecting there to be any further developments in the short term,' they were told by a senior detective named Paul Willis. 'We strongly advise that you head back to your respective homes, where a family liaison officer will stay with each of you overnight. You won't need to provide them with beds; they'll simply be on hand to offer support and to keep you updated on how the investigation is progressing.'

Ruth gave her car key fob to a detective who said he would arrange for her car to be picked up and driven to their home. She and Ethan were then taken to Bermondsey in a car belonging to the family liaison officer who had been assigned to them.

Her name was Tammy Robinson and Ruth guessed she was in her late thirties. She was wearing a white blouse over grey trousers and her hair was swept back in a knot that emphasised her pale, round face.

As soon as Ruth walked through their front door she felt a crushing sensation in her chest and broke down in tears.

Ethan put an arm around her waist and steered her towards

the living room while Robinson said she would find the kitchen and put the kettle on.

Just being in the house intensified the pain Ruth was feeling, and it caused dark shadows to form in her mind. This morning the rooms had echoed to the sounds of Liam's shrill laughter. But now the silence was heavy and oppressive and it engulfed her like a thick, malevolent fog.

She shivered as Ethan led her to the sofa and sat her down. He picked up a box of tissues from the coffee table and placed them on her lap.

'The police gave me the number of a doctor we can call out to give you a sedative or something,' he said. 'Do you want me to ring him?'

She shook her head. 'Nothing like that will help. And I need to stay awake in case there's news.'

She lifted her head to look at him and hot tears cascaded down her cheeks.

'Liam hasn't had his medication since before I took him out this morning,' she said. 'He must be in a terrible state by now and he can only get worse.'

Ethan just stared down at her, his expression unreadable, his lips pressed into a thin line. After a beat he started to say something but then changed his mind and stepped away from her. He went and sat in the armchair next to the sofa and used the remote control to switch on the TV.

Ruth could tell from his body language that he was still angry with her for not taking Liam to the Shrek Adventure. If she had, then their son would be here with them now. It was a cross she was going to have to bear, no matter how this ended.

But she knew that Ethan would also be feeling responsible

and it was tearing him up inside. After all, it was Ethan who had talked Ruth into letting Liam go to nursery school despite his cystic fibrosis. And it was Ethan who'd insisted they shouldn't give into pressure from people like Kenneth Tenant and take him out again.

Ethan worshipped his son and had never really forgiven himself for the fact that he and Ruth had passed on the faulty gene that had caused his illness. So Ruth could imagine how he too was being ravaged by guilt and trying desperately not to show it.

The sound of the television bled into her thoughts and her eyes were drawn to the big screen in the corner.

Ethan had tuned into Sky News and there was only one story dominating the agenda – the abduction of nine children from a nursery in South London by three armed men and a woman.

They were showing footage from the scene, which included exterior shots of the nursery and the crowd that had gathered in Peabody Street. There was a short CCTV sequence of the minibus as it was driven through Deptford on its way to Kent. And it looked exactly like the bus that Ruth had seen parked outside the nursery.

The report also included the short statement that Detective Tate had made to the cameras early on and it was followed by an update from a DCS Nash. Then came a mention of the nursery teacher Tasha Norris. According to the hospital her condition was critical but stable.

The reporter went on to name all nine children and showed their photographs, the ones that were in the nursery files. Liam's was the last photo to be put up and the reporter explained that he suffered from cystic fibrosis and that without his medication he was likely to become seriously ill very quickly.

Ethan reacted to this by shaking his head and getting to his feet. He turned to Ruth and fixed her with a long, steady stare.

'This shouldn't be happening to us,' he said. 'All you had to do was arrange to meet that bloke another time. Then you could have spent the day with your son. It would have been so fucking easy.'

With that he turned sharply and strode out of the room, brushing shoulders with Officer Robinson who was about to enter from the hall with two mugs of tea in her hand.

'Where are you going?' Ruth called after him.

'Out for a walk,' he yelled back. 'I need some fresh air.'

A second later the front door was slammed shut and Ruth dropped her face into her hands and started to cry again.

CHAPTER EIGHTEEN

'We've found something that could be significant,' said a suited-up forensic technician.

He was holding a clear plastic evidence bag for Anna to see. Inside was a half-smoked cigarette.

'It was found on the edge of the layby just a couple of feet in from the road,' he said. 'It's in pretty good nick for a discarded fag butt, which tells me it hasn't been here very long. Hours rather than days.'

'It could have been flicked from the window of a passing car,' DI Walker said.

Anna's eyes widened. 'Or it might have been dropped by someone who was waiting here for the minibus to turn up.'

Walker nodded. 'That's possible of course.'

Anna instructed the officer to get it checked for DNA. 'And tell the lab it has priority over everything else,' she said.

'Will do, ma'am.'

Anna had decided to stay on in Kent while the SOCOs

processed the scene and this was the first possible piece of evidence they had come across.

The minibus was still being examined for fingerprints, but nothing had been found so far to indicate that nine children had been on board – except for the note.

THE KIDS HAVE NOT BEEN HARMED – YET

It was a sinister and unnerving threat and one that Anna had decided to keep from the parents for the time being. It was hardly likely to provide any comfort in the circumstances and she saw no reason to pile on the agony for them.

The note suggested to Anna that the kidnappers would be in touch again – otherwise why bother to leave it? And if that was their intention, then it raised a whole bunch of new questions, none of which she could answer right now.

Having spent several hours at the layby, she told Walker that it was time to go. During that time the uniforms had canvassed people in the village and carried out a search of the area around the layby. But nothing had come of it.

TV crews had turned up along with a couple of newspaper hacks. Anna had answered a few of their questions and made another public appeal for information.

There was nothing more she could do here and darkness was encroaching fast. She told Walker to take her back to Wandsworth so she could pick up her car from the station. On the way she spoke to Sweeny in the mobile incident van at the community centre. The detective constable had been appointed the conduit for all updates. But there weren't many. Phil Green and Jonas Platt – the two fathers Anna wanted to speak to – still hadn't been tracked down.

There were no surprises so far from the forensic sweep of the nursery, and the e-fits of the three kidnappers had been produced and were in circulation. Sweeny said she would send the images to Anna's phone.

Background checks on the parents and staff were still being carried out and the parents had all returned to their homes.

Sweeny listed the names of the detectives who'd be on shift through the night and Anna told her to let it be known that the morning briefing would be held at seven sharp in the office.

'But I want to maintain a presence in Peabody Street so we leave the MIV there and you can station yourself there again after the briefing,' Anna said. 'Until then go home and try to get some sleep.'

Anna would have been prepared to work all night but she knew from experience that it was never a sensible thing to do. She had to be firing on all cylinders if she was going to be an effective team leader.

Already her eyes were weighted with fatigue and she was finding it harder to concentrate. She needed to recharge her batteries with a few hours' sleep.

But going home made her feel guilty because nine children were still at the mercy of four ruthless perps whose intentions were unknown.

By now they would surely be terrified and tearful and pining for their parents. And at least one of them – poor little Liam Brady – might well be struggling to survive without the medication needed to control his illness.

As she drove down to Vauxhall, Anna told herself that she would do everything in her power to save those children. She knew that if she failed them she would find it hard to deal with the consequences. Losing Chloe had almost destroyed her. If she wasn't able to reunite these poor little ones with their parents then it would add to the crushing weight of guilt that had been with her for the past ten years – ever since the night she arrived home and her mother told her that Matthew hadn't brought Chloe back.

CHAPTER NINETEEN

July 2009

'He was taking her to his sister's birthday party,' Anna said, as she stepped past her mum into the house. 'He's probably just stuck in traffic.'

Anna clung desperately to that possibility for the next couple of hours. That was how long it took her to conclude that the reason he hadn't yet turned up with their daughter was far more sinister.

First she discovered that Matthew's phone had been switched off and was no longer transmitting a signal. Then, from speaking to his sister, she found out that there hadn't been a birthday party and that Matthew had lied.

'I last spoke to him three nights ago,' his sister said, and Anna knew immediately that she was telling the truth. 'He told me he was moving abroad to start a new life with the money our mother left us. I haven't seen him or heard from him since then. He didn't mention Chloe.'

Anna had driven over to Matthew's flat where she learned that he had packed up and left, telling the landlord that he wouldn't be returning.

It was then that she raised the alarm and informed her colleagues in the Met that she feared her daughter was the victim of a parental abduction. An alert went out to ports and airports and Anna herself posted urgent appeals on Twitter and Facebook. She also contacted every one of Matthew's friends but all of them said they had no idea where he was, though she soon learned that he had packed in his job and sold his car.

Anna didn't even try to sleep that night; she paced the house, certain that if she thought hard enough, she might come up with an idea of where he'd taken Chloe. The following morning, she received a text on her phone from an unidentified number. The message was short, cruel and devastating.

You won't let us be a family again because I made a stupid mistake. So I'm starting my life afresh with my lovely daughter. Don't bother trying to find us because you never will. You have yourself to blame, Anna. You should have known that I wouldn't let you have a happy life if I couldn't be a part of it . . . M

CHAPTER TWENTY

She wasn't expecting Tom to be there when she arrived home. But he was and she was pleased.

'I know I told you that I was planning to stay in the flat tonight,' he said when he opened the door as she approached it. 'But I decided to come over and keep you company after I saw the news and realised that you've had the day from hell.'

'And I'm so glad you did,' she said. 'You can help me to wind down.'

He took her in his arms and gave her a tender kiss on the lips. As always, it made her feel loved and wanted and special.

'I've made you a sandwich,' he said. 'It's your favourite. Cheese, ham, pickle. And I opened a bottle of wine.'

Anna was always impressed at how thoughtful Tom Bannerman was. It was one of his most endearing qualities, and in that respect he presented a striking contrast to her ex-husband, who had tended to be pretty selfish and thoughtless for much of the time they were together.

But that wasn't the only difference between the two men.

Matthew was five six tall, white, and even before they met fifteen years ago he'd lost most of his hair. Back then he worked as a financial controller for a large catering company. He was mad about football, had the Chelsea logo tattooed on his chest, and his ambition was to one day move to Spain and run a beach bar.

Tom, on the other hand, was just over six feet tall, black, with thick, tightly curled hair that was greying at the temples. They'd met at the gym and there'd been chemistry between them from the start. Like Anna, Tom was divorced, and he had a nineteen-year-old daughter at university in Portsmouth. He had a cheerful disposition, and the hard, lean body of a much younger man.

He hated football and had been a council social worker for seventeen years, and it seemed his main ambition was to live with his girlfriend. And that was what they'd had an intense discussion about last night. The lease on his flat would soon expire and he was keen to move in with her. He'd actually been on about it for ages.

But for Anna the existing arrangement worked well. She still had a degree of independence but could spend time with Tom whenever she wanted. She loved being with him, and he clearly enjoyed being with her in spite of her mood swings and the distance she sometimes put between them on those occasions when she should have been celebrating milestones in Chloe's life such as birthdays and Christmases.

She was in no doubt that he was good for her. Indeed, he had helped her to reignite the spark of life that had been extinguished a decade ago. What's more, Tom was good-looking, charming and trustworthy, and he lived in a rented flat just a mile from her own terraced house in Vauxhall.

So she could understand his frustration, especially given that he was five years older than her at forty-seven and anxious to take the next big step in their relationship. And last evening she'd come close to telling him that she was ready, too. But instead she'd told him that she would think about it, and the crushed look on his face had made her feel terrible.

She didn't want to lose Tom, and it would tear her apart if he walked away. But she feared that if they lived together, and perhaps even got married, then her preoccupation with finding her daughter would eventually come between them. It had scuppered her last relationship with a man who'd been driven to distraction by what he called her 'unhealthy obsession'.

So far it hadn't been a problem with Tom because she'd had her own space. On those nights and weekends when she wasn't working or with him she could spend however long she wanted on the internet in what some of her friends and colleagues regarded as a futile attempt to trace Chloe.

But it didn't matter to her what people thought. There was no way she could ever give up searching, even if it did put an unbearable strain on her relationships.

Ten years on, the pain was still acute. It was with her every minute of every day. Work provided a refuge but there was no escape. Her daughter was always there, in her thoughts, in her dreams, in her prayers . . .

Tom poured her a glass of wine and sat opposite her at the table while she nibbled on the sandwich and told him about her day. He was a good listener and his warm brown eyes never left her face.

After she'd eaten, he poured two more glasses of wine and they went out onto the patio to have a smoke. He had one of his small cigars and she lit up a cigarette.

It was a mild night and the moon sat full and heavy in a cloudless sky.

'I can't stop thinking of those children,' Anna said. 'The poor little mites must be so scared.'

'Does it bother you that parts of the media are making a big thing of your own situation?' Tom asked her.

She shrugged. 'A bit, I suppose. But I guess it was inevitable. I just have to stay focused.'

It was ten o'clock when they came back in. Tom offered to clean up the kitchen while she got ready for bed.

She decided to shower in the morning and after brushing her teeth she stood naked in front of the mirror and exhaled an audible sigh.

Her reflection was not kind. She'd put on weight since she'd stopped going to the gym regularly. Her tummy was no longer flat and she'd lost muscle tissue on the arms and thighs. Her eyes were drawn to the caesarean section scar which served as a constant reminder of where Chloe had entered the world.

Anna remembered that day as though it were yesterday. But it was twelve years ago and for her the world had been a very different place then.

Matthew had captured the moment the nurse had placed Chloe in her arms. The photo was in a frame on her dressing table. She'd put it there so that it would be the last thing she looked at before she went to bed at night and the first thing she saw when she woke up in the morning.

She slipped on her towelling robe and told Tom she was going to check her emails before turning in.

He smiled. 'I'll wait up for you.'

He knew she would be a while because she always did more than just check her emails. She would also check the

113

social media sites dedicated to finding missing people. Chloe's name and photos – including the age-progression picture – were on every one of them.

There were also the sites she had set up herself – notably the FindChloe website and Facebook page, plus the dedicated Twitter account. Unfortunately there was little activity these days because after so long people had lost interest. Only the most high-profile cases – such as that of three-year-old Madeleine McCann, who'd been snatched from a holiday apartment in Portugal in 2007 – continued to attract attention for years afterwards.

But the Chloe sites had generated hundreds of responses ranging from possible sightings to claims from people who said they knew where Chloe and her father were living.

Anna had done her best to follow up every lead and had spent a small fortune employing a private investigator named Jack Keen to help her. But nothing had ever come of it, and it was as though Matthew and Chloe had disappeared into thin air.

Anna strongly suspected that her ex had taken her abroad, which was what he'd told his sister he was going to do. Spain was the most likely country since he'd worked there for a time in his early twenties and had always said he wanted to return. He even had a basic grasp of the language.

Anna had used her police contacts – including a friend who worked for Interpol – to try to trace them, but without success.

Until her death in a road accident four years ago, Matthew's sister Charlotte had always insisted that she had no idea where they were. And she managed to convince Anna that she was telling the truth. Anna went to Charlotte's funeral in the hope that Matthew would turn up; she had been his only sibling, and as both his parents were dead, he had no other family. But he didn't. Although she hadn't really expected him to, it still came as a bitter blow. And it had served to increase her fears that something might have happened to him. Or to both him and Chloe. After all, it was hard to believe that he had done such a good job of covering his tracks for so long.

Anna's study was at the front of the house overlooking the road. It had been Chloe's bedroom during the two years she lived in the house but seven years ago Anna had moved the cot and all the baby stuff into the loft and replaced them with a desk, chair and computer.

She'd covered the walls with photos of Chloe but not those that included Matthew. The age-progression photo had pride of place on the wall above the desk. Anna couldn't know, of course, if Chloe would resemble the young girl in the picture. But she hoped so because the face was soft and open and gorgeous.

As soon as Anna sat at her desk the walls closed in on her and the photos took her back in time. There was Chloe wrapped in a blanket in the hospital shortly after she was born. Chloe in her high chair with her face covered in yoghurt. Chloe crawling across the living room floor. Chloe taking her first steps in the garden. Chloe surrounded by her Christmas presents only months before she was taken.

Before long Anna could feel the throb of tears behind her eyes and she fought to hold them in.

Just concentrate, she told herself. Tonight you need to get to bed at a reasonable hour because tomorrow is going to be a tough day.

It didn't take her long to get through the routine of checking the various sites. And as usual she typed the names of Chloe and her father into Google in the hope that it might throw something up. But it didn't.

Finally, she opened up her FindChloe Facebook page and saw that there were no new posts. But to her surprise there was a private message, the first she'd received in ages, and it had been sent only a few hours ago.

When she opened it up her heart leapt into her throat.

I saw you on the news today and I was reminded of something. So call me because I have information about your daughter and her father.

There was a mobile number below the message and within seconds Anna was ringing it from the landline on her desk. But it didn't go through because the phone was switched off. She was offered the opportunity to leave a voicemail.

'This is Anna Tate,' she said. 'You left a message on my FindChloe Facebook page. If you're serious then please ring me.'

She left her mobile number and then went on to write what she'd just said as a reply to the message.

After that she sat there for a while with her eyes closed and her heart thumping. She didn't know what to make of the message. She was used to having her hopes raised only for them to be dashed again. And it wouldn't be the first time that some sick bastard had contacted her falsely claiming to know where Chloe was.

She checked the time again. Almost eleven. Too late to follow it up tonight. It would have to wait until the morning.

But as she sloped off to bed, Anna prayed to herself that this time it wasn't a false alarm or a cruel hoax. And that the message was from someone who had genuine information to impart about her missing daughter.

CHAPTER TWENTY-ONE

Ruth didn't know what to do with herself, or even how she would survive the night. There was no point going to bed because she wouldn't be able to sleep. The fear had coiled itself into a tight knot in her stomach and her head was swamped by negative thoughts.

She sat in the living room, staring at the TV and hoping that the presenter would suddenly announce that the children had been found safe and well. She didn't bother to pray; she'd stopped believing in God after Liam was diagnosed with CF. She simply couldn't accept that a divine being could be so cruel as to inflict such a debilitating illness on her precious child. She saw the abductions as more evidence that the Bible was all bollocks and faith was for fools.

At least Ethan had changed his tune and was being more supportive. After returning from his walk he'd held her hand and told her that he was sorry for snapping at her – and that he didn't really blame her for what had happened to their son.

But she didn't believe him, just like she hadn't believed him three months ago when he'd denied that he was having an affair. Now, as then, she could tell from the look in his eyes that he was hiding the truth.

He'd told her that the affair was a figment of her imagination, that he still loved her and would never be unfaithful. It was true that she'd had no proof of infidelity on his part. But she'd strongly suspected it, based on a marked change in the pattern of his behaviour.

He'd stopped initiating sex with her at weekends and become withdrawn and quiet. He'd bought new underwear for himself and darkened his hair with a shampoo dye. At the same time, he'd started coming home late from work and going on 'business' trips that entailed overnight stays in hotels.

He'd made time to pick Liam up from the nursery as often as possible and to take him to the hospital for his regular appointments. Ruth began to wonder if he was finding reasons to be alone so that he could speak on the phone to whomever he was seeing.

She'd checked his mobile a couple of times and his personal email account but neither had contained anything incriminating.

Finally, she'd confronted him with her suspicions and he'd reacted with shock and outrage, not speaking to her for several days.

But since then he'd made a point of coming straight home from work on most days, and when he didn't he'd call and tell her where he was. He had also cut back on the business trips and had even tried to initiate intimacy at every opportunity.

Ruth was still convinced that he'd had an affair but she

wanted to believe that it had been short-lived and was now over.

She still loved her husband and she was sure he wouldn't want to break up the family, if only for Liam's sake. That was why she hadn't broached the subject with him again. And why she'd been hoping that they'd be able to get on with their lives and she could eventually find a way to trust him again.

But now Liam had been taken and the family had been plunged into another crisis. Only this time the stakes were higher and she had a horrible feeling that the outcome was going to be far more devastating.

CHAPTER TWENTY-TWO

Day two

Anna managed a couple of hours of fragmented sleep, during which she dreamt about the last time she was with her daughter. It was the day before Chloe went to stay with her father and two days before he abducted her. They only had a short time together before Anna had to go to work. She had bathed and dressed her and Chloe had blown her a kiss as she walked to the car.

As always, the dream was so vivid, so real, that Anna was hot and breathless when she woke up.

It was only five o'clock and Tom was out cold. She gave him a gentle kiss on the forehead before getting up and stepping out of the bedroom.

The first thing she did was check her phone. There were no calls or messages, which meant there had been no significant developments in the case overnight. Though this initially made her sigh with relief – she hadn't missed anything while she'd been in bed – the realisation that twenty hours had now passed since the children were reported missing made her stomach drop to her feet. She knew that as each minute passed, they were less and less likely to find the children unharmed, especially little Liam.

She called the office to let them know she was up and would soon be making her way in for the briefing. Then she showered and dressed and made herself a cup of coffee.

At five thirty she called the number that had been left the previous evening on the FindChloe Facebook page. There was still no answer so she left another message asking the anonymous caller to ring her back.

At five forty-five she took a cup of tea in to Tom and woke him.

'How long have you been up?' he asked her.

'Not long. I have to be in at seven so I'll be leaving soon. Have you got a busy day ahead?'

'Not as busy or as stressful as yours is going to be. I'll be keeping my fingers crossed for you and those kiddies, Anna. And take care.'

'Will I see you tonight?'

'Do you want to?'

'Of course.'

'Then I'll come over and wait up for you whatever time you're back.'

Before leaving the house she switched on the TV in the kitchen to catch the six o'clock headlines. The stolen children were still the biggest story and the BBC had managed to get sound bites from Sarah Ramsay and two of the parents.

Sarah was shown speaking to a reporter outside her home, saying she was praying for the children and still could not believe they'd been kidnapped. When asked why the nursery hadn't been secure enough to protect them, she replied, 'Those men had guns and they threatened to shoot the children as well as the staff. There was simply nothing we could do to stop them. My colleague who tried was badly beaten.'

Kenneth Tenant didn't hold back when a microphone was shoved up against his face as he stepped out of his car.

'Those nursery people let us down,' he said. 'They were supposed to look after our kids. Now I don't know if I will ever see my darling daughter again.'

Justine Brooks's mother, Rachel, was interviewed over the phone and made an emotional appeal to the kidnappers to let the children go.

'You're breaking our hearts,' she said. 'I beg you not to hurt our babies. They don't deserve it and neither do we.'

It was all very upsetting, and Anna was as moved by it as she knew most viewers would be. In three more hours they'd hit the twenty-four-hour mark, and they were still no closer to finding the children. It wasn't a good sign.

Anna was about to switch the TV off when the presenter announced that they were crossing to the newsroom for some breaking news.

A second later a male journalist appeared. He was sitting on the edge of a desk with a notebook in his hand.

He began his report by saying, 'In the last few minutes there has been an extraordinary development in the child abduction story.'

As Anna listened to what he had to say she felt a shudder crawl up her spine and the blood drain from her face.

As soon as the journalist finished his report she dashed out the door and headed for her car.

CHAPTER TWENTY-THREE

It had been the longest and most harrowing night of Ruth's life. She'd flitted between staring at the TV and looking at the photos of Liam that now scattered the floor of their living room, while her imagination dragged her into the deep, dark depths of despair.

Her widowed father had phoned from his home in Eastbourne, wanting to come straight to London, despite the fact that he was wheelchair-bound following a stroke. She'd persuaded him not to and had promised to keep him updated.

She had no siblings and neither did Ethan. Her husband's parents were on holiday in Greece and were frantically making arrangements to return home. His mother had insisted on speaking to Ruth on the phone and had told her that she was thinking of them both and praying for Liam.

Both Ruth and Ethan took calls from their friends, and their phones pinged constantly with social media notifications. They discovered that a Facebook page had already been set up dedicated to the nine children, and it contained all their photos. The woman behind it was a parent herself who lived in Rotherhithe. She said she wanted to use the page for the exchange of information which she hoped would help the police.

The page had already generated hundreds of posts, mostly from people saying that they hoped the kids would soon be found and expressing sympathy for the parents. But there were those who took the opportunity to say what they thought of the kidnappers.

'*The men who did this are vile creatures who should receive the death penalty,*' said one.

'*I guarantee this is the work of child sex traffickers and those kids will never be seen again,*' said another.

There was a lot of activity on other social media sites as well, and it was clear that people all over the country, and especially those living in South London, were rallying in support of the parents.

Just before dawn Ethan had disappeared upstairs, leaving Ruth and Officer Robinson in the living room. An hour later Ruth had gone up to see what he was doing and had found him asleep on Liam's bed with his arms curled around their son's favourite teddy bear.

He was still there now, mumbling in his sleep, while Ruth sat in the chair clutching the pyjamas that Liam had worn the night before he was kidnapped.

She found herself thinking back to when she and Ethan had first got together five years ago. She had been twenty-four and working as a journalist on a local paper.

Their relationship began with a slow dance at the wedding of a guy who turned out to be a mutual friend. She found out a lot about Ethan that day and in the weeks that followed.

He was the same age as her and worked as a programmer for a computer games company. He'd had one long relationship which had ended the year before. And he had a reputation as a bit of a wide boy, having spent much of his youth as part of a gang that terrorised the council estate in Peckham where he lived.

Luckily for Ethan, he was one of the few members of the gang who managed to avoid getting arrested and having their lives blighted by a criminal record.

By the time Ruth met him at the wedding, all that was behind him and she found it hard to imagine that he had ever been a tearaway. He was softly spoken, mild-mannered and very bright. And it wasn't long before she was in love with him.

A year after their friend's wedding, they tied the knot themselves and a year after that Liam was born.

But what followed changed them both. Life became less fun and far more challenging. They had to make the tough decision not to have any more children because they were both CF gene carriers.

And their lives revolved entirely around their son. The effort it took to keep him well had proved both physically and mentally draining. But it had been worth it because Liam was the centre of their universe, the bond that held them together. And Ruth could not imagine life without him.

Ethan suddenly rolled over and opened his eyes. When he saw her, he blinked a couple of times and said, 'What time is it?'

She glanced at her watch. 'Just after six.'

He heaved himself up on one elbow.

'I'm sorry I dropped off. I didn't intend to. It was just . . .'

He was interrupted by a light tap on the door and Officer Robinson asked if she could come in.

'Yes, of course,' Ruth said. 'We're not sleeping.'

Robinson opened the door and Ruth's heart turned inside out when she saw the solemn expression on the woman's face.

'What is it?' she said. 'Has something happened? Is there news?'

Robinson gave a curt nod and her mouth straightened into a tight line.

'I'm afraid so,' she said. 'And you need to prepare yourselves for what I'm about to tell you.'

CHAPTER TWENTY-FOUR

The Major Investigation Team's open-plan office was now one of two official incident rooms, the other being the hall at the community centre in Peabody Street.

Anna made it clear at the start of the briefing that officers would be working out of both.

'The centre is where we'll bring the parents together to update them and interview them,' she said. 'It's convenient for them because they all live quite close to it. And it'll save us a lot of hassle.

'It's also where we'll be staging the first press conference later today. We'll need to give an official response to this latest development, and try to convince the parents and the public that it should actually be seen as a positive sign.'

She was standing at one end of the room between a white-board and a large TV mounted on the wall. The room was full to bursting and there were quite a few faces she didn't recognise. She knew that several detectives from Scotland Yard's Kidnap Unit and Anti-Terrorism Command were among those drafted in to work with MIT on the case. The Kidnap Unit would normally have been assigned the case, but its team was already overstretched because of a recent wave of gang-related abductions, along with manpower cuts.

'I'm assuming that you all know by now what happened this morning, but nonetheless I'd like DI Walker to talk us through it,' she said. 'I then want to hear where we are with all other lines of enquiry.'

Walker stepped up to the front of the room. He was already clutching the remote control and he used it to switch the TV on. A colour photograph filled the screen and even though Anna had already seen it she felt a tightness clench at her chest.

'This is the picture that was emailed this morning to three national newspapers, the BBC and Sky News,' Walker said. 'It was also sent to a couple of online news operations. It shows eight of the children who were taken from the Peabody Nursery yesterday morning. They're wearing the same clothes they were wearing then.

'The identities have been confirmed by staff members and several parents. The only child who is not in the photo is Liam Brady, the three-year-old boy who has cystic fibrosis. It raises the unsettling possibility that he was too ill to be there or that he's no longer alive. I understand his parents have been told about the picture.'

Walker cleared his throat and left it a beat before carrying on.

'As you can see, there's a message across the bottom of the photo that spells out what the motive is for the kidnappings.'

The children were sitting on the floor of a large room and all looking at the camera. None of them was smiling and at least two looked visibly upset.

The message printed across the bottom in bold letters read:

THE KIDS WILL DIE UNLESS WE RECEIVE £6M. PAYMENT MUST BE IN CRYPTOCURRENCY – I.E. BITCOINS. FURTHER DETAILS WILL FOLLOW SHORTLY. THE FIGURE IS NOT NEGOTIABLE SO SOMEONE NEEDS TO DECIDE WHO IS GOING TO COME UP WITH THE MONEY.

'The picture was attached to an email that appears to have come from a – so far – untraceable account,' Walker went on. 'The kidnappers must know that the parents will struggle to raise that amount of cash by themselves. They're obviously assuming that it will be paid by the authorities or by a bunch of wealthy people who'll feel compelled to save the kids.

'It's likely that when they give us the account number they'll demand that it's paid immediately. That'll enable them to transfer it straight away into another anonymous account and a string of other accounts after that until it becomes impossible to track even by the experts.'

'Six million quid doesn't seem an awful lot considering there are so many children,' one of the detectives said.

Walker nodded. 'I'm guessing it's a shrewd calculation on their part. Six million can probably be raised fairly quickly and easily and used to purchase the digital currency. And the public perception will probably be that it's not an unreasonable amount in the circumstances. So the government will be expected to demonstrate a moral obligation to stump it up.'

'But surely no amount of money should be paid over until we're certain the kids will be released?' the same detective said.

'And that's why these things are always so fucking tricky,' Walker said. 'At the end of the day you face a stark choice – pay up and trust that the kidnappers will keep their word, or refuse and face the consequences, which could be dire.'

He went on. 'In this case the kidnappers are in a strong position because they have multiple hostages. Refuse to pay and there's a risk they'll kill or disfigure one or more of the children just to show that they're serious. It's an established business model and time and again it's been proven to work.'

'And technology has made it easier for them to get away with it,' Anna pointed out. 'There's no need to execute the old-fashioned ransom drop where a bag stuffed with cash is left somewhere to be picked up. Now it can be transferred using digital currencies and there are ways of doing this so that the recipient can't be traced. The Bitcoins can then be sold on various exchanges and the cash that's generated put into various offshore accounts. By the time the perps get their hands on the money it's impossible to locate them.'

Anna went on to say that at least they now knew what they were dealing with and the odds on returning the children to their parents had been shortened.

'But that's assuming the decision is taken to pay the ransom,' she said. 'And that part of it is out of our hands. It's not even as if we can try to deal with them discreetly. The kidnappers have opted to maximise publicity and that has to be so the pressure to come up with the money will be considerable. The parents will make sure that pressure is sustained. Anyone stupid enough to point out that the UK government's policy is never to pay ransoms will be shot down in flames.

'It'd be different if the hostages were military personnel or aid workers in a war zone teeming with terrorists. But these are innocent toddlers taken from a nursery school in South London.'

Just listening to herself speak had made Anna's heart pound. The ransom demand, while not entirely unexpected, was going to throw up a whole new set of complications and involve many more people.

Who, for instance, would be ultimately responsible for deciding whether the ransom should be paid? What would happen if the parents couldn't raise the money? Would the government step in and pay it, thus setting a dangerous precedent?

Thankfully these were issues that Anna and her team would not have to deal with. It was their job to focus on finding the children and bringing the kidnappers to justice.

The first update was that all the parents had now been informed, including Phil Green, the father of Simone, the man who had lost the child custody battle with his ex-wife.

'I called at his flat in Camberwell last night,' DC Mark Shepherd said. 'He wasn't in so I waited around and he eventually turned up just after midnight. He'd clearly been on the booze and was slurring his words. He said he hadn't answered his phone to his ex because he lost it whilst out drinking on Sunday night. Anyway, he let me in and the place is a real mess. He said he's been struggling to get back on his feet since the divorce.'

'Was he aware that his daughter had been kidnapped?' Anna asked.

'No, he wasn't. I broke the news to him and he did seem genuinely shocked.'

'So where had he been all day? And how is it possible that he didn't know what had happened when it's been plastered all over the news?'

'He claims he got rat-assed on Sunday evening and had a stinking hangover the following morning. So he stayed in bed most of the day and when he eventually got up in the afternoon he didn't bother switching on the TV or radio. He says he went out to buy a new phone and after that he went out drinking again.'

'Do you think he's telling the truth?' Anna said.

Shepherd shrugged. 'I'm not sure. He doesn't have form but he strikes me as someone who's on the edge. Like he's angry with the world and blames everyone else for the state he's got himself in. That's why I'm checking out his alibi. I've requested footage from street cams around his flats and I'll visit the pub he says he went to on Sunday.'

'Have you spoken to his ex-wife again?'

Shepherd nodded. 'She reckons that Phil Green is a bad-tempered bloke and that his addiction to gambling has got him into a lot of debt. She says he drinks too much, and when he drinks he gets violent. She claims he hit her several times and that was one of the reasons she kicked him out and filed for divorce. She also claims that he's made all kinds of threats against her since she was awarded sole custody of their daughter.'

'Does she think he'd be capable of taking part in a crime such as this?'

'She says she can't imagine that he would, but I did speak to her before we knew about the ransom demand. So maybe the guy sees it as a way of getting out of debt and getting back at his ex-wife at the same time.'

'OK, then run a check on his finances,' Anna said. 'And find out as much about him as you can. If he is somehow involved then there's a slim chance that his heavy drinking has made him careless.'

Anna then asked where they were with the other suspect, Jonas Platt.

She was told that he'd finally been tracked down earlier this morning to a caravan park at Dymchurch on the Kent coast.

'He owns a static caravan there,' DI Bellingham said. 'He says he arrived late Friday and was intending to stay for a week. He's been alone so there's no one to corroborate his story. Kent police want to know what they should do with him.'

'I want him brought back here for questioning,' Anna said. 'And get them to search his car and caravan for anything that might link him to the kidnappings.'

Anna was then told that none of the parents or staff had criminal records and that no useful forensic evidence had been found in the nursery.

Meanwhile, the half-smoked cigarette discovered in the layby next to the abandoned minibus was still in the lab being checked for DNA traces.

'We've also drawn a blank on CCTV footage,' someone said. 'None of that so far viewed shows any minibuses in and around Farningham yesterday afternoon. So they managed to avoid the cameras on the way to the layby and when they left it.'

Anna's next question was going to relate to Sarah Ramsay

and her nursery chain, but she never got to ask it because DI Walker raised his hand to get her attention.

He looked up from his mobile phone and said, 'I've just had a message from the hospital. Tasha Norris died from her head injuries a few minutes ago. It means we're now investigating a murder as well as multiple kidnappings.'

CHAPTER TWENTY-FIVE

Ruth was all cried out, but she was still in shock. As she stared at the photo that was frozen on the TV screen the questions whirled through her mind.

Why wasn't Liam sitting with the other children? Was it because his condition had rapidly deteriorated and he was too ill? Or was her little boy dead?

And how the hell were she and the other parents expected to raise six million pounds?

Ethan was out in the garden on the phone again, and she assumed he was talking to his parents and colleagues.

Officer Robinson was sitting next to her on the sofa, attempting to put a positive spin on this latest development.

'Try not to think the worst, Mrs Brady,' she was saying. 'Your son could well have been resting up in another room when this photo was taken. And at least the kidnappers have established contact. It means that we can ask them about Liam and get them to show us that he's all right.'

'But he won't be all right,' Ruth snapped. 'Without his

medication he'll be struggling to breathe. And he needs regular physiotherapy sessions to clear his airways. Those bastards won't know about any of that so they'll just let him suffer. Or maybe they've decided he's a nuisance and they've locked him in another room to die.'

Her voice trembled as she spoke, and her stomach was clenched so tight she almost doubled over. The fear and frustration was overwhelming and her suffering had been taken to a whole new level by the photograph.

'Is there anything I can get for you?' Robinson asked. 'Tea, coffee, water perhaps?'

Ruth shook her head. 'All I want is my son back.'

She stood up then, scattering some screwed-up tissues on the floor. She grabbed the remote control from the table and pressed play to move beyond the frozen photo on the screen. She then started tapping the programme button so the TV jumped through the various news channels on the Sky menu.

On most of them, including CNN and Euronews, the ransom demand from the kidnappers was the main story. Ruth stood in the middle of the room, transfixed by the coverage, while her heart hammered in her chest.

There were chilling references to the fact that only eight children appeared in the photo and yet nine had been abducted. Liam was named, his picture shown, and there were brief descriptions of his illness.

There were also short clips of interviews with several of the other parents, including Kenneth Tenant and Rebecca Chandler, mother of four-year-old Toby. Sarah Ramsay also made an appearance, defending the safety measures that were in place at her nurseries.

'Nothing we could have done would have prevented what

happened,' she said, and Ruth knew that she was probably right.

But on another channel a London MP called for greater security measures at all nurseries in the UK.

'To my mind this was a crime that was waiting to happen,' he declared. 'Nurseries are easy targets for terrorists and criminal gangs who may have decided to view them as an opportunity to extort obscene amounts of money from desperate parents.'

The ransom itself raised lots of questions. Should it be paid? Who would pay it? Why six million pounds? What would happen to the children if it wasn't paid?

It was all becoming too much for Ruth so she switched the TV off. The worry was like a raging storm inside her.

Officer Robinson said something to her but she ignored her and walked over to the patio doors to look outside.

Ethan was standing on the lawn with his mobile phone against his ear. When he saw her he gave a little wave.

But as he did so something caught Ruth's eye: her husband was clutching a second phone in his other hand. A frown creased her brow and she felt her throat catch.

As far as she knew Ethan had only ever had one phone – a black Samsung Galaxy. That was stuck to his ear. The other phone he was holding was white.

The first thought that sprang into Ruth's mind was that the phone was probably a pay-as-you-go and he must have used it to communicate with the woman he had the affair with. The second thought was that the affair must still be going on and he was feeling the need to tell the bitch what was happening.

Ruth took a deep breath to get a handle on her emotions.

She knew she would have to confront the bastard, but was now the right time? They had more important things to worry about and a major spat would be a distraction.

A voice broke into her thoughts and she realised that Robinson was trying to get her attention again. She turned to find the woman standing right behind her.

'I've just been given some news that I need to share with you, Mrs Brady,' she said. 'But it's not about Liam.'

'What is it then?'

Robinson clenched her jaw and said, 'The teacher who was attacked at the nursery – Tasha Norris. I'm sorry to have to tell you that she died in hospital a short time ago.'

An image of poor Tasha flashed in Ruth's mind. She had been by far the best teacher at the nursery. Always smiling, always kind, always full of praise for Liam. It was such a terrible, terrible tragedy.

And along with Ruth's fears for Liam it put into perspective her own marriage woes.

Confronting her cheating slug of a husband about that other phone would have to wait. There was only so much grief and heartache she could deal with at any one time.

CHAPTER TWENTY-SIX

It took a few minutes for the team to absorb the news of Tasha Norris's death. It added another dimension to the case and would pile more pressure on Anna.

They couldn't even be sure that Tasha was the only fatality. A big question mark hung over little Liam Brady. The fact that he hadn't been photographed with the other children was a bad sign. There seemed to be only two plausible explanations – that he'd been taken ill or he was no longer alive.

Anna's heart went out to Liam's mother and father, Ruth and Ethan Brady. She could only imagine how worried they were right now.

'I want all the parents to be brought together,' she said to the team. 'They'll have questions that we'll need to do our best to answer.'

DI Bellingham asked who would take responsibility for responding to the ransom demand.

'I'll talk to DCS Nash about that,' Anna said. 'I'm pretty sure he's already raised the subject with the Commissioner, who in turn will have referred it up to the Home Secretary. It's bound to have caused a right old stir in the corridors of power. They won't want to be seen to hand money over to hostage-takers, but equally they won't want to see children murdered. To quote a cliché – they're caught between a rock and a hard place.'

'There's nothing to stop the parents from seizing the initiative and paying the ransom themselves,' someone said.

'I don't think that will happen,' Anna replied. 'They appear to be comfortably off, but I very much doubt they can raise that amount of money between them in a short space of time. Sure, they can sell their homes if they own them but that will take time and I think it's reasonable to assume that the kidnappers will want to conclude the transaction in hours or days rather than weeks.'

'And I suppose this is where the government comes in,' Walker said. 'It can pay the money on behalf of the parents, but if it does there's a real danger it'll open the floodgates to organised criminals and terrorists.'

The meeting carried on for another twenty minutes during which Anna assigned tasks and set timetables.

After winding up she phoned Nash, who was just about to go into a meeting with the Met Commissioner. The news about Tasha Norris hadn't reached him yet and he muttered a loud curse when Anna told him that she had died.

'That's all we bloody well need on top of everything else,' he moaned.

Anna bit her tongue so as not to react to such an insensitive, yet not untypical, remark from her boss. Instead, she quickly summarised the state of the investigation for him and told him of her plan to stage a press conference.

'We need answers to the questions that are going to be asked, sir,' she said. 'For starters, what's our official response to the ransom demand?'

'There isn't one yet,' he said. 'I'm about to discuss it with the Commissioner. Have you had any reaction from the parents?'

'Not yet. I'm getting them all together, hopefully within the next couple of hours. But it's obvious they'll want the ransom to be paid. I know I would in their position.'

'But it's not as simple as that, Anna.'

'I realise that, sir. For one thing, they'll struggle to come up with six million.'

'Precisely. And they'll no doubt expect help from the government. If they don't get it there will be an almighty shit storm.'

'Which is further evidence that these guys are pretty smart,' Anna said.

'That's why I'm banking on you being even smarter, Anna,' Nash said. 'Find those children before an ugly situation gets a thousand times uglier.'

After coming off the phone to Nash, Anna announced that she was going to the community centre in Peabody Street. It was where she was expecting to spend most of the morning and part of the afternoon. She planned to talk to the parents and ask the media liaison team to set up a press conference.

After that the plan was to return to the office to question Jonas Platt, who would now be on his way back to London from his caravan in Dymchurch.

He and Phil Green were the only persons of interest in the frame, and yet they weren't exactly grade A suspects. For sure, they both bore grudges. Jonas Platt blamed Sarah Ramsay for the death of his daughter. And Phil Green was angry with his ex-wife because she'd taken sole custody of their daughter. He was also in debt and hitting the bottle in a big way.

But were either crazy enough to pursue such an extreme form of revenge? If they were, then in what capacity? Neither was involved in the actual abduction, that was clear. But that could have been because they were both known to Sarah and the teachers.

So maybe one of them had decided to organise it when he realised how easy it would be. He had the inside track on the nursery, knew how many staff to expect, roughly how many children, what time to strike, and the best way to take the kids away.

Anna knew that it was just one of dozens of possible scenarios, but that didn't mean it wasn't perfectly feasible.

'I want you to come with me to Peabody Street,' she said to Walker. 'And we'll take DI Bellingham and DS Granger with us.'

'I'll get the pool car,' Walker said.

As Anna walked into her tiny office to pick up her bag, her phone rang.

'DCI Tate,' she answered.

A woman spoke, her voice barely above a whisper.

'Oh hello, Ms Tate. My name is Janet Russell. You rang this number last night and this morning and left voicemails for my husband.'

As the woman's words registered, Anna felt her entire body stiffen.

'Is your husband the person who contacted my FindChloe Facebook page?'

'He is, but I wasn't aware of it until a short time ago when he told me. And I've only just switched his phone on. It's been off since yesterday evening.'

'Then is it possible for me to speak to him?' Anna asked. 'He said in his message that he has information about my missing daughter Chloe.'

'Well, he's sleeping right now and I'm not able to disturb him.'

'So do you know what your husband wants to tell me, Mrs Russell?'

'I do, but I would rather it came from him.'

'Then can you wake him please? I really need to know what information he has.'

'Paul has been given a sedative, Ms Tate. He's out to the world and won't be stirring for several hours.'

'Is he unwell?'

'He has terminal cancer, I'm afraid. It's why he decided to contact you. He saw you on the television and it made him remember something that happened ten years ago. He wants you to know about it before it's too late.'

Anna's pulse quickened. 'In that case I'd like to speak to him face to face. Would that be possible?'

'Of course.'

'Then give me your address and I'll drop by the first chance I get.'

'Paul is no longer at home, Ms Tate. He's receiving palliative care in a hospice in Dulwich. And for your information, he's possibly only got days to live. But let me tell you where we are. I'm sure Paul will want to see you.'

CHAPTER TWENTY-SEVEN

Anna didn't say a word to her colleagues in the pool car. She just sat there staring through the windscreen, oblivious to the conversation the others were having between themselves.

They probably assumed she was thinking about the case. But she wasn't. Instead, her mind was consumed by what Janet Russell had said. Was it really possible that her husband had information on Chloe dating back ten years? And, if so, what kind of information?

Anna had Googled the hospice in Dulwich before leaving the office and it did indeed exist. She'd also called them to see if they had any patients named Paul Russell. They did. But that was the only information she could get out of them over the phone.

She kept going over what the woman had told her. She'd seemed genuine and for that reason Anna couldn't suppress a ripple of hope.

She wanted to tell Walker to change direction and drive to the hospice in Dulwich. She was desperate to know what

Paul Russell wanted to tell her. But she couldn't just abandon the investigation, and just thinking about it made her feel guilty because right now she needed to focus on those nine missing children. Not on Chloe. And besides, she still couldn't be sure that it wouldn't be a waste of time.

'Are you all right, guv?' Walker said. 'You seem unusually quiet.'

They were passing through Clapham on their way to Rotherhithe. Traffic was heavy and the sun was already warming up the day.

'I'm fine,' Anna lied. 'Just trying to get my head around all that's happened this morning. The photograph of the kids, the ransom demand, poor Tasha Norris.'

Walker nodded. 'It is a lot to take in.'

Anna knew she had to stop thinking about Paul Russell. But it wasn't going to be easy. The man was now inside her head and she was desperate to go and see him. The questions she wanted to ask were piling up and one in particular was causing her stomach to twist in an anxious knot.

Did he know where Chloe was now?

When they arrived at Peabody Street it was at the centre of a febrile media circus. There were now camera crews, photographers and reporters from all over the world. Most were gathered at either end of the street beyond the cordons. Some were filming and taking photographs from the balconies of the three-storey block of flats overlooking the nursery school. Others had set up camp in front gardens, no doubt having paid the owners and tenants for the privilege.

The SOCOs had finished their work in the nursery and

come up with a big fat zero. The building was now empty, but nobody was being allowed in.

People were already gathered in the community centre. Several parents had arrived, along with their appointed FLOs. There were more reps from the media liaison department, and the reception area was buzzing with beat officers in fluorescent yellow jackets and civilian support staff.

Anna was asked what time she wanted to stage the press conference.

'Let's say eleven o'clock here in the hall,' she said. 'It wouldn't be fair on anyone to wait any longer. And by that time I'll hopefully have spoken to all the parents.'

She took from her pocket the list that DC Sweeny had given her with the names and photographs of all the children. She wanted to remind herself who they were and who their parents were.

It suddenly occurred to her that if the children hadn't been abducted then Paul Russell wouldn't have seen her on the television. And, whatever he remembered from ten years ago, he would have taken to his grave.

Stop it, she told herself. *You can't allow yourself to be distracted by a man who might well turn out to be a fantasist. You need to get on and do your job.*

But this wasn't the first time that her obsession with finding Chloe had interfered with her work. Six years ago, while working on a murder investigation, she'd received a tip that Chloe and her father were living in a flat just outside Benidorm on Spain's Costa Blanca.

She'd called in sick and taken the first available flight to Alicante. But it had turned out to be a wasted journey. There was a man who resembled Matthew and he was with his daughter who was about Chloe's age. But his wife was also living with them in the apartment and they were French, not English.

Somehow her boss at the time found out that she had lied about being ill. Luckily he gave her a bollocking instead of an official reprimand. Since then she'd been more careful when it came to following up leads, of which there'd been precious few.

And none had sounded as promising as the one from this man who seemed to hold valuable information, but had only days to live . . .

CHAPTER TWENTY-EIGHT

Ruth and Ethan were taken to Peabody Street in Officer Robinson's car. They'd been told that DCI Tate wanted to talk to them along with the other parents.

Before leaving the flat they'd both showered and put on fresh clothes. But it made no difference to how Ruth felt. Her thoughts were moving like thick, muddy water, and she was swamped by a sense of isolation, having convinced herself that her husband was still cheating on her.

The temptation to confront him about that other phone was still bubbling away beneath the surface. But she resisted, telling herself that it would serve no useful purpose other than to allow her to get it off her chest.

When he'd come in from the garden earlier she'd asked him who he'd been speaking to. He'd told her his parents and his accountant.

'Dad and mum have offered to give us their entire savings,' he'd said. 'And I asked my accountant how much he thinks we can add to the mortgage. But the most we can raise is about sixty thousand, which is nowhere near enough. Six million divided by nine is almost seven hundred grand. I don't see how any of the other parents can come up with that amount of money either.'

So at that moment it hadn't mattered to Ruth that she believed he was being unfaithful. All that mattered was getting their son back. And that was still how she felt.

Her darling Liam was her number one priority. Her marriage came second to that.

A bout of trembling gripped Ruth as they turned into Peabody Street.

Dozens of press people and onlookers were gathered on the pavements. Officer Robinson was able to drive up to the cordon, which was lifted to let them through, and she parked her car at the kerb in front of the community centre.

Before getting out, Ruth took a moment to compose herself. She willed her body to stop shaking and fought down the tears that were gathering in her eyes and stinging in her throat.

Ethan squeezed her fingers and said, 'We don't know why Liam wasn't in the photo, Ruth. And because we don't know we can't give up hope that he's alive and well. The people who have him will know by now what's wrong with him. So it's possible that they're taking steps to look after him.'

'You can't really believe that, Ethan,' she said.

He gave a sharp intake of breath, almost a sob.

'I'm making myself believe it,' he said. 'The alternative is too horrendous to contemplate.'

Ruth felt her chest expand as she took a deep breath.

'If you're not up to going inside I can go by myself,' Ethan said. 'I'm sure that Officer Robinson will look after you.'

Ruth shook her head. 'We both need to find out what's happening and ask questions. Let's just get it over with.'

As she climbed out of the car a cold chill crept over her shoulders and down her neck. She was sure that if the police had some good news to share they would have done so by now. In which case it was unlikely they were about to reveal anything that would ease her fears.

Two uniformed WPCs were waiting to greet them as they entered the community centre. They were then taken to the same room they'd been in the day before. It turned out they were the last to arrive. The other parents were already there and the discussion they were having ceased abruptly when they saw Ruth and Ethan.

'Detective Tate will be with you shortly,' one of the WPCs said, before they both took up position with their backs against the wall either side of the door.

Daniel's mother, Belinda, got up from her chair and gave Ruth a sympathetic look.

'How are you holding up, Ruth?' she said.

Ruth's throat tightened and for a few seconds she couldn't speak.

Ethan answered for her: 'She's not good, Belinda. We're both struggling with this.'

'We all are,' Belinda said. 'But I can only imagine how you must be feeling—'

'We're hoping it doesn't mean anything,' Ethan interrupted, as he put an arm around his wife and squeezed her shoulder.

'He was probably just feeling unwell when the photograph was taken.'

A low murmur spread around the room and most of the parents, including Belinda, nodded in agreement, even though it was obvious from their expressions that they didn't believe it.

After an awkward silence the discussion resumed and several of the parents gave emotional accounts of the last time they saw their children.

James Chandler sobbed as he described how his son Toby had misbehaved on Sunday evening.

'I told him off and made him cry,' he said. 'But all he did was spray a wall with his water pistol. So why did I have to make a big fucking deal of it?'

Wendy Ryan was ravaged by guilt because Simone hadn't wanted to go to the nursery on Monday morning.

'She claimed she wasn't feeling well and I didn't believe her,' she said. 'I told her she had to go because I couldn't have more time off work.'

The conversation then switched to the ransom and it quickly became evident to Ruth that they weren't the only couple who wouldn't be able to make a significant contribution towards the ransom demand.

'It doesn't matter because the fuckers know we're in no position to pay it,' Kenneth Tenant said. He was standing next to one of the windows, his face radiating hostility. 'They're assuming the government will come up with the money. And it will bloody well have to if it doesn't want the blood of our kids on its hands.'

It was the first time Ruth had agreed with anything Kenneth Tenant had said. But she wasn't convinced the government would cave in so easily and pay the ransom on their behalf. And even if it did, and the children were released, she couldn't be sure that Liam would be among them.

CHAPTER TWENTY-NINE

'All the parents are here except one,' DC Mark Shepherd said.

'So who's missing?' Anna asked him.

'Phil Green. Simone Green's dad. I've tried calling his phone but he's not answering.'

'Has he been in touch with his ex-wife since you visited him last night?'

'He rang her about two hours ago. She told him she was coming here and he said he would meet her.'

'Then maybe he'll soon turn up.'

'Possibly. But what concerns me is that I've just found out that he lied to me about where he was yesterday morning.'

'What do you mean?'

'Well, if you remember, he told me he got drunk on Sunday night and had a hangover which kept him in bed until yesterday afternoon. That was why he didn't know what had happened to Simone and the other children.'

'Are you telling me he wasn't at home?

Shepherd nodded. 'He went out at about nine yesterday morning, just after the kids were taken. We know because one of the CCTV cameras I had checked out is right across the street from his flat. I just viewed footage from it which shows him getting into his car and driving off.'

Anna rolled out her bottom lip and frowned.

'Does he have a job?'

'No. He's been out of work for months. And the thing is there's a good chance he knows he's been rumbled and that if he turns up here he'll be put on the spot. I told him last night we'd be checking his movements. He must realise that includes street cameras.'

'Then I suggest we send a patrol to his flat to see if he's there. And at the same time, if his phone is still on, it'll be emitting a signal. So try to get a fix on it.'

'I'll do it right away, ma'am,' Shepherd said. 'But do you really think the guy could actually be involved in what's happened?'

'Anything is possible,' Anna said. 'Especially as Green is someone with huge personal problems. He lost the custody battle for his daughter, he hasn't got a job and has big debts apparently. And according to his wife he's a violent alcoholic. So I reckon he'd be capable of pretty much anything.'

Anna was suddenly reminded of something her late mother had said to her shortly after Matthew abducted Chloe.

He was a terrible husband to you, Anna, but he's always been such a good, caring father. I can't believe he would do something that will cause so much pain and suffering.

Anna could only tell her what she had long known to be true – that everyone has a monster inside them. And there's always the possibility that, given the right set of circumstances, it can be let loose to cause mayhem and misery on a grand scale.

Before going to speak to the parents, Anna put in another call to DCS Nash. He was still in a meeting with the Met Commissioner, other senior officers at Scotland Yard, and officials from the Home Office.

'The issue of the ransom is still under discussion,' he said in answer to Anna's first question.

'So is that what you want me to tell the parents and the press?' she replied.

'I'm about to text you a statement from the Commissioner,' he said. 'The Prime Minister herself has been involved in what we should put out.'

'Will it be enough to reassure the parents that the ransom will be paid?'

'That depends what they're expecting. But right now that's all we've got. The view from on high is that it's too soon to give a full and unqualified commitment. The fear is that it could encourage others, including terrorists, to carry out copy-cat crimes involving groups of young children.'

'I fully understand that, sir. But I'm guessing it won't be long before we hear from the kidnappers again, and when we do it'll be crunch time.'

'Then all we can do is play it by ear. You just focus on the investigation. We will provide whatever you need in terms of resources and manpower – just ask for it. If anyone can find those bastards then it's you, Anna. Meanwhile, I'll handle this side of things and we will keep each other updated.'

The parents had grown impatient waiting for Anna to

arrive. When she entered the room the first voice she heard belonged to an irate Kenneth Tenant.

'About fucking time,' he growled. 'We want to know what's going on.'

Then someone else shouted, 'And who's going to pay this ransom that's being demanded? We sure as hell can't.'

More questions were fired at Anna by the other parents, and one woman, Molly Wilson's mum, Janet, screamed hysterically and accused the police of not doing enough to find her daughter.

It was a while before Anna could get a word in.

'Please just listen up, everyone,' she said. 'I'll try to answer all of your questions. But as you can appreciate things have developed rapidly in the last few hours and we're responding as quickly as we can.'

It took a few more minutes for them to settle down, and it gave Anna an opportunity to see what the ordeal was doing to them. Without exception their faces were grey and stiff with shock. The haunted expressions in their eyes reflected the anguish and uncertainty that was tearing them apart inside. She was only sorry that she couldn't give them a firm assurance that things would be all right.

It was fairly obvious that none of them had slept much, if at all. Poor Ruth Brady looked as though she had aged several years overnight. Her eyes were teary and bloodshot, and without make-up the skin around them appeared dark and tender.

Wendy Ryan, Phil Green's ex-wife, kept rocking back and forth in one of the front row chairs, while clutching her handbag close to her chest. Next to her Sahib Hussein's father, Rafi, was bent forward, elbows on his knees, face buried in his hands. Every couple of seconds his shoulders moved as he choked out a sob.

Anna began by telling them what they already knew – that Tasha Norris had died.

'Mrs Norris's death is being treated as murder,' she said. 'Despite a six-hour operation the surgeons were unable to save her life because the head injuries she received were so severe.'

There was resounding silence as the parents contemplated Tasha's fate and the kidnappers' brutality – probably fearing for their own children even more now.

Anna continued, 'I can tell you that a meeting of senior Scotland Yard officers and officials from the Home Office is now underway,' she said. 'The Prime Minister is also taking part via telephone from the United States where she's attending trade talks. Meanwhile, the Met Commissioner has just released a statement condemning what's happened to your children and promising to do everything he can to ensure that they're returned to you unharmed. To that end every law enforcement agency in the country is involved in some way in the investigation. Specialist teams have been sent to ports and airports and a huge operation is underway to try to trace the vehicle the children were transferred to.'

'But will the government pay the ransom?' Kenneth Tenant asked. 'That's what we want to know.'

'What response there should be to the ransom demand is top of the agenda, Mr Tenant. And the Commissioner wants it to be known that under no circumstances should you parents be expected to pay it.'

'That's not really an answer,' Tenant said. 'It's more like a fudge.'

'The position will be clarified in due course, Mr Tenant,' Anna told him. 'But from experience we know it would not be wise to rush into making a decision on a situation such as this. First we need to establish a dialogue with the kidnappers, and then involve trained negotiators who can help secure the most positive outcome.'

Anna realised that it must have sounded like she was reading from a press release. But at the same time she knew that it was important to manage expectations at this stage. They didn't want to give the parents the impression that everything would turn out fine if the government stumped up the cash. And they didn't want the kidnappers to think that if it was so easy to extort six million pounds then they might as well ask for twice as much.

Ethan Brady then asked her if the kidnappers had established contact since the photo of the children was posted online and emailed to the media.

Anna shook her head. 'We've heard no more, I'm afraid. But we expect them to get in touch again soon. And let me say that if you're contacted individually by someone claiming to have your child we strongly advise you not to enter into discussions with them. And please don't be tempted to hand over money. You won't know for sure who you're dealing with and you could well place yourselves in danger.'

Anna then explained that all the divisions of the Met were involved in the investigation. Forensic evidence was being analysed, computer technicians were trying to trace the source of the email that contained the photograph, and hours of CCTV footage were being examined.

'You may also be aware of the huge social media campaign that has swung into action,' Anna said. 'Facebook and Twitter accounts have been set up with the aim of stimulating interest and gathering information. #Peabodykids is being used across a range of social media platforms and these are being closely monitored by the Met.'

'Is it true that you already have a couple of suspects?'

The question came from James Chandler, father of four-year-old Toby.

'We've spoken to a number of people but only because they need to be ruled out of our enquiries,' Anna said. 'However, you should know that we still haven't identified the three men and woman who actually came here and took your children away. But e-fits that the teachers helped us put together have been widely circulated.'

There were more questions relating to the investigation and what the police were expecting to happen next. Anna answered them as best she could, but the one that really threw her came from Ruth Brady.

'My son was the only child not in the photograph,' she said, as she fought to keep her voice steady. 'Do you think that means he's dead?'

Anna felt her breathing stall, and the silence that suddenly descended on the room was deafening. Before speaking she had to swallow to clear the lump in her throat.

'There's no evidence to suggest that, Mrs Brady,' she said. 'He could have been excluded for any number of reasons.'

Ruth just stared at Anna, her eyes glistening, her chest rising and falling dramatically with every breath.

Her husband reached out and took her hand, but she reacted by snatching it away, which struck Anna as odd. Ethan then leaned across and whispered something in her ear that she appeared to ignore.

Anna experienced an overwhelming wave of sympathy for the woman. She had to do something more; she couldn't leave it like this.

'I've had an idea, Mrs Brady,' she said. 'In a little while I'll be holding a press conference in the hall. Why don't you come and say something, perhaps appeal to the kidnappers to let you know how your son is? It might prompt a swift response.'

A frown gathered on Ruth's forehead and she twisted her lips in thought. Then she lifted her chin and pushed back her shoulders.

'I'll do it,' she said. 'I'll do anything that will help get my boy back.'

Before leaving the room, Anna informed the parents that when they were ready to go home cars would be on hand to take them.

She then made her team aware that Ruth Brady would be taking part in the press conference. It was due to start in half an hour and the hacks outside were already bemoaning the fact that they'd been waiting around for so long.

She decided there was just enough time for a short catch-up meeting with her detectives. She summoned them into one of the other rooms and told them what the Commissioner had said in his statement.

'Basically they're stalling,' she said. 'For obvious reasons they're reluctant to make it known that they'll probably have to pay the ransom. They're hoping that we can find the children before it comes to that.'

She then told them that after the press conference she'd be returning to the office to interview Jonas Platt.

'He's still one of our persons of interest because of his

grudge against Sarah Ramsay and the nurseries,' she said. 'He's being brought back from Dymchurch where he's been staying in a static caravan he owns. Do we know if Kent police found anything incriminating there?'

'No, they didn't,' DC Prebble said. 'They searched the caravan and his car. But they haven't yet come across any witnesses to confirm that he's been there since Friday. And they're still checking through CCTV footage.'

Anna brought them up to date on where they were with Simone Green's father, Phil.

'DC Shepherd has discovered that he lied to us about where he was yesterday. He told us he was at home in bed recovering from a hangover, but we now know he went out in the morning. And this morning he said he was planning to come to the community centre to see his ex-wife but he hasn't shown up.'

'There's been a development since I spoke to you, ma'am,' Shepherd said. 'Green was involved in a minor accident this morning not far from his home. He crashed his car into the side of a bus. He wasn't hurt, but officers who attended realised he was drunk and tried to breathalyse him. But he became abusive and so he was arrested. He's now in a cell at Camberwell nick. They contacted us because he told them he was the father of one of the abducted kids and that he was on his way here when he crashed.'

'Then tell them to keep him there,' Anna said. 'I'll drop by on the way back to the office to see what he has to say for himself.'

Anna ended the meeting by reminding everyone that Sarah Ramsay was also a potential suspect because she had allowed the kidnappers into the nursery without checking their credentials. DI Bellingham had been instructed to look into her background and find out what he could about her.

'I've actually come across something that puts her firmly in the frame,' he said. 'I made various enquiries, and in the last ten minutes I got a call back from someone at OFSTED. For those who don't know what that is, it's the government Office for Standards in Education and Children's Services, which covers nurseries.

'This official told me that Sarah Ramsay put her Peabody Nursery chain up for sale six months ago. She's asking for three million pounds, which includes the freehold on several of the properties.'

'She failed to mention that to me when I spoke to her,' Anna said.

Bellingham nodded. 'And I suppose she also failed to mention that she's in the shit financially and needs to raise a huge amount of money to get her out of it. Hence the sell-off. But the problem is she's been unable to find a buyer.'

Anna gave a slow nod and said, 'So perhaps she decided to give up the ghost on that and try to raise the money by unlawful means.'

CHAPTER THIRTY

The media liaison team had placed a table and three chairs on the small stage in the hall. Anna sat between Ruth Brady and Kenneth Tenant. The latter had insisted on taking part so that he too could appeal to the kidnappers.

'We're all in the same boat on this,' he'd said to Anna. 'So I don't see why the Bradys should be treated any differently to the rest of us.'

So as not to exacerbate the friction that obviously existed between the two families, Anna had said it wouldn't be a problem. She intended to invite both to speak after she had outlined the state of the investigation and taken some questions.

There were about fifty members of the media in the room, including reporters, photographers and TV camera crews, two of which were providing live coverage of the event. Yet there were only about thirty chairs, so many of them were standing at the back and to the sides.

She began by saying how sorry she was to learn this morning that Tasha Norris had died.

'It means that as well as this being an investigation into the abduction of nine small children, it's now also a murder enquiry,' she said. 'Mrs Norris, who was just twenty-three, was brutally beaten as she bravely tried to protect the children who were in her care. It was a callous and unnecessary attack and it's left her husband without a wife. Her killer is one of the three men who entered the Peabody Nursery yesterday morning to kidnap the children. It's our intention to bring all three of them to justice, along with the woman who was waiting outside in the minibus. We also aim to reunite those children with their parents.'

Anna then referred to the Commissioner's statement and outlined where they were with the case. She also said that discussions were underway at the highest level to decide how to respond to the ransom demand. She confirmed that several people had been questioned in relation to the case but they did not have a leading suspect. She steered clear of naming Sarah Ramsay, Jonas Platt or Phil Green.

But she did say that the identities of the kidnap gang were still not known.

'We want to hear from anyone who believes they might have information that would be helpful to us,' she said. 'It could be that someone you know has aroused your suspicion. Or that the e-fit pictures of the three men remind you of a person or persons you're acquainted with, or have seen some-where before. It's hard to believe that a crime such as this has been carried out in the UK. The victims are small, defenceless children and we need all the help we can get if we're to find them.'

The questions came thick and fast then.

Were the police making any progress?

Was any evidence found on the minibus that was abandoned in Kent?

Was it possible that the kidnappers were part of a terrorist cell operating in this country?

Should other nurseries across the UK step up security or close down completely until a major review of safety was carried out?

Ruth Brady and Kenneth Tenant sat quietly and patiently with their heads bowed throughout the Q and A session. Anna then introduced them and said that they would both like to speak briefly but would not be taking any questions.

Ruth went first and in a faltering voice said, 'I beg whoever you are to let us have our children back. And please don't harm them. My son Liam has a condition called cystic fibrosis, and he needs specific medication to keep him alive. I'm so worried because he wasn't in that photograph you took. He's only three years old and we love him so much and I don't know what . . .'

That was as far as she got before she stopped and shook her head, her eyes filling with tears.

'That's all I have to say,' she said and stayed where she was, staring down at the table.

Kenneth Tenant took this as his cue to start speaking, and Anna watched his tough exterior collapse as he described his daughter Grace as a happy, beautiful little girl who had her whole life ahead of her.

'Please don't take her away from us,' he pleaded, looking directly at one of the TV cameras. 'She's all we've got and if we don't get her back we won't want to go on living.'

Anna decided that it was the obvious point at which to draw the conference to a close. And she was about to do so when one of the journalists standing at the back abruptly called out to attract her attention. When she looked at him he started waving his mobile phone in the air.

Anna recognised him as Luke Dennis from the *Evening Standard*, the hack she'd come across the day before.

'My office just called to tell me that the kidnappers have posted something else online,' he said. 'This time it's a video clip.'

There was a collective intake of breath followed by one hell of a commotion as virtually everyone in the hall – including those parents who had hung around – either reached for their phones or dashed outside.

A few minutes later Anna and DI Walker viewed the video together in the mobile incident van.

It was enough to bring tears to Anna's eyes and cause a fierce rage to ball like a fist inside her.

'We need to catch these cunts,' Walker said, and the words hissed out through his teeth. 'But if and when we do I strongly advise you not to leave me alone with them. If you do I swear I will kill them with my bare fucking hands.'

CHAPTER THIRTY-ONE

The video clip lasted two minutes. The first thirty seconds was shot in a room that was in semi-darkness. The camera panned across the floor to reveal nine empty sleeping bags, each with a pillow.

An electronically distorted voice provided a sinister commentary:

'This is where the noisy little brats spent the night. Most of them cried themselves to sleep. Those who made a fuss were punished.'

The shot changed to show another room. This one was brighter, and the carpeted floor was littered with toys. There was also a black leather sofa and a large TV on a stand.

There were six children in the room and they were wearing the same clothes they'd had on the day before.

Anna recognised them all from their photographs – Daniel Neville, aged three, Toby Chandler, aged four, Simone Green, aged four, Abdul Ahmed, aged four, Justine Brooks, aged four and Molly Wilson, aged five.

All six were sitting quietly while watching a *Peppa Pig*

animation programme on TV. The three girls were on the sofa and the boys were on the floor.

The boys had their backs to the camera, but the girls' faces were visible and they weren't smiling. It was obvious that they had slept in their clothes and that their hair hadn't been brushed.

After a couple of seconds the commentary continued:

'This is the quietest they've been but that's because they now know what to expect if they piss us off. The sooner they're back with their parents the better for all concerned.'

Before the shot changed again, Molly Wilson turned to face the camera and you could see that she was trying desperately not to cry. She was gritting her teeth and her whole body was trembling.

Another shot, another room. This one was smaller and less bright, and contained a single bed pushed up against a wall.

Five-year-old Sahib Hussein was sitting on the floor with his back against the bed. His knees were drawn up to his chest and his face was tucked between them. His muffled sobs sent Anna's heart into freefall.

There was another child on top of the bed. Grace Tenant, aged four, had her back against a pile of pillows and the expression on her face was one of sheer terror.

The commentary continued:

'These little bastards are the ones who've given us most of the problems. They won't stop crying and they've both shit themselves. So they don't get to watch television.'

The camera zoomed in on Grace's face and a voice out of shot asked her what she wanted to say to her mummy. Grace looked into the camera and as she spoke her voice was punctuated by sobs.

'I want . . . you . . . to save . . . me, mummy. Please . . . because I scared.'

The video then cut abruptly to a menacing-looking figure dressed all in black. It was clearly a man and he was sitting in a chair facing the camera, which framed his head and torso. He was wearing a balaclava and a roll-neck sweater and the only parts of him visible were his eyes and his mouth.

'*You now have until eleven o'clock on Thursday morning to sort out the money,*' he said in the same distorted voice. '*That should give you plenty of time. We will then make contact again. We'll expect the transfer of six million pounds worth of Bitcoins to be swift and efficient. If it doesn't happen the little girl you just saw will be the first to die. After that, for each day that the money isn't paid, another child will die and the ransom will go up by another million. And to prove to you that these are not idle threats, the killings will be carried out on camera and the videos posted online.*'

The man smiled then, revealing a set of small, sharp teeth. Moments later the image faded to black.

CHAPTER THIRTY-TWO

A long career in the Met had exposed Anna Tate to all kinds of upsetting sights and experiences. But the last time she'd felt so shaken was when she'd read the text message from her ex-husband telling her that he had abducted their daughter and she would never see Chloe again.

The video from the kidnappers was beyond evil and it had a profound effect on her and everyone else.

For the media vultures it was an exciting development in a story that just kept on giving. But for the parents it was yet another dose of sheer torture.

Understandably, Kenneth Tenant reacted badly to seeing his petrified daughter and being told that she would be the first to die if the ransom wasn't paid.

After viewing the video on a reporter's phone, he dropped to his knees and sobbed like a baby. His wife stood over him and cried with him.

The impact the video had on Ruth Brady was different but no less seismic. She gave a terrible anguished cry and then turned to her husband and said, 'Liam's not on the video. He's the only one missing. Oh my God Ethan, our baby must be dead. They killed him.'

For a while there was chaos in the community centre as officers tried to move the reporters, photographers and camera crews outside. But they carried on filming, taking pictures and interviewing as many people as they could, including parents, police officers and each other.

Anna called DCS Nash, who had viewed the press conference live on a television in the meeting room at the Yard. Even he couldn't disguise the tremor in his voice.

'It was like watching a horror film,' he said. 'The bastards staged it so that it would have the maximum impact. Is there any chance we can find out who uploaded it?'

'I very much doubt it, but we'll try,' Anna said. 'I gather it was also emailed to several newspapers, as was the photograph.'

'I got the impression it's a fairly large house.'

'And it's probably in the country somewhere,' Anna said. 'But that doesn't give us much to go on.'

'I can tell it's pretty manic there right now. Do you want me to come over?'

'There's no need. I'll be leaving after I've given a brief statement to the hacks. I don't want them thinking we're too freaked out to react to what's happened.'

'Well, be careful what you say, Anna. Every bugger out there will be latching on to your every word.'

Anna then spoke to each of the parents again before they were driven home. Most of them were too upset even to respond, including Kenneth Tenant and Ruth Brady. But Ruth's husband, Ethan, took her to one side and said, 'I'm just praying that my boy is still alive. But if he is he won't be for much longer without his medication. I beg you to do everything you can to make sure the ransom is paid. That monster on the video wasn't bluffing and you know it. If they don't get the money they'll carry out their threat.'

Anna was of the same opinion but she held back from telling him. Instead, she said, 'Just trust me, Mr Brady. Everything possible will be done to reunite you all with your children.'

It was another forty minutes before the police had the community centre to themselves again.

The parents had gone home and the media reps had been moved back out onto the street. Anna had told the reporters that she'd provide them with a short statement after she had spoken to her team.

By now there were six detectives and fifteen uniformed officers in the community centre, plus a dozen or so support staff. They were all keen to air their views about the video and reaffirm their commitment to finding the children.

One of the WPCs had actually been reduced to tears by what she'd seen and she spoke for everyone when she said, 'Those heartless bastards deserve to rot in hell for what they're doing to those kiddies.'

And one of the civilian staff members with the media liaison team said, 'My son is the same age as that little girl on the video. He goes to a nursery school in Forest Hill. I just phoned my wife and told her to pick him up and take him home. I'm not sure we can ever let him go back there now we know that he will never be safe.'

Anna didn't doubt that it was a sentiment that would be

shared by thousands of other parents across the country. The kidnappers had already raised huge question marks over safety measures at nursery schools. But the gruesome video would compound parents' fears and could even lead to a massive boycott of all pre-school establishments.

It made Anna think of Chloe. Just weeks before Matthew abducted her they'd discussed sending her to a nursery school two streets away from the house in Vauxhall. But back then what had happened in Peabody Street would only have been the stuff of nightmares. Now it was a hideous reality and had the potential to impact on society in the same way that terrorist van attacks had.

The whole of the pre-school sector would be expected to respond to this new threat. And it was a threat that was likely to become even more credible if the kidnappers achieved their objective and walked away with six million pounds.

Having listened to what her team members had to say about this shocking development, Anna issued a list of instructions.

'I want that video examined frame by frame and every detail logged,' she said. 'You're looking for any clues that might suggest where it was taken. Zoom into every object and listen for background sounds that you weren't aware of when you first watched it.

'And set the cyber analysts to work on it. The emails were probably routed through hundreds of proxy servers, but I refuse to accept that it renders them completely untraceable.'

She then said she was going to return to the office to question Jonas Platt. On the way she would interview Phil Green at Camberwell police station, then call on Sarah Ramsay at her home.

'We're looking at those three because it's just conceivable that they were somehow involved in planning the crime. But we have to accept that there's no hard evidence linking them to it. They're in the frame because each of them has a possible motive and, let's be honest, because we don't have any other suspects.

'We therefore need to up our game. Keep looking at everyone who is linked in any way to the nursery and the parents. And get me an update on where we are with the organised outfits. Could one of the London gangs be behind this? We know they're fond of kidnapping each other's people but maybe one of them has decided to branch out.'

A few more issues were discussed and tasks assigned. Then Anna wound up the meeting and went outside to talk to the media.

She told them that the video of the children and the masked kidnapper had come as an enormous shock.

'We're doing our best to find out who posted it online and sent it as an email attachment to several newspapers,' she said. 'And we're continuing to follow up every lead in an effort to locate the children. Meanwhile, we're also providing round-the-clock support to the parents who've been traumatised by this latest, cruel development.

'In respect of the ransom demand, nothing has changed since I addressed that question during the press conference. What response there should be has still to be determined.'

One of the reporters raised a hand in the air to draw attention to himself.

'Does that mean you're not aware, DCI Tate, of the story that broke in the last ten minutes?' he said.

Anna arched her brow at him. 'And what story is that, sir?'

'An anonymous businessman has offered to pay the six-million-pound ransom to the kidnappers,' he said. 'And he's calling on the police to arrange the transfer on his behalf. Do you think that will be possible?'

It was another unexpected turn of events that Anna wasn't prepared for. She twisted her lips in thought and remembered what Nash had told her about being careful what she said. For that reason she decided to duck the question.

'That's news to me,' she said. 'It's something that will have to be considered by my superiors and officials at the Home Office.'

She turned sharply on her heels and walked away, hoping she wouldn't look flustered and out of her depth when the footage appeared on the television news.

CHAPTER THIRTY-THREE

Sarah Ramsay lived in a terraced house just half a mile from Peabody Street. But when Anna and Walker turned up there she wasn't at home. Anna had her mobile number so she rang it, but there was no answer. She decided to leave a message.

'It's DCI Tate here, Miss Ramsay. I need to talk to you again. Will you please get back to me as soon as possible so that we can arrange a time and a place later today?'

It was only a short ride from Sarah Ramsay's house to Camberwell, and Anna and Walker spent it discussing the anonymous tycoon's offer to pay the ransom.

'It's no great surprise to me,' Walker said. 'If I had more dosh than I could spend I'd do the same after seeing that bloody video.'

As he spoke he gripped the steering wheel so hard his knuckles turned white.

Anna could tell that the case was getting to him. He wasn't usually one to let his emotions show but, as the father of two little girls, he empathised with the parents of the kidnapped children.

'I suspect that by the end of the day people will be queuing up to pay all or some of the ransom,' Anna said. 'The problem is it will play right into the hands of the kidnappers and make it difficult, if not impossible, to negotiate with them.'

'I have to admit that those guys, whoever they are, have played a blinder,' Walker said grudgingly. 'It's not as if this job would have taken much planning either. All they had to do was nick a minibus or two and find somewhere secluded to hide the kids. And children of that age are relatively easy to control. You just have to feed them, scare them and keep them quiet.'

'Well, from what we saw on the video, it seems like they've got things well and truly under their control,' Anna said.

Walker nodded. 'And I reckon it's safe to assume that they've also got everything organised in respect of the money transfer. Using a digital currency is a clever move on their part. In fact, kidnappers are frequently opting for it now to ensure that ransoms can be paid anonymously. But Christ knows what will happen once it's paid. They might well keep the kids and ask for more. Or some other gang could jump on the bandwagon and grab a bunch of kids from another nursery.'

Both were terrifying prospects. And for Anna a stark reminder that this case was tough, emotive and dangerously unpredictable.

The duty inspector at Camberwell police station was expecting them. He explained that Phil Green had been charged with drink driving and hadn't objected when told that he would have to remain in custody for a while.

'We've set aside an interview room so I'll have him brought up right away,' the inspector said.

'Has he been offered legal representation?' Anna asked.

The inspector nodded. 'He has but he turned it down. He reckons he doesn't need a lawyer.'

The interview room was small and gloomy, and contained a table and four chairs. A fluorescent light hummed on the ceiling.

Phil Green was brought in by a uniformed officer. He was a big man, out of condition. He had a drinker's bloated face and dark, untidy stubble lined his jaw. He was wearing an open-neck shirt and black jeans, and it looked like he hadn't changed in a week.

Anna gestured for him to sit opposite them. 'I'm Detective Chief Inspector Tate and this is Detective Inspector Walker, Mr Green. We're investigating the abduction of your daughter and the other children from the Peabody Nursery in Rotherhithe.'

Once seated he tilted his head back and appraised Anna with his flint-grey eyes.

'I'm confused,' he said, and the agitation was obvious in the tenor of his voice. 'First that detective came to my flat last night and questioned me like I was a frigging suspect. And now this. You should be out there looking for Simone. Not giving me a hard time just for the sake of it.'

Anna could smell the booze on his breath and it made her stomach turn.

'Tell us what happened this morning, Mr Green,' she said.

He blew out air through puckered lips and shrugged.

'I should have stopped at a T-junction, but I didn't and rammed into the side of a ruddy bus. And yeah, I was over the limit. But who can blame me for hitting the bottle after being told that my daughter had been kidnapped? I was in a right state. I couldn't sleep all night and the whisky was all I had for company.'

'So where were you going?' Walker asked.

He licked his lips, swallowed hard. 'To Peabody Street. I told my ex-wife I'd meet her there in the community centre. She told me you lot were going to update all the parents.'

'When was the last time you saw your daughter?' Walker asked.

'What's that got to do with anything?'

'Just answer the question.'

Green shrugged. 'It's been weeks. My ex has been keeping her away from me. She got custody and thinks . . .'

A light seemed to go on inside his head suddenly and he thrust out his jaw.

'It's that bitch, isn't it?' he said, leaning forward, elbows on the table. 'She's made me out to be some kind of nutter. What has she told you? That I might have been involved in kidnapping my own kid just to get back at her? Is that it?'

'She's told us you've threatened her and been violent towards her,' Anna said. 'She also claims you're an alcoholic with a serious gambling addiction that's left you in considerable debt. Now, to my mind, that suggests you're quite capable of doing something pretty wild and very nasty because you're desperate for money or set on revenge. But that's not why we're having this conversation.'

His eyebrows snapped together in a frown. 'So why are we having it then?'

'Because you lied to the detective who came to your flat. You told him you were in bed most of yesterday. You said you had a hangover and didn't go out until the afternoon. But you were caught on CCTV leaving your flat shortly after the children were snatched from the nursery. So that tells me you went somewhere and didn't want anyone to know about it.'

He challenged her with a sneer.

'Firstly I don't have to account for my movements to you or anyone else,' he said, his speech now fast and clipped. 'And secondly there is no way I would ever hurt Simone. She means the world to me. Why do you think I'm so pissed off that her mother makes it so hard for me to see her? I admit to being a pathetic arsehole but I'm not a baby snatcher.'

'So you're saying you had absolutely nothing to do with what happened to those children,' Anna said.

'I've told you that. The Peabody staff know me. So they must have told you that I wasn't one of the three fuckers who did it.'

'That doesn't mean you weren't involved in some other capacity. You could have helped plan it.'

He shook his head and laughed. 'For fuck's sake you must be desperate. Is it not obvious to you by now that I couldn't organise a piss-up in brewery?'

'So what exactly is your problem?' Walker asked him.

'I thought you knew that,' he replied. 'My ex-wife is my problem. She's turned my life into a living hell, and it's because of her that I drink too much and I'm living on the fucking breadline.'

'So maybe it's time you took responsibility for your own actions,' Anna said.

He glared at her and produced a crooked smile.

'That's easy for you to say, copper,' he said. 'You strike me as someone who's sailed through life without anything bad happening to her. So don't you dare lecture me.'

Anna felt Walker's body tense beside her so she put her hand on his arm to stop him reacting. As much as she felt like telling Green how wrong he was, she decided it just wasn't worth the effort.

'Let's get back on track here,' she said. 'I want to know where you went yesterday and why you lied about it to one of my officers.'

'I went for a drive,' he said. 'And as far as I know there's no law against that.'

'So where did you go?'

'I can't remember.'

'Is that because you were drunk?'

'I wasn't drunk.'

'So you didn't have a hangover from drinking too much the night before.'

He cleared his throat and his eyes seemed to go out of focus.

'I was just feeling miserable. And when I feel like that driving around helps me to get my head straight.'

'So why didn't you say that to Detective Shepherd? Why make up a story about staying in bed?'

He licked his lips and squinted.

'I don't know. I was upset and confused after he broke the news to me about Simone. It was a lot to take in and I just said the first thing that came into my head.'

Anna's eyes flared with impatience. She leaned forward across the table and her voice took on a hard edge.

'It's so bloody obvious that you're lying,' she snapped. 'You're hiding something and I won't leave you alone until I know what it is. But if it has nothing to do with the kidnappings then you really ought to tell me because every minute I waste talking to you is time that could be better spent trying to find your daughter. And if you really love her like you say you do, you will stop pissing us around and tell the truth.'

Green sat back in his chair, his reddened eyes struggling to find focus. He was considering his options, weighing up what he should and shouldn't say. It made Anna want to grab him by the neck and shake it out of him.

For several long seconds he just sat there, his lips clamped together, a vein pulsing at the side of his head.

Then he blew out his cheeks resignedly and said, 'OK, I'll tell you and face the consequences, but only because I don't want any harm to come to my daughter.'

CHAPTER THIRTY-FOUR

'So what did you make of that?' Walker said as they hurried out of Camberwell police station. 'Was the scumbag telling the truth?'

Anna shrugged. 'I think so, but we won't know for sure until we've checked out his story.' She held out her hands and asked him for the car keys. 'I'll drive while you get on the phone and put Shepherd on the case.'

In the car Walker called DC Shepherd and told him they had just interviewed Phil Green.

'He fessed up to lying to you last night,' Walker said. 'But not before we told him he was caught on CCTV leaving his flat yesterday morning. He claims he went to his ex-wife's house because he knew she'd be out at work after dropping their daughter off at the nursery. He's still got a key because he used to live there. He apparently let himself in and stole some cash and jewellery. You need to come to Camberwell and pick Green up. Then take him to his flat. He's agreed to give back what he took. At the same time search the place for anything that might link him to the kidnappings. He's given us permission so you won't need a warrant and I doubt you'll find anything anyway.

'After that, speak to his ex-wife to see if she wants to press charges, and check CCTV cameras around her house so we can confirm the times he gave us.'

Anna had nothing but contempt for Phil Green, but he'd convinced her that he wasn't involved in the abductions, partly because she didn't think he had it in him to pull off something so daring. The man was a good-for-nothing toerag who had hit rock bottom.

'I'm pretty sure his story will check out,' Walker said when he came off the phone. 'So at least we won't have to waste any more time with him. He doesn't even seem overly concerned about his own daughter. Makes you wonder why he's been kicking up such a fuss about losing custody of her to his ex.'

'I suspect that's all about control,' Anna said. 'The woman he bullied and threatened finally got one over on him and he can't handle it.'

In a way, Green reminded her of Matthew: he'd never come to terms with the fact that Anna had divorced him, despite the fact he was the cause. And when she wouldn't have him back he set out to get revenge using their child as his weapon of choice.

The thought would have lingered but for the sound of Anna's phone ringing. She whipped it out of her jacket pocket and handed it to Walker.

'You'll have to take it,' she said.

He took it from her and answered it.

'DCI Tate's phone,' he said. 'This is DI Walker.'

He listened and then said, 'So where are you now? Right. In that case we'll come to your house later. Will you be in all afternoon? I see. We'll call with a time then.'

After hanging up, he said, 'That was Sarah Ramsay. She wasn't at home earlier or able to answer the phone because she was with Tasha Norris's husband. She picked him up from the hospital after his wife died and took him home. She's now busy informing her customers that the Peabody Street Nursery will be closed for the foreseeable future.'

'We'll go and see her after we've talked to Jonas Platt,' Anna said. 'The more I think about that woman the more suspicious I'm becoming. How did she strike you, Max?'

He shrugged. 'She's smart and attractive and seemed genuinely upset over what's happened. But I've not had a one-to-one conversation with her like you have.'

'Well, she is intelligent,' Anna said. 'There's no question about that. But it wasn't a very smart move letting those men into the nursery without first checking their credentials. And as for being upset – that could be an act.'

'She definitely has a motive,' Walker said. 'Sounds like there's a good chance she'll go bankrupt if she can't sell her business.'

'And with all this bad publicity that will become increasingly difficult.'

Walker nodded. 'So it could be she did opt for the nuclear option. If so, then six million quid would be enough to dig her out of the shit and provide ample reward for those people who agreed to help her.'

'We need to run a check on everyone she knows. Does she have any dodgy friends? And let's get access to her phone records and emails.'

'I'll get on to it as soon as we're back in the office.'

Walker was still holding Anna's phone when it pinged with a text message.

'Can you see who it's from?' she asked him. 'It could be important.'

He opened up the message, and as he read it a deep frown scored his forehead.

'So that's why you've been a bit distracted,' he said.

She took her eyes off the road to look at him.

'What are you on about?'

Walker held up her phone. 'Well, the message is from someone named Paul Russell. He says, and I quote: "I know from the news how busy you are, but I can't do this over the phone. If you have time, please come visit me so I can apologise for the part I played in what happened ten years ago."'

Anna felt something lodge in her throat, and every muscle in her body seemed to contract.

'So who the hell is Paul Russell and what is it he knows about Chloe and Matthew?' Walker said.

It was several seconds before Anna could speak, and when she did it sounded as though her voice was being squeezed out of her.

'All I know about him is that he's dying of cancer,' she said. 'He sent me a message yesterday via my FindChloe Facebook page. He said he had information from ten years ago and he wanted to pass it on to me before he died.'

She told Walker about the conversation she'd had with Russell's wife and how she'd found out that a man with that name was indeed spending his last days at a hospice in Dulwich.

'What does he mean when he says he wants to apologise for the part he played in what happened?'

'I have no idea,' Anna said. 'It wasn't in the first message.'

'So shall I respond to him for you?'

'Not yet. I need to think about this.'

She felt nauseous suddenly, and hoped it didn't show in her expression.

'Look, I know how important this is to you, guv,' Walker said. 'Why don't you go and see him? I can cover for you. It shouldn't take long.'

'That wouldn't be fair,' she replied.

'Why not? I'm more than capable of—'

She cut him off. 'I don't mean fair on you. I'm talking about those nine children and their parents. They're my priority right now and I can't allow myself to be distracted by this.'

'But you are distracted, guv. And with good reason.'

'I accept that, but this level of distraction I can manage. If he tells me something that blows my mind then I'll never be able to concentrate on this investigation. I'd be letting those kids down and I can't do that.'

'But what if he dies?' Walker said. 'If he's in a hospice with cancer then he must be on his last legs.'

'He won't die before I get to see him.'

'How do you know that?'

'I just do. Now will you please just let it go, Max, before I decide to do something I will later come to regret?'

Walker dropped it but the latest message from Paul Russell was stuck on repeat mode inside Anna's head.

If you have time, please come visit me so I can apologise for the part I played in what happened ten years ago.

It made no sense to Anna. What possible role could he have played in Chloe's abduction? She was sure she had never heard Matthew mention his name. So who was he? And what

exactly had he done that was so bad he felt the need to apologise for it on his deathbed?

At any other time Anna would have rushed straight over
to the hospice. But these were exceptional circumstances. She
was heading up an investigation in which every second
counted. The kidnappers had imposed a deadline. The lives
of nine small children hung in the balance. Their parents
were counting on her doing all she could to save them, and
she was determined not to let them down.

CHAPTER THIRTY-FIVE

Back at MIT headquarters, Anna was told that Jonas Platt was waiting to be interviewed. He had asked to be represented by the duty solicitor but had not once objected to being brought in.

'According to the officers from Kent who drove him here he's keen to talk to you,' DI Bellingham said. 'He apparently wants to sound off about Sarah Ramsay and her nurseries.'

Before meeting Platt, Anna called the team together to see where they were and to tell them what they'd got from Phil Green.

Unfortunately very little progress had been made since the last briefing. No new suspects had emerged and the Cyber Crime Unit hadn't managed to find out who had posted the video and photo of the children.

They were still waiting for the DNA results on the cigarette butt found next to where the minibus was dumped in Kent. And they'd received very few calls so far in response to the e-fits of the three kidnappers. Half of all those that had come in had already been followed up and proved to be false alarms.

But it wasn't all negative news. Scotland Yard's Serious and Organised Crime Command had appointed a team of officers to work full-time on trying to establish whether one of the big London gangs might be involved. And in the last few minutes the Met Commissioner had issued a public statement in which he appealed to the kidnappers to get in touch with him personally so that he could discuss the ransom demand.

'So what's to stop every nutter in the country from calling in?' someone asked.

DI Bellingham explained that before being put through they would be asked if the kidnappers had left anything inside the minibus when they abandoned it.

'We haven't made public the fact that they left a note on the front seat so that should be enough to establish credibility,' he said.

There was nothing for Anna to get excited about, and as she headed off to interview Jonas Platt, her head started to pound with the effort of thinking about it all.

Jonas Platt was waiting for them in the interview room. He sat next to the duty solicitor, and a ceiling fan circled lazily above them.

Platt was in his forties, with a pock-marked face and pale eyes with dark shadows beneath them. He was wearing a tight brown T-shirt that clung to his thin frame and had a big, dark stain on the chest.

Anna could feel him sizing her up. When she introduced herself and Walker he responded with a sharp nod and a tepid smile.

For the benefit of the tape recorder she then named everyone in the room and said that Mr Platt was being interviewed as part of the investigation into the Peabody Street kidnappings.

The duty solicitor intervened at this point. His name was Ray Thomas and he was a sharply dressed man aged about fifty. Anna knew him well and had a lot of respect for him.

'Before we start, I would like it to be recorded that Mr Platt has not been arrested or charged with any offence and came here of his own free will,' he said.

'Duly noted,' Anna replied. Then she turned to Platt and said, 'Is there anything you would like to say before we start asking questions, Mr Platt?'

He pressed his lips together while he thought about it and said, 'Only that as soon as I heard what had happened at the nursery in Peabody Street I knew that it wouldn't be long before you lot were knocking on my door. But that's OK because it's got nothing to do with me. I admit I hate Sarah Ramsay with a vengeance and want to see her nurseries closed down. But abducting a bunch of children is not how I'd go about it.'

'Can I ask you where you were yesterday morning, Mr Platt?' Anna asked him.

'You should know this already. I went to stay at my caravan in Dymchurch. Got there on Friday night aiming to stay for about a week.'

'And you were alone?'

'That's right. I'm between jobs so I've got plenty of time on my hands and I get bored in London.'

'So the first you heard about the kidnappings was when the police contacted you.'

'No. I'd already heard it on the news.'

Anna took out her notebook and placed it on the table. She flicked through it until she came to the notes she'd made about the man sitting opposite her.

'I just want to remind myself why your name is at the top of our list of suspects, Mr Platt,' she said.

His eyes flared with impatience as she scanned the page and clucked her tongue in response to what was written on it.

'Let's start with your criminal record, shall we?' she said. 'Eight years ago you were jailed for fifteen months for assaulting a man. Before that you did a spell of community service for drug offences. So we know you're not averse to breaking the law.'

'That was in a previous life,' he said. 'After I met Angela I changed. I got a job and put all that stuff behind me. Then we married and had Kelly and there was no going back. I was made up and happy with life.'

'But then you lost Kelly,' Anna said, her tone gentler.

Platt nodded. 'That was nineteen months ago in January, three weeks after her third birthday.'

'It's my understanding that her death was a tragic accident, Mr Platt.'

'That depends how you look at it,' he said. 'Everyone knows that it's dangerous to give children whole grapes to eat. There have been plenty of warnings over the years that they should be cut up. Other kids have died in the same way that Kelly did. So as far as I'm concerned those nursery staff who were supposed to be looking after her were to blame. They put out a bowl of grapes for the children to share. Kelly choked on the first one she put into her mouth. All attempts to revive her failed.'

There were tears in his eyes now and Anna couldn't help but feel sorry for him.

'Was Sarah Ramsay there when it happened?' she asked.

'No, but that doesn't mean she wasn't ultimately responsible,' he said. 'It was her business and so she should be held accountable. I learned afterwards that there was nothing in the staff guidelines about potentially dangerous foods.'

'So you set out to make her pay for what happened.'

'Well, I couldn't let her get away with it, and if I hadn't decided to do something she would have. So I made sure everyone knew what I thought.'

'She says you threatened her on a number of occasions,' Anna said. 'You even went to her house and said you would make her suffer. And you stood outside one of the nurseries with a placard that accused the staff of murdering your daughter.'

He wiped his eyes on his bare arm, then laced his hands together on the table.

'I lost it. I know that. I was so angry when I learned that her nurseries wouldn't be closed down. All she got was a fine. It wasn't right.'

'So you continued your campaign of threats and abuse until the court issued a restraining order against you.'

He nodded. 'That's correct, but by then I'd had enough anyway. My obsession with it all impacted on my marriage and Angela eventually left me. But I'll never apologise for my actions. What's happened in Peabody Street shows that I should have been listened to. If the authorities had closed all the nurseries then those poor kiddies wouldn't have been snatched.'

'Were you aware that Miss Ramsay is being forced to sell the nurseries because business is so bad?'

He dredged up a smile. 'I didn't know but I'm glad. I only hope I had a part to play in her downfall. And I hope to God she loses all her money.'

'When was the last time you spoke to her?' Anna asked.

'A week or so after she got the restraining order. I phoned her to tell her she'd ruined my life and that I would never let her forget it.'

'What did she say?'

'She told me that if I contacted her again she would phone the police and have me arrested. But then that same night I got a call from a man who said that if I didn't leave her alone he'd come round and cut me up.'

'Did he use those exact words?'

Platt nodded. 'I'll never forget the way he spoke to me. He sounded like a right nut job.'

'Do you know who he was?'

'He said he was her partner but he wouldn't give his name. And he also told me that he knew I'd split from my wife and that if I didn't back off he'd pay her a visit.'

'Is his number still on your phone?'

'No number came up and I got the impression he was calling from a phone box.'

Anna looked at Walker and raised her brow. She thought back to her chat with Sarah Ramsay and reminded herself what the woman had said.

I don't have a family and there's been no man in my life for some time. So I had to deal with it by myself and it really freaked me out.

So did she lie or simply forget to mention the mystery man who leapt to her defence by threatening Jonas Platt?

The interview lasted another twenty minutes, with Walker

asking most of the questions. Platt continued to deny any involvement in the kidnappings and the duty solicitor pointed out that there was no evidence to justify holding him in custody.

It was five o'clock when Anna called a halt after Platt gave permission for his home to be searched and his phone records checked.

As he walked out of the interview room his parting words to Anna were, 'Sarah Ramsay should be locked up. She's already got my daughter's blood on her hands and now these other nine children will in all likelihood turn up dead because of her.'

CHAPTER THIRTY-SIX

Ruth was lying on Liam's bed, hugging his pillow. She didn't know what else to do with herself.

They had arrived home hours ago and she was still unable to contain her anguish. The video had convinced her that she would never see her son again. If he was alive then surely he would have featured in it along with the other children.

Ethan was still in denial, telling her to have faith, be positive, that there was no reason to assume the worst. But the fear was like a crushing weight in her chest.

The constant presence of the family liaison officer had been more unsettling than helpful so they had asked her to give them some privacy. Officer Robinson said she understood and gave them her contact details. She told them to call her whenever they needed to and that she would be in regular contact by phone.

'As soon as there's a development I'll let you know,' she'd said.

Even the word development caused the blood to thunder

in Ruth's head. So far every 'development' had added to her suffering. The dumping of the minibus. The photograph. The video. The ransom demand from the man in the balaclava.

Ruth found herself in the not unfamiliar position of resenting the other parents. Only now it wasn't because their children didn't have a life-threatening condition. It was because they knew that their sons and daughters were alive. They had seen them in the photo and on the video. So if the ransom did get paid then they would get them back.

But Ruth was denied even that tiny crumb of comfort. She knew that Ethan felt it even more than she did. After Kenneth Tenant had reacted tearfully to seeing his terrified daughter on the video, Ethan had leaned over and whispered in her ear, 'It's about time that smug git had something to cry about.'

It was a nasty thing to say but Ruth understood where it came from. For ages Kenneth Tenant had treated Liam almost like a leper, even suggesting once that he shouldn't be allowed to play with 'normal, healthy' kids.

'Is there anything you want, Ruth?'

Ethan broke into Ruth's thoughts, peering into the bedroom for the third time in the last hour.

'I want Liam back,' she said. 'And I want us to be a family again.'

'We will be,' he said. 'Just as soon as the ransom is paid.'

She pushed the pillow to one side and swung her legs to the floor.

'You can't be certain of that,' she said, louder than she'd intended. 'And even if it does get paid it doesn't mean that . . .'

'Don't bloody say it again,' he snapped at her. 'You're like a prophet of fucking doom and I don't want to hear it.'

She leapt to her feet so fast that her glasses came off and fell on the carpet.

'But I'm not like you,' she said. 'I can't convince myself that everything will be all right just by telling myself it will be.'

He gritted his teeth and shook his head.

'I'm as scared as you are, Ruth, but the only way I can handle it is with positive thinking. There's still no proof that our son is no longer alive. So I refuse to believe that he isn't.'

Ethan's face was a blur so Ruth reached down to pick up her glasses. When she stood up again he was no longer standing in the doorway.

She put her glasses back on and stepped out of the bedroom. Her mind was in turmoil as she walked down the stairs and her legs felt heavy and weak.

Ethan was in the kitchen, pouring himself a glass of wine from the fridge.

'Do you want one?' he asked her.

'It's too early for me,' she said. 'I think what I need is some fresh air.'

'Then go into the garden. It's still warm out.'

He turned to face her and she was surprised to see the pity in his eyes.

'We need to accept that we have different ways of coping with this,' he said. 'And we will only get through it if we stick together and support each other.'

He put the glass down on the worktop and came towards her, and when he took her in his arms she lost it again and sobs wracked her body. But he held onto her until she stopped and it made her realise that she still loved him and did not want to lose him.

But was he still in love with her? she wondered. That was

the million-dollar question. His love and loyalty had been cast into doubt by her suspicions that he was cheating on her. But she still didn't know for sure that he was. So was it possible she was a victim of her own paranoia?

She thought about his other phone, the one she hadn't known about. Had she leapt to the wrong conclusion? Was there an innocent explanation, after all?

'You have to stop blaming yourself,' Ethan said. 'I think that's the main reason why you're being so negative.'

She was taken aback, and for a moment she actually thought he'd been reading her mind. But then he clarified the remark with: 'I've forgiven you for not taking Liam to the Shrek Adventure instead of to the nursery so you could see that editor bloke. It's time you forgave yourself.'

A red mist descended and she pushed him away with a hard shove.

'You bastard. How dare you say that? It wasn't my fault.'

Instead of apologising, he shook his head and reached for his glass of wine. His body was stiff, jaw clenched, eyes hard.

'The fact is, he wasn't supposed to have been there, Ruth,' he said. 'I just can't shake that thought out of my mind. I wish I could.'

Ruth felt her throat constrict and dry up. She stood in the middle of the kitchen, paralysed by a blast of hot anger. She wanted to say something to him as he walked through the open kitchen door into the garden. But the words just wouldn't come.

She looked around, unsure what to do next. Her eyes settled on her handbag that was lying on the table. Without thinking she grabbed it and hurried into the hall where she slipped into her shoes.

'I'm going out,' she yelled back at Ethan, but as she stepped through the front door she wasn't even sure that he heard her.

She wanted to flee from her thoughts but she knew that wasn't going to be possible. The next best thing, she decided, was to walk the streets for a while in the hope that it would help subdue the whirlwind of emotions that was raging through her.

She was angry, upset, fearful. And her stomach was cramping with nerves.

As she walked she ran her hands through her hair, digging her fingers into her scalp. The streets were busy with the tail-end of the rush hour and there were people out walking just because they wanted to make the most of the sunshine. Some of them stared at her, but that was no surprise because she must have looked a mess as well as distressed.

Myriad thoughts and images continued to crowd her mind. Liam's cute little face. Ethan's insensitive expression. The man in the balaclava on the video.

They were grinding her down, freezing the blood in her veins. She wasn't sure how much more she could take.

She came to the corner shop where she often took Liam to buy him sweets and ice creams. Saw a pile of newspapers on the floor just inside the door. The latest edition of the giveaway *Evening Standard*. The headline screamed at her.

NURSERY KIDNAPPERS
DEMAND £6M RANSOM

Beneath it was the photograph of the children and an image from the video of balaclava man.

Ruth picked up a copy and read the sub-heading.

Parents' anguish as kidnappers
threaten to kill their children

The story stretched across the first five inside pages. There were more images from the video, photographs of the nursery, the scene in Peabody Street earlier in the day, the abandoned minibus, shots of police officers working the case – including Detective Anna Tate, to whom several quotes were attributed.

There was even a boxed-off section about Tate's own missing daughter, Chloe, and how the detective had been searching for her for ten years. It included a picture of the girl taken at the age of two shortly before she was abducted by her father, who was believed to have moved to another country with her.

On another page there were individual photos of the nine children, including one of Liam. Then Ruth saw a picture of herself at the press conference. A whole half page was devoted to Liam and his condition and the fact that he was the only child missing from the photograph and video posted by the kidnappers.

'His parents and the police fear that the three-year-old may have been taken ill or even that he could have died because he doesn't have his medication,' wrote the reporter, who was named as Luke Dennis.

Ruth folded the paper and stuffed it into her bag. Then she started walking again, and it struck her as strange that around her life was going on as normal. People were laughing, chatting, going about their business completely oblivious, it seemed, to the nightmare that had engulfed nine London families. It didn't seem right. Or fair.

She walked aimlessly for about an hour, eventually arriving back at her house.

She was still distraught and, if anything, angrier than she'd been when she'd started out. And that anger was directed at her husband. He should have been helping her through this instead of making her feel bad about herself.

It then occurred to her that while she'd been out he had probably been on the phone to his bit on the side, pouring out his heart to her and telling her that it was all his wife's fault.

Bastard.

She decided to confront him and to hell with the consequences. She would ask him why he had a second phone. And demand to see who he'd been calling on it.

But just as she was approaching their front door she noticed that their car was no longer in its parking bay.

And when she let herself into the house she discovered that it was empty. Ethan had gone out. But where?

She groped in her bag for her mobile, speed-dialling his number.

And then she heard it ring and seconds later she saw that he had left it on the worktop in the kitchen. There was no sign of the other phone, of course; she assumed that the bastard had taken that with him.

CHAPTER THIRTY-SEVEN

Sarah Ramsay was drying her hair with a towel when Anna and Walker arrived at her house. She explained that she had just had a shower and then led them through to the living room.

It was bright and modern with contemporary furniture and glass doors leading to a smart patio.

'I needed to freshen up,' she said as she gestured for them to be seated. 'I never slept last night and I didn't get the chance to shower this morning.'

'Another bad day, I take it,' Anna said.

Sarah finished drying her hair and dropped the towel on top of a side cabinet.

'That would be an understatement,' she said. 'When I heard about Tasha I went straight to the hospital to be with her husband. It was unbelievably distressing. Then I had to fend off the press who've been phoning and turning up at my door. I also had to inform all the parents whose children attend Peabody Street that the nursery won't be open for a while.

But in all honesty I don't expect to be seeing them again anyway. Not after what's happened.'

She did appear tired, Anna thought, but even without make-up, her flawless skin glowed and her eyes sparkled. It was hard to believe she'd been through such a traumatic ordeal.

She was wearing shorts and a baggy brown blouse. As she stood there asking them if they wanted drinks, Anna noticed Walker couldn't take his eyes off her bare legs.

'I wouldn't say no to something cold,' Anna said. 'I'm gasping. That's the trouble with an investigation as big as this one. You too often forget to eat and drink.'

'What about you, detective inspector?' Sarah said to Walker.

Walker raised his eyes to her face. 'Same for me if that's OK,' he said, a little awkwardly.

'I've got lemonade or Diet Coke.'

They both opted for lemonade and Sarah disappeared into the kitchen.

'I saw you ogling her,' Anna whispered to Walker. 'Did you have to make it so bloody obvious?'

He grinned. 'Actually I was just admiring her shorts and thinking how good they would look on my wife.'

Anna shook her head at him but couldn't help smiling back. It was a rare – if misplaced – moment of levity that lifted her spirits slightly.

Sarah returned with their drinks on a tray. She placed them on the coffee table and sat down on an armchair opposite the sofa on which Anna and Walker had made themselves comfortable.

'I've been keeping abreast of events,' she said. 'But I still can't believe what's happening. It's so horrible, especially for those poor parents. But at least there's some good news.'

Anna frowned. 'And what's that, Miss Ramsay?'

'Well, the offer from the anonymous businessman to pay the ransom, of course. The parents must be so relieved. They wouldn't be able to raise that kind of money.'

'Payment of the ransom is no guarantee that the children will be returned safely,' Anna said. 'It's never that easy. Kidnappings are unpredictable crimes. A lot can – and often does – go wrong.'

'But if those men get what they want, why wouldn't they just hand the children back?' Sarah said.

Anna blew out her cheeks. 'There's a very simple answer to that. Those men are not decent and honourable. We can't take their word as gospel. For all we know those nine children have already been sold on as sex slaves. Or they're being abused as we speak by a bunch of paedophiles who think Christmas has come early.'

Sarah was clearly shocked, or pretending to be, Anna thought.

'That didn't occur to me,' Sarah said. 'I just assumed that . . .'

She didn't finish the sentence because the words got stuck in her throat.

'Take a minute,' Anna said. 'And don't imagine for a second that you're the only one who thinks those things are straightforward. It's a popular misconception when it comes to kidnappings and ransom demands.'

Sarah picked up her glass and drank some more of her lemonade, while at the same time sneaking a peek at her watch.

'Are we keeping you from something, Miss Ramsay?' Anna asked her.

She shook her head. 'It's just that I have to make some

calls to the staff at the other nurseries. They need to know what's happening.'

'In what respect?'

'Well, they're all naturally concerned about the abductions. And most of them knew Tasha so they're also extremely upset. I've had messages from some of them who think I should close the other five nurseries until the children have been returned home.'

'And do you think you will?'

'I've already decided to.'

'So it will be another blow to your business?'

Sarah nodded. 'Obviously. But it can't be helped and I'm afraid I've grown accustomed to financial set-backs. This year has been a bad one.'

'Actually, that's what we wanted to talk to you about,' Anna said. 'Why didn't you tell me that you were having to sell up?'

Sarah's brow shot up. 'Well, I didn't think it was relevant. And I still don't. What has the state of my business got to do with the kidnappings?'

'We understand that you're in considerable debt and you're unable to sell the nurseries,' Anna said. 'A lot of people who've been in a similar position have resorted to desperate measures in a bid to sort their problems out. And a great many have ended up in prison as a result.'

Sarah drew in a loud breath and her eyes widened in shock and anger.

'I don't believe it,' she gasped. 'You actually think I had something to do with it. I'm a bloody *suspect*.'

'At this stage everyone with links to the Peabody Nurseries is a potential suspect, Miss Ramsay,' Anna said. 'I'm sure you can understand why.'

'No, I can't. It's ridiculous to think that I could be involved in abducting my own young charges just to get myself out of debt.'

'It's not just that, Miss Ramsay. We believe it's likely that the kidnappers knew what to expect before they entered the nursery. It seems they knew roughly how many kids would be attending, hence the size of the minibus they used. They also appeared to be aware of the interior layout. The description you and your colleagues gave us of what happened suggests they had a detailed plan that included putting the children in the Quiet Room so as not to alarm them when they herded the staff into the storeroom. And, of course, there's the fact that you yourself saw fit to let those men into the building without checking their credentials.'

'But I thought they were police officers,' she said. 'They held up their warrant cards.'

'Anyone can lay their hands on fake ID cards,' Anna said. 'Surely you know that. The men told you they were from Rotherhithe CID. It wouldn't have taken you long to confirm that by phone.'

'But that didn't occur to me. The man who spoke sounded genuine and we've never had police officers call at any of the nurseries before.'

'But, as the owner, security should be paramount. As you well know, a great deal of criticism has been levelled against you by parents who claim your establishments are not as safe as many others.'

'That's not fair,' she said. 'I take security very seriously. I was planning to introduce a whole raft of new measures. But that was before the business took a downturn after Kelly Platt died and her father set out to destroy me. Then came the three-hundred-K fine that knocked me for six.'

Her eyes were brimming with tears now and she was shaking all over.

'Yesterday you pointed the finger at Jonas Platt,' Anna said. 'For your information we spoke to him earlier. He admits that he still harbours a serious grudge against you and wants to see your business collapse. But he denies knowing anything about the abductions.'

'Well he would, wouldn't he? He's hardly likely to admit it. Just like he kept denying that he was phoning me up and making threats even after I got the restraining order against him.'

'You mentioned something else yesterday that I need you to clarify,' Anna said. 'You told me that you were single, having divorced some years ago, and that there's no man in your life now.'

'Which is true,' Sarah said. 'Are you now accusing me of making that up?'

'Not at all. But Mr Platt alleges that after he last made contact with you by phone he received a call from a man claiming to be your partner. This man, who didn't give a name, warned him to leave you alone and said that if he didn't he would go to his home and cut him up.'

'And you believe him?'

'Well, is it true? Do you have a business partner or a boyfriend?'

'Of course not. I would have told you if I had. Platt is making it up. He sees this as an opportunity to kick me while I'm down.'

Her voice was rising now, her face taut with indignation.

She suddenly slammed her glass down on the table, splashing some of it over the wooden surface.

'I've had enough of this,' she declared, and abruptly stood up. 'Are you going to charge me with anything?'

'Of course not,' Anna said. 'This is an informal interview. We just needed to clear up certain matters.'

'In that case I want you to go. You've upset me with these outrageous suggestions, allegations, or whatever they're supposed to be. I'm not going to listen to any more of it. You're out of order and wasting time here when you should be out there looking for those children.'

Anna knew that they had no choice but to leave, having pushed her as far as they dared.

She was about to apologise for upsetting her, but Sarah started sobbing and hurried out of the room.

'Maybe you should go after her, guv,' Walker said.

Anna shook her head. 'I don't think that would be a good idea. Let her calm down. We can talk to her again tomorrow if need be.'

When they were back in the pool car, Walker said, 'I'm not sure we handled that well.'

Anna hunched her shoulders. 'The questions needed to be asked.'

Walker started the engine, engaged gear, said, 'So what do you think? Is she as innocent as she's making out?'

'I really don't know,' Anna said. 'If she just put on an act for our benefit then it was a bloody good performance. But the fact remains that she had a motive and if you choose to believe Jonas Platt then she's lying about not knowing who threatened to cut him up.'

They discussed it during the drive back to MIT headquarters, where Anna checked in with the team to see if there were any updates. There weren't.

It was only eight o'clock but it felt like much later and Anna's eyes were heavy and sore.

'We need to call it a day,' she said. 'Go home, Max, and try to get some sleep. We've got a unit working through the night so if anything happens we'll be across it. Tomorrow is going to be just as hectic, and we have the kidnappers' deadline to look forward to.'

'Can I make a suggestion, guv?' Walker said.

'I'm listening . . .'

'That you take the long way back to Vauxhall via Dulwich. There's a man in a hospice there who you really need to go and see before it's too late.'

CHAPTER THIRTY-EIGHT

Anna had already made up her mind to go and see the mysterious Paul Russell at the hospice in Dulwich. The day was almost over so she saw no reason to feel guilty about it. And it would just be a short stop on her way home.

Even so, she was still well aware that it probably wasn't a good idea.

The temptation was too great, though. She needed to know if this was a genuine lead or yet another false alarm in her quest to find her daughter.

If it was something to get excited about she would have to make sure that it didn't prove to be a major distraction. She was in no position to follow it up even if it was worth doing so. Still, she had an answer to that and his name was Jack Keen. He was the private investigator she had employed in the past at huge cost. He knew almost as much as she did about Chloe and Matthew.

She made two calls from the car after leaving MIT HQ. The first was to the number she had for Paul Russell. It was his wife who answered, and Anna expected to be told that her husband wouldn't be able to see her so late in the day.

Instead, she said, 'He's been waiting for you to respond to his text, Ms Tate. And he's still awake. So I'll tell him you're on your way over.'

The second call was to Tom who, as she suspected, was already at her house.

'There's a jacket potato in the oven with your name on it,' he said. 'And I brought over a bottle of your favourite red wine.'

'You're a star, Tom, and I don't know what I'd do without you.'

'So when are you going to let me move in?'

He said it jokingly so she ignored it and told him where she was going. He warned her not to build up her hopes.

'I won't,' she said, but he knew better than to believe her.

On the way to Dulwich she switched on the radio and channel-hopped until she came to a news bulletin. From the sound of it there was nothing else going on in the world. She hadn't known a story fill up so much airtime since the last royal wedding.

But then it was hardly a surprise. Stories involving children always captured the public's imagination. And this one was in a league of its own.

Nine small children. A six-million-pound ransom demand. A sinister figure in a balaclava. And a police investigation that seemed to be going nowhere.

Anna had hoped that by now they would have made more progress but the lack of solid evidence, including the forensic kind, was hugely frustrating. And they were fast running out of suspects.

213

She had already decided that Phil Green was no longer in the frame, unless it turned out he'd lied again, this time about breaking into his ex-wife's house to steal cash and jewellery.

And Jonas Platt had more or less convinced her that he wasn't involved, even though he harboured an unhealthy grudge against the Peabody Nursery chain.

That left Sarah Ramsay, and as far as Anna was concerned the jury was still out on her. She just wasn't convinced that the woman had offered them the complete truth. It was partly down to intuition, and partly down to years of experience interviewing people who didn't want you to know what they'd done.

Money was always the most obvious motive when it came to major crimes, or rather the need or desire to obtain large amounts of it quickly.

And Anna found it hard to believe that the kidnappers had been able to pull it off without inside help. Of course, they had to keep an open mind in respect of the other staff members and even the parents. Any one of them could have colluded with a bunch of experienced London villains with the balls to walk into the nursery posing as coppers.

It wasn't the first time Anna had set foot inside a hospice. Her own father had received palliative care after he was diagnosed with terminal lung cancer.

That was fourteen years ago, and she could still remember visiting him and being astonished at how upbeat everyone was, even though the wards were filled with people who had only days, weeks or months to live.

The hospice in Dulwich boasted a view of the famous park.

When Anna arrived she gave her name to the receptionist and told her that Paul Russell was expecting her.

'Mr Russell's wife is with him now,' the woman said. 'I'll let her know you're here and she can come and get you.'

'Can you please tell me how long Paul has been a patient here?' Anna asked as the receptionist picked up the phone.

'Two months,' she said. 'As you probably know, he has pancreatic cancer and is receiving end-of-life care here. It's a real shame because he's such a lovely man.'

Anna stepped back from the desk and the receptionist spoke briefly into the phone. Outside it was getting dark and a few pillows of cloud had appeared in the sky.

She started breathing deeply to calm herself. But her nerves were jangling and her heart seemed ready to burst through her ribcage.

She took out her purse and flipped it open to reveal the photo of Chloe that she kept there, the one where her daughter was sitting in her high chair with a big, beaming smile on her face.

'Please God I'm about to take a step closer to you, sweetheart,' she said aloud.

Talking to Chloe was something she occasionally did. It was odd, she knew, but strangely comforting. In those early years after Matthew took her Anna did it all the time. It was one of the behavioural issues that had given her friends and colleagues cause for concern. Another was that she frequently thought she saw Matthew and Chloe on the streets. On one occasion she actually ran after a bus, having mistaken another father and daughter for them. Over the years she had learned to control her imagination and tone down her emotional responses to events. But it was never an easy thing to do

215

when the thought of eventually finding Chloe was all that kept her going.

Mrs Russell appeared after about a minute. She was a slight woman with a cap of grey hair and looked to be in her late seventies.

She smiled when she saw Anna and walked straight over to her, holding out her hand for Anna to shake.

'I'm pleased to meet you, Ms Tate,' she said, and Anna detected a slight Irish lilt to her voice.

The woman was wearing a light summer dress that revealed sallow skin stretched tight across her bones.

'And I you, Mrs Russell,' Anna said. 'I'm sorry I couldn't get here any earlier.'

'Oh, that's quite all right. I'm really glad you could make it seeing as how busy you must be with this dreadful kidnapping business.'

'I'm just hoping I haven't wasted my time coming here,' Anna said. 'During the ten years I've been looking for my daughter a great many people have given me false hope.'

'Only you can be the judge of whether what Paul has to say is useful to you, Ms Tate. But I really hope it is.'

Anna followed her along a wide corridor where the corrosive smell of disinfectant assaulted her nostrils. They passed a couple of small wards where most of the beds were occupied. Again she was reminded of her father, whose life had ended in just such a ward with Anna and her mother at his bedside.

Seven years later her mother had died after a heart attack while out shopping. To this day Anna believed it was caused by the stress and heartache caused by her granddaughter's abduction. And for that Anna would never forgive her ex-husband.

'Here we are,' Mrs Russell said. 'Paul is lucky enough to have his own private room.'

It was a small room with a bed, a TV on a stand, and an array of medical equipment.

Paul Russell was sitting up on the bed, bare-chested and linked up to a heart monitor and IV drip. He was pale and gaunt, almost skeletal under the harsh light, and about the same age as his wife. His grey hair was all but gone, and when he smiled Anna saw that most of his teeth were too.

'When I didn't hear back from you I began to think that perhaps you weren't going to take me seriously,' he said, his voice deep and scratchy.

Anna stepped further into the room and Mrs Russell closed the door behind them.

'I was curious,' Anna said. 'Especially after you wrote in your text that you wanted to apologise for the part you played in what happened to my daughter.'

He nodded. 'It's late in coming, I know, but I sincerely hope you'll accept it. At the time I was a very different person and I did not take account of the consequences of my actions. There was a point nine years ago when I did contemplate getting in touch with you. Your case was still attracting publicity thanks to your own efforts. But to my eternal shame I decided not to.'

Mrs Russell sat on the chair next to the bed and reached over for her husband's hand.

Anna shuffled forward so she was standing at the foot of the bed looking down. Her mouth was dry and her heart was pounding.

'Over time I pushed what I did to the back of my mind because that was the easiest way to deal with it,' Russell continued. 'Plus, I didn't want to risk the police finding out. That would have landed me in big trouble, which in turn would have made life difficult for my wife.'

He glanced at her but she sighed and looked away to avoid eye contact.

Turning back to Anna, he said, 'By chance, I saw you on the news being interviewed outside that nursery after those children were taken. The reporter asked you if you were the same person whose own daughter was abducted ten years ago. It rang a bell with me so I used my phone to Google your name. I came across all the news stories, the Facebook page you dedicated to your daughter and the magazine interview you did recently to mark the tenth anniversary of her disappearance. It all came flooding back to me and I decided I ought to tell you what I know. I've got nothing to lose now, and there's a chance, albeit a slim one, that the information will help you find your daughter.'

A shiver convulsed Anna's body and her head started buzzing relentlessly.

'I'm listening,' she said. 'What is it you want to tell me?'

Paul Russell ran his tongue over his few front teeth and shifted position slightly on the bed, which seemed to cause him a little discomfort.

Then he said, 'Four years ago at the age of sixty-eight I retired from a long career as a master craftsman. In London I was known as one of the best in the business when it came to forging documents. I ran a very successful business supplying counterfeit documents to criminals, refugees, migrant workers and anybody else who was willing to pay for them. I provided driving licences, diplomas, receipts, court papers and letters of endorsement. But mostly I produced sophisticated fake passports and that's why your ex-husband turned up on my doorstep ten years ago, weeks before I read in the paper that he had abducted his own daughter.'

Anna's mind screamed and her heart raced. She sensed straight away that this wasn't a made-up story. Paul Russell was the real deal and he had a genuine story to tell.

'Your ex, Matthew Dobson, had been put in touch with me by someone we both knew,' Russell said. 'The chap in question was a pub landlord named Chris Foreman and he had various underworld connections. But alas he died two years ago. Anyway, your ex wanted me to provide him with fake passports for himself and his daughter. He gave me the photographs I needed along with six thousand pounds.'

'How did you know he was telling the truth when he told you that Chloe was his daughter?'

'He showed me paperwork relating to your divorce and the custody arrangement in respect of your daughter. He also showed me your daughter's birth certificate and a number of other documents and photographs. The pub landlord I mentioned, who was apparently paid handsomely for his discretion, also confirmed it for me.'

'And it didn't bother you that he was obviously planning to abduct Chloe?'

'Like I said at the outset, I was a different person then. I was without a moral compass. And besides, I'd produced counterfeit papers for other men who used them to leave the country and vanish with their own children.'

Anna shook her head. 'But how could you have done that? Don't you understand what it's like to have a child, and then to suddenly lose him or her for the rest of your life?'

He held her gaze. 'We never had children, Ms Tate, so the

answer to your question is that I can't possibly understand what it's like. And back then I didn't try to. But like I said, I am no longer the person I was.'

Anna sighed and shook her head again.

After a beat, Russell said, 'The reason I wanted to see you, Ms Tate, is because I can remember clearly the false names your ex wanted me to put on the passports. They were James and Alice Miller.'

Shock flooded Anna's system and in her mind's eye she saw Chloe's face.

Had her daughter really been known as Alice Miller for the past ten years?

It took a few seconds for her to find her voice.

'Did Matthew tell you where he was taking Chloe?'

He shook his head. 'No. And I didn't ask. It was none of my business.'

Anna closed her eyes to let it sink in. She was shocked and elated in equal measure. This was the first time in ten years that she had something concrete to act on.

'What I've told you is the absolute truth, Ms Tate,' Russell said. 'And I'm so very sorry that I've waited so long to give you this information. I can't begin to imagine how much you've suffered because of what your ex-husband did.'

She opened her eyes, looked at him, and found herself wishing that he didn't have cancer because then she could have leapt onto the bed and beaten the shit out of him.

'But there's also something else I have to tell you,' he said, and Anna felt the hairs rise on the back of her neck.

'What is it?' she asked.

He exhaled a breath. 'After providing your ex with the passports I heard nothing from him for seven years. Then

220

three years ago he contacted me out of the blue and said he was returning to live in the UK. He had a list of fake documents he wanted produced, including driving licence, job references and bank statements. Plus a birth certificate and other papers for his daughter, who by then was nine. But I had to explain to him that I'd retired from the forgery business and couldn't help. He asked me if I could recommend someone else but I chose not to. Then he hung up and I've heard nothing from him since.'

Anna was too stunned even to react. She just stood there, trying to take it all in. The names – James and Alice Miller. The fact that they may well have moved back to the UK three years ago.

'Since you're a detective you might be able to trace where they are now,' Paul Russell said.

His words snapped her out of herself and she stared down at him, and then at his wife who had started to cry.

The sight of them caused the anger that had boiled up inside her to evaporate. She decided there was no point telling Paul Russell what she thought of him. The poor sod would soon be dead and his wife would be a widow.

She told herself that she just had to be grateful that the man had finally shown remorse and opened up about what he knew.

'I believe your story, Mr Russell,' she said. 'And I thank you for telling me. I don't suppose it was easy for you.'

She thought about telling him that she forgave him for what he'd done, but couldn't bring herself to do so. It would be a lie.

Her own eyes were filling with tears now and she desperately wanted to leave the room and the hospice. But before she did she shook both their hands and said, 'I'm truly sorry that your time together is being cut short. My own father ended his days in a place similar to this, so I know what you're going through.'

As she walked towards the door, Mrs Russell said, 'I wish you all the luck in the world, my dear. And please know that I will be praying for you.'

CHAPTER THIRTY-NINE

Anna had made a rule never to smoke in the car but she desperately needed a nicotine hit so she lit up as she drove away from the hospice.

Her mind was still trying to wrap itself around what she'd been told. It wasn't easy because Paul Russell's deathbed confession was so huge and filled her with a sense of hope she hadn't experienced in a very long time. If only the old bastard hadn't waited a decade to tell her.

It was a major breakthrough in terms of her search for her daughter, one that could be followed up. She had the identities that Matthew had adopted for himself and Chloe. James and Alice Miller. She could search for those names, check to see if there was any record of the fake passports being used. She could scour the internet, Facebook, Twitter, and other social networking sites.

Was it really possible that her daughter had been living in the UK for the past three years? Anna had always assumed that Matthew had taken her abroad to begin a new life in a place where there was little risk of Chloe finding out who she really was. And if he had brought her back he must have had a reason.

She dragged heavily on the cigarette and blew the smoke out of the open window. This was the first meaningful lead she'd had in ten years and she had a dying man to thank for it.

The adrenalin was pumping through her now at a rate of knots. She would have given anything to be able to assign a team of detectives to the task of finding James and Alice Miller. But that wasn't going to be possible. This was a cold case that even ten years ago had only briefly involved the Met because she'd been one of their own. A lot of senior officers were against committing resources to what they regarded as a domestic dispute that had got out of hand. And it was widely assumed then that Matthew would eventually return and hand their daughter back to her mother.

So Anna was on her own, and in her head she was already making a list of what needed to be done and what questions she needed to find the answers to.

She was so deep in thought that when her phone rang she actually considered not answering it. But she did, and because she hadn't attached it to the hands-free device it meant pulling over to the side of the road and cutting the engine.

It was DCS Nash, and just the sound of his voice came as a sharp reality check.

'Where are you, Anna?' he said.

'On my way home, sir. There's nothing more I can do tonight so I thought it best if I tried to get some shut-eye.'

'Well, I called the office and they said you left there over an hour ago.'

'I did, but I had to go to the shops. Is there a problem? I was planning to update you on the investigation first thing in the morning.'

'I'm calling to update you,' he said. 'I take it you were told about the press release the Commissioner put out asking the kidnappers to contact him personally?'

'I was told, sir. Yes.'

'Well, it worked and they did. An hour ago a man called the Yard and said he was responding to the request. He was asked the question that was aimed at sifting out time-wasters – did the kidnappers leave anything on the minibus? Well, he gave the right answer and was then given the number to the mobile phone that the Commissioner had been given. The Commissioner was told to expect the call but when it came through the man refused to let him speak and reiterated their intention to start killing the kids if the ransom isn't paid.

'He then said that he would call back on the same number with the transfer details when the deadline is reached. He said the Bitcoins will need to be in place by then and transferred immediately. He also said that if we want to pay the ransom sooner all we have to do is announce it on the TV and he'd be in touch. Then he hung up before the call could be traced.'

'Shit,' was all Anna could think of saying.

'I thought you ought to know,' Nash said.

'So what will happen now, sir?' she said. 'Will the ransom be paid?'

'Not if you can find those evil fuckers before they call

again. There are just thirty-seven hours on the clock until their deadline. And you don't need me to tell you, Anna, that if we're forced to hand over six million pounds, then every school and nursery in the country will become vulnerable to similar attacks.'

The call from Nash had the same effect on Anna as a slap around the face. It woke her up to the fact that her attention had already shifted away from the investigation. And that was exactly what she'd told herself she wouldn't allow to happen.

She couldn't focus on trying to find the nine abducted children while pursuing the new lead in the search for Matthew and Chloe.

By the time she arrived home she'd decided to once again employ the services of Jack Keen. She would ask the private investigator, who was himself a former police officer, to try to track down James and Alice Miller. That way she'd be free to concentrate on the investigation.

Before calling him she discussed it with Tom, who agreed it was a no-brainer.

'I know how long you've waited for a breakthrough like this, Anna,' he said. 'But you have to push it to the back of your mind until this case is resolved. If you don't you'll be letting those children down and at the same time making yourself ill.'

Anna nodded. 'Then I'll phone him while you get my potato out of the oven and pour me a glass of my favourite red. I've gone virtually all day without food and I'm famished. Then while I stuff my face I can fill you in on the rest of my day.'

'And is it really the sort of thing I want to hear just before bedtime?' he asked.

She grinned. 'Of course it is. You're always on about how much you enjoy listening to horror stories.'

CHAPTER FORTY

While waiting for Ethan to return home, Ruth came close to ending her own life. After downing four neat vodkas she spent an hour sitting on the bathroom floor rearranging a line of sleeping pills over and over again.

The choice she grappled with was whether to kill herself now so that she wouldn't have to suffer any more hurt if she found out that Liam had died. Or stay alive just in case he was and would need her more than ever.

Eventually she decided to embrace hope rather than despair.

She was now back in the living room, slouched on the sofa with her feet resting on the coffee table. She'd been watching the same rolling news bulletins for what felt like hours and every word and every image had taunted and tormented her.

She heard the front door open and close, but when Ethan called out her name she didn't bother to respond.

A moment later he entered the living room and his eyes moved from her face to the half-empty bottle of vodka on the table.

'As you can see, I had to resort to finding some comfort in the bottle,' she said, her face puce with rage. 'I had little choice seeing as my husband decided to fuck off for the entire evening without telling me where he was going.'

'You were out yourself,' he said. 'So I didn't think it would be a problem, especially since you were cross with me. And I didn't actually expect to be so long, so I'm sorry.'

'Where have you been?'

There was a moment of hesitation, then, 'I went to see my parents. They'd just arrived back from Greece and were going to come over. I told them it'd be best if I went to them. I was going to pop out to the shop anyway to get some fags.'

So far so good, Ruth thought. His parents lived only a couple of miles away and she knew for a fact that he was telling the truth about visiting them.

'So how long did you stay at their house?' she asked him.

He stepped further into the room and cleared his throat.

'I was there until twenty minutes ago when I left and came straight home.'

And there it was. The big fat, fucking lie.

'Did you know you left your phone here?' she said.

He sat on the arm of the sofa and shrugged. 'I didn't until I got to my parents'. It was a silly thing to do given what's going on.'

Ruth squinted at him. 'But I take it you didn't forget your other phone.'

He frowned. 'What other phone?'

'The white mobile you use to talk secretly to the bitch you're having an affair with behind my back,' she said. 'You made the mistake of letting me see it when you were busy talking to her in the garden.'

The blood drained from his face and to Ruth his expression was as good as a confession.

He started to speak, but she got in first.

'Don't dig a deeper hole for yourself by telling another lie,' she said. 'You see, I already know that you only stayed with your parents for an hour. They phoned here to see how I was and they told me you left there two hours ago. And you're forgetting the GPS on the car. According to the app on my phone it's been parked outside a pub in Gulliver Street, Rotherhithe, for the past two hours.'

Ethan closed his eyes and sucked on his top lip. Ruth could tell that he knew the game was up. He had been entrapped by a combination of lies and rank stupidity.

She reached for the bottle and poured herself another generous helping of vodka.

'I've suspected for some time that you were cheating on me,' she said. 'When I confronted you before, you denied it. But you lied because you've been sneaking off to see her only hours after your son was abducted. You disgust me, Ethan. Liam might be dead, or it could be that he's being abused. Or maybe he's desperately ill. But you don't seem to care and I really don't understand it. I thought you loved him. And me. But it's clear that you don't, and right now I hate you more than I thought I could ever hate anybody.'

She gulped at the vodka to stop herself crying, but it didn't work and she broke down, spluttering it all over the carpet.

Her lungs started struggling for oxygen and it felt like her mind was coming apart.

Through her tears she saw Ethan stand up and move towards her. His breath was heavy and rasping and she realised that he was also crying.

What happened next she didn't expect and it both shocked and confused her.

Ethan put his hand on the back of her neck and gently squeezed.

Then he said, 'It's true, my love. I have been seeing someone and I met her tonight. But I can't put into words how sorry I am that you've had to find out now while we're going through such a desperate time. So it's only fair that I tell you everything. I should have done so before now. But you're not going to like it, so please try to find it in your heart to forgive me.'

And so the story came out – a story that Ruth found almost impossible to believe.

CHAPTER FORTY-ONE

Day three

Anna had spent most of the night wrestling with her duvet and staring into the darkness. There was just too much to think about and fret over.

She and Tom had gone up to bed at midnight in the hope that they could both get a decent amount of sleep.

It hadn't been much of an evening for Tom. She'd talked for half an hour on the phone to Jack Keen, who had been only too eager to do some more investigative work for her.

She had passed on all the information that Paul Russell had given her and they'd agreed a fee. It irritated her to pay money for a job that she could have done herself if only she had the time, but what choice did she have?

'Let me know as soon as you have something,' she'd told him.

'Of course, Anna. And good luck with the case. You're really going to need it – if things go wrong and there's no fairy tale ending, then you'll be the person everyone blames.'

'Thanks, Jack,' she'd said, and cursed under her breath because she knew it to be true.

As the SIO, she was the one in the firing line, the one who would be named and shamed if there wasn't a successful resolution.

Anna had then talked non-stop during dinner about Paul and Janet Russell, the video from the kidnappers, the tycoon's offer to pay the ransom, and the fact that they were making slow progress with the investigation.

It didn't occur to her until afterwards that she hadn't once asked Tom about his day. Not that he'd seemed to mind. Her man was one of the most patient people she had ever known. But then he would have to be to put up with a woman like her who found it so hard to relax.

He'd had his moments, of course, such as when they went on that long weekend to Gibraltar and she spent an inordinate amount of time on the phone, either calling the office or surfing the web.

'Fuck me, Anna,' he'd ranted at her as they left a restaurant. 'Can't you switch off for even a couple of days?'

But that was the problem. She couldn't. Or at least she hadn't been able to since Matthew had created such a big, dark hole in her life, a hole that she felt the need to keep filling. If she wasn't busy with work or seeking clues to Chloe's whereabouts, she became anxious, agitated, and sometimes even guilt reared its ugly head.

And to make matters worse, there were the constant flashbacks to those precious years she'd had with Chloe. Not a day went by when she wasn't reminded of something her daughter did or said.

There was the first time she uttered the word *mummy*. The

toothy grin when she managed to poo on her potty for the first time. The mess she made at virtually every mealtime. The way she splashed about in the bath and threw a tantrum when it was time to get out.

Whenever Anna had a flashback it left her feeling bereft and tearful. At such times she was so glad she was a copper because every case drew her in and provided a distraction.

And to think that, up until the age of twenty, her heart had been set on becoming a teacher. But that was the year her father had been beaten up and left for dead by two thugs employed by a West End drug dealer. At the time he'd been working as an undercover cop for the Met, but the injuries he sustained were such that he'd been forced to take early retirement.

It had compelled Anna to think again about her future, and she'd convinced herself that she owed it to her dad to follow in his footsteps. The fact that his attackers had never been arrested filled her with a burning sense of injustice. She imagined herself tracking them down one day and putting the cuffs on their wrists.

That day still hadn't come, but she had no regrets about the decision she'd taken to join the force.

For a change she didn't dream about Chloe. This time her sleep was haunted by images of the nine abducted children. And it wasn't a dream. It was a hellish nightmare because they were no longer alive.

Their bodies were sprawled across the blood-soaked floor of an anonymous room. Through a large window could be seen the anguished faces of their parents, who were crying and screaming and asking why the police had failed to save them.

Anna came awake with a start, her face covered in sweat. She couldn't move for a full minute because it took that long for the dreadful images and sounds to recede from her mind.

Finally, she turned over and looked at the digital display on the bedside clock. It was four a.m. She had set the alarm for five so that she could get to the office early, but rather than lie awake for another hour she decided to get up and spend the time doing something useful.

She switched off her alarm and left Tom snoring as she slipped out of bed and into her dressing gown.

Her intention was to go over her case notes in advance of the morning briefing in the hope that she might spot something she'd missed. But inevitably she was drawn to her laptop – and Google and Facebook and Twitter.

An hour later she realised why Matthew had chosen to adopt the names James and Alice Miller. They were among the most common in the UK. She came across scores of James Millers, including accountants, business executives, actors, doctors and writers. But none of their photos bore any resemblance to Matthew.

There were fewer Alice Millers, and again those whose photos she saw looked nothing like the age-progression picture she had of Chloe.

Jack Keen certainly had his work cut out for him, she realised. But the man was good at what he did and had contacts in most police forces and government departments, as well as on the staff of all the national newspapers. He could probably get to see documents that even she couldn't get access to without going through official channels.

She would leave it to him and hope for the best. And try hard not to keep thinking about it, which wasn't going to be easy.

She took a shower in the downstairs bathroom so as not to wake Tom, turning the water as hot as she could without burning herself. Then she had a coffee, thick and black, and watched the morning news on the TV in the kitchen.

The kidnapping story was still getting wall-to-wall coverage. There was only one development that she hadn't been aware of. Kenneth Tenant had been interviewed in his home and had made it known that he was contacting the other parents to get them to stage their own press conference at the Peabody community centre later that morning.

'I want us to make a joint appeal to the kidnappers not to hurt our children,' he said. 'And at the same time we'll plead with the authorities not to prevaricate over payment of the ransom. This is not a terrorist situation so the principle that ransoms should never be paid should not apply.'

It was a move that was sure to cause a stir in the corridors of power as they grappled with the situation, Anna thought. And any attempt to stop the press conference, or to stop it being held in the community centre, would be asking for trouble.

When she heard Tom's alarm go off at six she took him in a cup of tea and a couple of his favourite chocolate biscuits.

'I didn't realise you were up,' he said.

'I couldn't sleep. And I'm sorry I have to rush out again so early.'

'No need to apologise, for Christ's sake. It's your job.'

'Well, when this is all over we'll spend some quality time together. My mind and body will be all yours.'

'Is that a promise? I can't remember the last time we had sex.'

'Then your memory must be failing you, Thomas

Bannerman. It was last Friday night and we used that new toy you bought for me.'

He laughed, and his straight, white teeth positively glowed against his dark skin.

'Oh, that's right,' he said. 'Now I remember. You told me yet again that I'm the best lay you've ever had.'

'In your dreams, big boy,' she said. But it was true, and it wasn't just because of the impressive size of his manhood. He was a tender, passionate lover who always aimed to please her before pleasing himself. A stark contrast to the way Matthew had performed between the sheets. To her ex-husband, fore-play had been something to get out of the way as quickly as possible. She had often wondered if he'd put in more effort with his mistress.

'I won't be able to come over tonight,' Tom said. 'I told my mother I'd go and see her. It'll be late by the time I get back.'

Tom's mother was in a care home and he visited her as often as possible.

'No worries,' Anna said as she started to get dressed. 'I'll probably be back late myself. I'm sure it's going to be another hellish day.'

'Well, focus solely on the investigation,' he said. 'You need to try and just concentrate on one thing at a time. If you don't, you'll do your head in.'

'I'll try,' she said.

The morning briefing kicked off at seven and even DCS Nash turned up for it. He took the floor first and told everyone about the phone call the Commissioner had received the previous evening.

237

'We failed in our objective to engage with the kidnappers,' he said. 'They've made it clear that they're not prepared to negotiate in secret with us. And they know that will ramp up the pressure. When their deadline is reached they want a speedy, uncomplicated transfer of funds.

'They're aware that if it's dragged out there's a chance that they'll come unstuck. Plus, they won't want to hang onto nine kids for longer than is necessary.

'For your information, despite strong reservations, the government now accepts that the ransom will have to be paid. The purchase of the digital currency is already in hand. But we won't make that known yet and we won't make the money available before the deadline because discussions are still taking place as to who will pay it. Should the anonymous businessman be taken up on his offer or should it come from taxpayers? That side of things is all very political and will likely have an impact down the line.

'But we have been talking to the businessman in question, who is a father himself and runs a hedge fund. He's agreed not to go public with his name and not to deal directly with the kidnappers. So far no other individual or organisation has offered to pay the full amount.'

He paused there for several seconds and scratched his chin thoughtfully before continuing.

'I'm aware that the parents are to stage their own press conference this morning. I've decided to come along and answer questions myself directly afterwards.' He looked at Anna. 'This will leave you free to crack on with the investigation, DCI Tate. It's been agreed that I'll respond to the parents by saying that we'll arrange for them to have a meeting later today with the Commissioner himself. That will buy us

238

some time and mean that we won't have to announce our decision on the ransom.'

It was Anna's turn then to provide an update on the interviews conducted with Phil Green, Jonas Platt and Sarah Ramsay.

'Instinct tells me that the Ramsay woman is hiding something from us even if she hasn't told us an outright lie,' she said. 'So she stays in the frame as a prime suspect.'

There were more updates from the team. Phil Green's story that he was breaking into his ex-wife's house when the children were being snatched had checked out. He had her cash and jewellery in his flat and he'd been caught yet again on the prying eyes of CCTV cameras. Nothing had been found in his home to connect him to the abductions.

Copies of a document were handed round. It contained a list of fifteen people who were going to be called on and questioned today. Ten of them had links to the Peabody Nurseries and included other staff members, cleaners and various outside contractors. The other five were men who had been brought to their attention because they looked like the e-fit images of the three kidnappers.

A detective from the Serious and Organised Crime Command said that his officers had so far found no evidence pointing to any of the London gangs.

'We're already monitoring the movements and communications of the capital's most notorious villains,' he said. 'And there's been nothing to link them to this. The snouts we've spoken to say they've heard nothing and they reckon it's probably a one-off stunt by either a terror cell or a bunch of desperate amateurs.'

Anna was then told that information was still pouring in

239

from members of the public, but most of it either hadn't yet been followed up or had turned out to be spurious.

And she was made aware of an unofficial online poll which asked the question: *Should the six-million-pound ransom be paid to secure the release of the Peabody children?*

So far thirty thousand people had taken part and, if the poll was to be believed, then the vote was only sixty/forty in favour of paying it.

Hundreds of people had posted comments. Most of those opposed to giving in to the hostage-takers gave the reason that it would turn other groups of children into potential targets. It was an old debate with a new twist and Anna had no doubt that it would continue to rage whatever the outcome.

She spent a bit of time talking about the video of the children. Close examination of every frame hadn't offered up a single clue as to the location of the house or the identity of the man in the balaclava.

'The sequence is disturbing in several respects,' Anna said. 'The children are obviously terrified, and we get the impression that they've already been subjected to verbal and perhaps physical abuse. And little Liam Brady is noticeable by his absence. He's the boy with cystic fibrosis and we can only hope that he hasn't had a serious turn for the worse.'

Finally, she said they would carry on using the Peabody community centre as another base of operations.

'I'm going back there now because I want to talk to some of the parents again,' she said. 'I'm not convinced we've pumped them enough for information. And I'm hoping there's something important we haven't been told because we haven't asked the right questions.'

CHAPTER FORTY-TWO

On the way to Rotherhithe, Walker asked Anna if she had gone to the hospice to see Paul Russell. She said she had and gave him a detailed account of the meeting.

'It sounds promising, guv.'

'I know, and I've already engaged the services of a private investigator to look into it,' she said. 'But I'd rather not talk about it, Max, because it'll make it hard for me to concentrate on the case.'

He nodded. 'Understood. But if there's any way you think I might be able to help, then just ask. I'm one of those people who can't compartmentalise things so if I was in your shoes I'd be in a right quandary.'

Inside she was, but she was trying hard not to show it.

The scene in Peabody Street hadn't changed. The press were still there in force, the SOCOs were still in control of the nursery building, and the community centre was still a hub of activity when they entered.

'I fancy a coffee,' Walker said, pointing to the café. 'Would you like one, guv?'

'No thanks. I want to single out a few of the parents before the press conference starts.'

It was scheduled to begin at ten. It was nine fifteen now and already most of the parents had arrived and were discussing among themselves who would speak and what they would say.

Kenneth Tenant was acting as their self-appointed spokesperson and when he saw Anna he came over.

'Don't try to talk us out of it, detective,' he said. 'We're doing this and if you won't let us do it in here we'll take it outside on the street.'

Anna shook her head. 'There's no need. We're fully supportive. I've come to tell you that we'll help you organise it.'

'We'd rather you told us that the ransom will be paid and then get on and sort it out,' he said. 'You heard what that bastard said on the video. If you fuck them around over the money my daughter will be the first one they kill.'

'The Commissioner is giving the ransom demand the utmost priority,' Anna said. 'And he's planning to meet you all later today to discuss it. But you should know that we all have just one objective and that is to bring your children home.'

Tenant was then approached by one of the media liaison people who wanted to talk to him about the press conference and who would be attending.

Anna said she would catch up with him later, and was about to go and speak to Phil Green's ex-wife, Wendy, when she spotted Ruth Brady and her husband Ethan entering the community centre.

They were both wearing sombre expressions, and Anna could see that, behind her glasses, Ruth's eyes were red and swollen from crying.

Anna felt a frisson of guilt at not having spent more time with the poor woman, but with so many parents involved in the case it would have been impossible.

She could tell that the ordeal was having a brutal impact on both of them. They moved as though they were carrying a huge weight on their shoulders.

Anna crossed the reception and caught them before they reached the other parents, who were being moved into the hall.

'Hello, Mr and Mrs Brady,' she said. 'Are you here for the conference?'

Ruth stopped abruptly and caught her breath, and her husband instinctively reached out and grabbed her arm, as though to stop her falling over.

'I'm sorry if I startled you,' Anna said. 'Are you all right?'

Ruth just stared at her, and when she didn't answer, Ethan stepped forward and said, 'My wife is finding it increasingly difficult to cope the longer this goes on, Detective Tate. It's really hard not knowing what's happened to Liam.'

'I can appreciate how tough it must be,' Anna said. 'But try not to lose hope.'

'That's why we came here this morning. We think a press conference just for the parents is a good way to get more people rooting for us. This time I'll be the one taking part and Ruth will be watching from the wings.'

He let go of his wife's arm and placed his own around her shoulders. She winced, as though it was something she didn't want him to do. It was a strange reaction, but Anna recalled how Ruth had snatched her hand away the day before when Ethan had tried to hold it. She assumed the situation was causing tension between them, which sometimes happened when couples were plunged into a crisis and began to take it out on each other.

'Have you got anything new to tell us?' Ethan said, and it seemed to Anna as though the question was an attempt to divert attention away from his wife's reaction.

'I really wish I did,' Anna said. 'Hopefully I'll have something positive to pass on by the end of the day. A lot's going on, and the response from the public has been tremendous. We're following up dozens of leads.'

Ruth suddenly spoke up, and it caused phlegm to rattle in the back of her throat.

'Why don't you just tell the bastards that they can have the money?' she said. 'It's not that much, after all – just under seven hundred thousand pounds per child. Surely our kids are worth that.'

'The amount of the ransom is not an issue and I'm confident that if we haven't found your children by eleven o'clock tomorrow then it will be paid,' Anna said. 'But then we have to hope that the kidnappers will stick to their word and release the children straight away.'

'I'm sure they will,' Ethan said. 'They'd have no reason to hold onto them.'

Without warning, Ruth abruptly shifted her attention away from Anna and made a sneering shape with her mouth.

'Nobody told me that bitch would be here,' she exclaimed, and her voice cracked with fury.

Anna followed her gaze and saw that Sarah Ramsay had just walked into the building. This was unexpected, but it shouldn't have come as a total surprise because the woman had as much right to be here as everybody else.

Nevertheless, a twist of panic wrenched through Anna's gut because she knew the parents were going to be none too pleased to see her.

Anna turned back to Ruth and was shocked to see that her face had morphed into a mask of pure hatred.

'Just calm down, Ruth,' Ethan said to his wife. 'We don't have to stay. We can go home.'

'I'm not going anywhere,' Ruth snapped. 'She's the one who should go.'

Ethan removed his arm from around her shoulders and stood in front of her.

'Please don't make a scene, Ruth,' he pleaded. 'Not here. Not now.'

But she wasn't listening to him. Her face remained taut, brimming with hate.

Anna turned again and saw that Sarah was making her way towards two women who were sitting at a table on the edge of the café. She recognised them as Emma Stevens and Paige Quinlan, the teachers who'd been locked in the storeroom with Sarah.

'Let's just go into the hall with the other parents,' Ethan urged his wife. 'Please, Ruth. Now is really not the time.'

Ruth responded dramatically by pushing him aside and rushing forward. She moved so quickly that by the time Sarah saw her coming she wasn't able to defend herself.

Ruth went straight up to the nursery owner and slapped her hard around the face.

Sarah howled in pain and staggered sideways, clutching her cheek.

'You fucking whore,' Ruth cried out. 'My husband has told me that you've been having an affair with him. Well, it's over. Do you understand? Stay away from him and me. I won't let you break up my family.'

Ruth leaned towards Sarah, closing the space between them, and before Anna could reach her she lashed out again, striking Sarah on the shoulder and sending her hurtling into a wall.

'That's enough,' Anna yelled, grabbing Ruth by the arm and pulling her away.

Ruth didn't resist. Her body sagged and she allowed Anna to move her across the room to where Ethan was standing, as though frozen to the spot.

'Take her into one of the other rooms,' Anna told him. 'Sit her down and then wait for me. You've both got some explaining to do.'

She hurried back to Sarah, who was now surrounded by a group of people, including Emma and Paige. Her right cheek was red and tears were trailing from the corners of her eyes.

'Are you OK?' Anna asked her.

Sarah nodded. 'I'll live. And just so you know, I don't want to press charges. I had that coming.'

'We'll talk about that,' Anna said. Then she called over one of the uniformed officers and told him to take Sarah into one of the private rooms.

Turning back to Sarah, she said, 'I'll be with you in a minute. Don't leave here until we've spoken. The officer will fetch you a tea or coffee.'

DI Walker appeared at her side and together they got the people who had gathered, including a couple of the other parents, to disperse.

'The show's over,' Walker told them. 'It's no big deal.'

But Anna didn't necessarily agree with that. If it was true that Ethan Brady had been having a relationship with Sarah Ramsay then it was potentially pretty significant.

It would prove that Sarah had lied about not having a man in her life and it would raise one particular question: was Ethan Brady the man who had phoned Jonas Platt threatening to cut him up?

'Well, that was an unexpected bit of light entertainment,' Walker said. 'I'm glad we didn't miss it.'

'I'll let them both calm down before I talk to them,' Anna said. 'And while I'm doing that I want you to get the team to dig a lot deeper into the backgrounds of the Brady couple and Sarah Ramsay.'

Walker raised one eyebrow. 'Do you actually think that what just happened here could be relevant to the case, guv?'

'I really don't know,' she said. 'But I intend to find out.'

CHAPTER FORTY-THREE

The community centre manager, who had witnessed the drama in reception, told Ethan that he could take his wife into the office.

Once inside, Ethan shut the door behind them and turned on Ruth.

'I can't believe you did that,' he said. 'What were you thinking?'

Ruth ignored the question, sitting down on one of the two chairs facing the large cluttered desk. A feeling of desperation consumed her and dilated blood vessels pounded inside her head.

She concentrated on her breathing, eyes closed, trying to calm her racing heart.

Ethan stood over her, seething.

'You promised you wouldn't say or do anything until this is all over,' he fumed. 'We have enough to worry about with Liam. Now we'll attract attention for the wrong fucking reason.'

Ruth opened her eyes and looked at him, her face full of emotion.

'I couldn't stop myself,' she said. 'As soon as I saw the bitch I wanted to hurt her. I'm only sorry I didn't get more blows in.'

'Well, now everyone will know about the affair. And it wasn't necessary because I told you that I was ending it.'

'And why should I believe you? You haven't stopped lying to me. And not just about screwing that cow. You've lied about everything else and now our lives are completely fucked up. And to top it all you actually expect me to forgive you, which would be really funny if it wasn't so frigging tragic.'

A sob exploded out of her throat and her mouth flooded with saliva. There was so much of it she thought she would vomit.

'Please can you hold your temper in until we get home?' Ethan said. 'You can lay into me again then. Kicking off here just makes us look pathetic and selfish. The only issue on our minds should be our son. Not our bloody marriage, which has been less than perfect for a long time, as you well know.'

That was one of the things he sprung on her last night – that their marriage had become stale and difficult, and the only thing holding it together was Liam.

He'd told her that it was why he'd started flirting with Sarah Ramsay on the days he drove their son to and from the nursery school.

'*One thing led to another,*' he'd said between sobs. '*And before we knew it we were seeing each other. It wasn't meant to happen. It was a mistake on both our parts. I do regret it,*

Ruth. I still love you and I think you still love me, despite everything. I'm sure we can get our relationship on track again so long as we get our son back.'

He'd admitted that when he'd claimed he was working late and away on business he was really with her. It was the reason he'd bought the second phone, so that they could stay in touch without Ruth finding out.

So her suspicions hadn't been unfounded after all, which was why his admission of an affair had come as really no great surprise.

But the other thing he'd confessed to last night had come as a massive shock. It had taken her breath away, almost as if she'd been winded. She was still struggling to believe it, and the more she thought about it, the more the nausea roiled in her stomach.

Ethan shot Ruth a warning look as Detective Tate stepped into the manager's office. It made her want to spit in his face.

'You'll be pleased to know that Miss Ramsay does not intend to press charges,' Tate said.

'That's big of her,' Ruth replied, her voice laced with sarcasm. 'But I don't care if she does.'

Tate sat behind the desk facing them. 'Well, for what it's worth, she told me that she feels she deserved what you did to her.'

'She deserves more than a single slap around the face,' Ruth said. 'She's been fucking my husband, and they've been having secret little chats on the phone when they should have been looking for my son.'

Detective Tate turned to Ethan. 'I take it this is true . . .'

He nodded, shamefaced. 'It is, but it's really got nothing

to do with you or anyone else. It's a private matter and I don't want it to serve as a distraction. I want you to focus on finding our son, not the problems in our marriage.'

'But I'm afraid I can't ignore it, Mr Brady,' the detective said. 'Firstly I need to know how long this affair has been going on because it could have a bearing on the investigation.'

Ethan looked puzzled. 'I don't see how.'

The detective hesitated, then glanced at Ruth.

'Whatever it is you want to say you can say it in front of my wife,' Ethan told her. 'We've got no more secrets. And, just to be clear, my relationship with Sarah Ramsay started six months ago. My wife knows because I told her last night after she confronted me with her suspicions.'

Tate leaned forward, lacing her fingers together on top of the desk. 'I'm sure you're both aware of a man named Jonas Platt whose daughter choked to death at the Peabody Nursery in Lewisham.'

'Of course we've heard of him,' Ethan said. 'A lot of people think he could be involved in the kidnappings.'

'Well, he denies that, but he does admit to making threats against Miss Ramsay because he blames her for what happened to his daughter. And he told me that a man claiming to be Miss Ramsay's partner threatened to hurt him if he didn't leave her alone. I want to know if that man was you, Mr Brady. And before you answer, you should know that I'll be speaking to Sarah Ramsay in a moment and I will get to the truth.'

Ruth looked at Ethan and noticed the sweat beading above his top lip.

'Yes, it was me,' he said. 'But so what? The bloke was making her life a misery.'

251

Ruth bridled, but this time she reined back her anger. Last night he said he'd told her everything, but he hadn't mentioned threatening Jonas Platt on Sarah Ramsay's behalf. Or that he regarded himself as the bitch's *partner*.

'Did Miss Ramsay ask you to call Mr Platt to warn him off?' Tate asked.

Ethan shook his head. 'No, she didn't. I did it to help out because he was scaring her and doing what he could to damage her business. And he seemed determined to carry on even after the courts got involved.'

'But was Miss Ramsay aware that you were going to threaten Mr Platt?'

'Of course. I told her. She didn't try to stop me.'

The detective asked a few more questions of both of them.

Had their son ever gone this long without his medication before?

Had they themselves ever been threatened or intimidated by Jonas Platt?

Had they recently been approached by any strangers who asked them about the nursery in Peabody Street?

Having had time to dwell on it, was there anyone they could think of who might be involved in the abductions?

Finally, Tate sat up straight in her chair and said, 'I think that about covers it. But before I leave you, is there anything you haven't told me that you think I ought to know?'

Ruth and Ethan exchanged glances and then shook their heads in unison.

'Fair enough,' the detective said. She looked pointedly at Ruth, adding, 'I can understand how terribly upset you are, Mrs Brady. You've had one awful shock on top of another. But you really need to control your temper from now on.

Today you got away with slapping someone. But whatever your motivation it's still an assault and if it happens again you won't be so lucky.'

CHAPTER FORTY-FOUR

Anna came out of the manager's office feeling immensely sorry for Ruth Brady.

First her three-year-old son was kidnapped from a nursery, and then she found out that her husband had been cheating on her with none other than the woman who ran the place. At the same time she was having to deal with the very real possibility that her son was no longer alive.

Anna didn't blame her for lashing out at Sarah Ramsay. She would probably have done something similar if she had ever come face to face with the woman who had the affair with Matthew.

She hadn't seen the point in asking the Brady couple too many questions about their marriage and why it was falling apart. That was really none of her business. She did, however, come away with the impression that there were things they weren't telling her. Or perhaps she just sensed that Ethan was holding back on his wife.

It had been enough for Anna to establish that Sarah

Ramsay had lied. She'd been involved with a man for the past six months despite her denial. And she did know who had threatened Jonas Platt. It made Anna wonder if there were other things she had lied about.

She found Walker in reception and told him what she'd learned. He told her that the press conference had been delayed by half an hour because a couple of the parents were late turning up.

'That suits me,' Anna said. 'It'll give me time to have a word with Sarah Ramsay before it starts.'

Sarah had been taken to one of the side rooms and she was sitting at a table with Emma Wilson and Paige Quinlan. Anna explained that she wanted to speak to Sarah alone and the other two left the room.

'How's the face?' she asked, sitting down beside her.

'Still a bit sore,' Sarah said. 'How's Ruth?'

'In a mess. She obviously didn't expect to see you here.'

'I didn't intend to come. But Emma and Paige persuaded me after they heard that Kenneth Tenant was arranging a press conference for the parents. They thought we should take the opportunity to tell our side of the story so that we're not made out to be a bunch of cowardly cretins. I assumed Ruth would be here but I had no idea that Ethan had gone and told her about us. Do you know why he did?'

'I gather that Ruth has suspected for a while that he's been cheating and last night she confronted him, probably because of the pressure they're under. He admitted it and said it had been going on for six months.'

Sarah swallowed hard and shook her head. 'I feel terrible. This wasn't meant to happen. We should have ended it ages ago.'

'So why didn't you?'

A troubled look clouded Sarah's features.

'I suppose because it was exciting and we were enjoying ourselves. But we both knew it wouldn't last. Ethan was never going to leave Ruth because Liam means too much to him.'

'Do you love him?'

She didn't even have to think about it. 'Unfortunately I do, but I'm not sure he has ever really loved me.'

Anna tried and failed to summon up even a smidgen of sympathy.

'So now tell me why you lied to me, Miss Ramsay,' she said. 'You told me there was no man in your life.'

'I'm surprised you're bothering to ask me that question, detective. Surely it's obvious. The man's married. I wanted to protect him.'

'And is that why you also lied about not knowing who threatened Jonas Platt?'

Sarah blinked back tears and said, 'Look, I'm sorry about that. But with all that's going on I really didn't think it would be an issue. And I'm still not sure why it is. Everything else I've told you is the truth. I had nothing to do with what happened and I have absolutely no idea who could be behind it.'

Anna sat back and threw out a long sigh.

'Well, let's leave it at that for now then,' she said. 'Can I suggest you go home? It's probably not sensible for you to hang around. Let your two colleagues speak to the press on your behalf.'

She nodded. 'Very well.'

'But I will ask you the same question I asked Mr and Mrs Brady,' Anna said. 'And I want an honest answer. Is there anything you haven't told me that you think I ought to know?'

Sarah dabbed at her wet eyes with the back of her hand, smearing mascara across her cheeks.

'That depends on whether Ethan revealed everything about our relationship to you,' she answered.

'All he told me is what I told you,' Anna said. 'But I did have the feeling that something was being held back.'

The lines around Sarah's eyes deepened.

'There is something that I suspect he didn't mention then,' she said.

'So what is it?'

Sarah fixed Anna with a long, steady stare.

'I'm pregnant with Ethan's baby,' she said. 'It was conceived nine weeks ago. I know that Ethan carries the defective gene that causes cystic fibrosis. And so does Ruth, which is why Liam has the condition. But I've been tested and I'm not a carrier, so the baby should be perfectly healthy. And for that reason I'm keeping it.'

'And does Ethan know?'

'He does. He was naturally shocked to begin with, but he's been very supportive, and I made it clear to him that I didn't expect him to leave Ruth. I said I was happy to bring the baby up by myself and that there was no need for her ever to know.'

'But it's possible he told her,' Anna said. 'And if so then I suspect that neither of them would want it to get out.'

'If he did come clean about the baby then I really do pity her,' Sarah said. 'What that poor woman is going through I wouldn't wish on my worst enemy.'

Anna had seen it before, how a serious crime can lay bare the secrets and lies of a town, village or small community of people.

Those linked to the Peabody Nursery represented a microcosm of life in London which, viewed from the outside, looked to be normal, carefree and straightforward.

But the abductions had acted like a pressure valve, revealing the truth behind the smiles and relationships.

This not only compounded the suffering of those involved. It also made the investigation process more complicated. Time was being spent trying to find out why someone had lied when it had nothing to do with the offence. Phil Green had been a case in point, and now Anna was wondering if she was barking up the wrong tree with Sarah Ramsay, too.

'How did it go?' Walker asked her as she came back into reception.

Anna shrugged. 'Well, the bullet points are these. She admits she's been having an affair with Ethan Brady. She says she loves him, and so in order to protect him she lied about not having a man in her life and about not knowing who threatened Jonas Platt. Oh, and she also happens to be pregnant with Ethan's baby.'

His jaw dropped. 'Jesus, I didn't see that one coming. She doesn't look like she's up the duff to me.'

'Well, she is. Just over two months and not showing yet.'

'So does his wife know or has he only confessed to having an affair?'

'I'm not sure. It didn't come up during my conversation with them. I'm sure there was something they weren't telling me. But look, as far as I'm concerned it's a side show and I don't want to waste time on it. The clock's ticking and we need to start getting somewhere.'

*

The press conference eventually got underway. Five parents sat behind the table on the stage in the hall and the event was compered by a media liaison official named Bruce Kemp.

He explained that the parents would be making a direct appeal to the kidnappers. He then gestured towards DCS Nash, who had arrived while Anna was with Sarah Ramsay, and was now sitting in one of the front-row seats with a crowd of up to forty reporters, photographers and TV camera crews behind him.

'Detective Chief Superintendent Nash will then provide an update on the investigation and take some questions,' Kemp said.

The five parents taking part were Kenneth Tenant, Ethan Brady, Rachel Brooks, Sabina Hussein and Janet Wilson.

Anna watched from the back of the hall and she found it hard to hold back her own tears because it was one of the most emotional spectacles she had ever witnessed.

Kenneth Tenant was the first to speak and pleaded with the kidnappers not to harm any of the children.

'We'll make sure that you get the money,' he said. 'But in the meantime please take care of our kids. We miss them so much and we want them back.'

He read out a note his wife had written but then had to stop because he was crying so much.

It was Ethan's turn next, and he asked the kidnappers to provide proof that his son Liam was still alive.

'For his mother and I this is a living nightmare,' he said. 'We just want our little boy returned to us. We miss him so much and we're desperately worried.'

Rachel Brooks held up a photograph of her four-year-old daughter Justine, and said, 'This is my little girl. She's done you no harm so please don't hurt her. When you get the ransom money just let her go. Please.'

Janet Wilson addressed the issue of the ransom and urged the authorities not to put politics and principles before children's lives.

'If you refuse to pay the ransom or you delay it and a child dies then you will also be guilty of murder in our eyes,' she said.

The Q and A session descended into chaos with the parents accusing the police and the government of not doing enough and claiming that Sarah Ramsay and the other nursery staff should be charged with neglect.

Janet Wilson got so worked up that she fainted and had to be carried out of the hall on a stretcher. And Kenneth Tenant stood in front of DCS Nash and demanded a guarantee that the ransom would be paid. For Anna it felt like events were spiralling out of control, which was the last thing they wanted. This was supposed to have been a media event aimed at helping the investigation, not a raucous side show.

She slipped out of the hall before the parents and reporters turned on her. As she entered the reception she bumped into DC Sweeny, who was clearly in a hurry.

'I was coming to find you, ma'am,' she said excitedly. 'Some news just came through from the lab and you need to know about it.'

'Go on.'

'It's to do with the cigarette butt that was found near the abandoned minibus in Kent,' Sweeny said. 'They've lifted the DNA, put it through the system, and finally come up with a match.'

Anna felt a rush of adrenalin.

'So we have a name.'

'We do indeed. Ross Palmer. He's a man with form. He was released from prison five months ago on licence, but he's already on the run having committed a further offence.'

'This sounds like the breakthrough we've been waiting for,' Anna said. 'Get me everything we have on him. And I want a photo as quickly as possible so that I can show the nursery staff.'

CHAPTER FORTY-FIVE

There were eight officers crammed into the mobile incident van outside the community centre, including Anna and Walker.

DC Sweeny was busy tapping at her keyboard and a picture suddenly appeared on the computer screen in front of her.

'This is Ross Palmer,' she said. 'It's the latest photo we have and was taken prior to his release from prison five months ago.'

Palmer was white, five foot ten and aged twenty-eight. He had a square face with hard features and a distinctive dimple on his chin. His light-coloured hair was shaved to a whisker and his eyes were slits beneath a heavy brow.

The first thing that occurred to Anna was that he did not resemble any of the e-fit images of the three kidnappers.

'There's a good chance he's changed his appearance by now,' Walker said, as though reading her mind. 'That's what I would do if I looked anything like him.'

'So what do we know about Mr Palmer?' Anna said.

Sweeny adjusted the mouse and Palmer's file replaced his photo.

'You need to read it out loud,' Walker said. 'I left my glasses in the car.'

'No problem,' Sweeny said. 'Let's start with the fact that he spent his formative years on a council estate in South London. He was part of a street gang and had his first brush with the law when he was eighteen. He was given a caution for a first offence of shoplifting. Then at nineteen he received a suspended sentence for possessing indecent images of children, or to be specific, young girls.'

'You can tell he's a nonce just by looking at him,' Walker said.

Sweeny ignored him and continued. 'Seven years ago, at the age of twenty-one, he was jailed for four years for a smash-and-grab raid on a jewellers in Tooting. He and an accomplice rode up to the shop on a motor scooter. They smashed the front window with a pickaxe and helped themselves to rings, watches and necklaces. But as they were getting away Palmer, who was the passenger on the scooter, fell off into the road. Passers-by grabbed him but his accomplice got away and Palmer never grassed him up.

'Anyway, he would have been released after serving just over half the sentence but while inside he sliced the face of a fellow inmate with a knife and had his sentence extended another two years.

'He was released five months ago. But then two months ago he failed to report to his probation officer. The reason became clear a few days later when police investigating an assault and criminal damage in a pub issued a warrant for his arrest. He'd been caught on CCTV and it didn't take long to establish his identity. So he disappeared before he was collared. He hasn't been seen since.'

'So where did he live after he got out?' Anna asked.

'According to the probation service he was staying with his parents,' Sweeny said. 'They have a house in Woolwich. But they told detectives who spoke to them that he packed up and left there in a hurry the morning after the incident in the pub. They claim he didn't tell them where he was going or why.'

'We need to find out if there's a link between this bloke and the Peabody Nursery,' Anna said. 'Does he have ties to any of the staff or parents?'

'Before we get too worked up about this we need to remind ourselves that it's quite possible that Palmer wasn't at the layby when the minibus was there,' Walker said. 'You said yourself, guv, that the cigarette butt could have been lobbed from a passing car.'

'For now we assume that that isn't the case,' Anna responded. 'It strikes me as far less likely than the scenarios in which he was either one of the kidnappers or he was waiting at the layby for them to turn up in the minibus. If so then he made a stupid mistake by having a smoke and dropping the butt right where it could easily be found. But stupid mistakes are what usually proves to be the undoing of most criminals.'

'So how do we play this, guv?' Walker said. 'If we go public with his picture it could cause Palmer and whoever is in this with him to panic. It's conceivable that they'll decide there's no point carrying on and let the children go.'

Anna shook her head. 'I think it's more likely that he'll take a more aggressive stance. If he is our man then he's got nothing to lose. He'll have to carry it through because presumably he needs the money to leave the country, which is almost certainly what he intends to do.'

'But we'll need to show his photo to Sarah Ramsay and the teachers,' Walker said. 'Hopefully they'll ID him as one of the three kidnappers. And the parents might know him or maybe they've seen him hanging around Peabody Street these past few weeks.'

Anna told Sweeny to print off a dozen of the Palmer photographs.

'We'll start with Emma Stevens and Paige Quinlan,' she said. 'They're hopefully still around. I'm guessing Sarah Ramsay will have taken my advice and left by now. But let's not let the media see it just yet.'

While the photos were being run off Anna asked Sweeny to look up the details of the incident in the pub which had led to Palmer fleeing.

According to the case file, he had been drinking in a pub near London Bridge with a woman who still hadn't been identified. They'd both had a lot to drink and Palmer was getting lippy. The manager politely asked them both to leave, at which point Palmer lost his temper and head-butted him. He picked up a chair and threw it at the shelves behind the bar, smashing a load of bottles. Then, before he and the woman left the pub, he punched another customer in the face.

He would have known that he'd been caught bang to rights on CCTV and that, if convicted of assault and criminal damage, he would end up back behind bars.

'If he is involved in the kidnappings then he surely has to be connected in some way to the nursery,' Walker said. 'Or perhaps he knows someone else who is linked to it and was invited to take part.'

'That ties in with my theory that at least one of the perps has inside knowledge of the Peabody Street set-up,' Anna said.

Sweeny picked up the photos from the printer and handed them to Anna.

But before leaving the mobile incident van Anna asked her to look up the details of Palmer's conviction for possessing indecent images. So Sweeny did and it made for uncomfortable reading.

Ross Palmer had been one of twenty men arrested as part of a police clampdown on the downloading of child porn. He was a member of an online group who shared photos and short video clips. He was traced after police hacked into one of the websites being used. His computer and phones were seized and found to contain no less than forty photos of young girls, some as young as three, plus five video clips.

As well as receiving a suspended prison sentence Palmer was put on the sex offenders register for ten years.

'So not only have nine children been kidnapped,' Walker said. 'We now know that they could be at the mercy of a fucking nonce.'

The back-to-back press conferences were over and the media scrum had moved back out onto the street. A few of the parents had remained in the community centre to talk to each other while several were being interviewed outside.

Anna asked a couple of uniformed officers to round them all up along with Emma Stevens and Paige Quinlan.

'Bring the parents back into the hall and take the teachers

into the manager's office,' she instructed. 'And see if Sarah Ramsay is still on site.'

She then briefed DCS Nash, who was in a foul mood because he'd just faced a barrage of hostile questions from the media. But news of a potential breakthrough brought a smile to his face.

'I plan to show the photo to the parents and staff,' Anna said. 'I don't want to make it public just yet. Then I'm going to see Ross Palmer's mum and dad in Woolwich. He's got no other relatives apparently and he's never been married.'

'I'm not surprised he hasn't got a wife if it's children who turn him on,' Nash said.

'Well, we can't be sure that he's still into that stuff,' Anna said. 'He was nineteen – it could have been a passing phase.'

Nash shook his head. 'That's wishful thinking, Anna, and you know it. Once a nonce always a nonce. And this increases the likelihood that if he is involved then the kids might not be handed back even if the ransom's paid. Or if they are, then heaven knows what state they might be in both physically and mentally.'

Anna knew that Nash was right and it gave her something else to worry about.

Images from the video posted online arrived unbidden in her mind. Those scared little faces. The electronically distorted voice of the narrator. The imposing figure in the balaclava. The words that sent a chill through her body.

Most of them cried themselves to sleep. Those who made a fuss were punished.

This is the quietest they've been but that's because they now know what to expect if they piss us off.

Anna was hoping against hope that none of the kids had

been assaulted in any way, that the kidnappers' claim that some of them had been punished was just a way of raising the fear factor.

The trouble was, she had no idea what type of men they were dealing with. Ross Palmer might or might not be one of them. And if he was then did the others share his taste for young flesh?

Was that one of the reasons they'd got involved in the kidnappings? After all, money didn't have to be the main motivation. Unimpeded access to nine innocent children could be just as appealing to certain warped individuals, and that included women as well as men.

'He definitely wasn't one of the three men,' Paige Quinlan said when Anna showed her the photograph of Ross Palmer.

Emma Stevens agreed with her. 'He looks nothing like any of them.'

'Are you sure?' Anna pressed them. 'Perhaps he had make-up on or something.'

Paige shook her head. 'I will never forget their faces. None of them had a dimple on his chin like that.'

Anna couldn't conceal her disappointment as she exited the manager's office.

'It doesn't mean for sure that he's not involved,' she said to Walker. 'He might have been the driver of the vehicle the kids were moved to.'

Next she went into the community centre hall. Four parents had been rounded up – Ethan Brady, Kenneth Tenant, Rachel Brooks and Sabina Hussein. Their other halves were either outside giving interviews and sound bites to the media or sitting in the café waiting to go home.

Anna showed the photo to each of them.

'We have reason to believe that this man might be involved in some way, but I must stress that it's only a possibility,' she said. 'We have no solid evidence to suggest that he is. However, we have to rule him out. What I need to know is if any of you are familiar with this man or if you've seen him hanging around.'

'I've never laid eyes on him,' Rachel Brooks said and Anna got the same response from the others.

'So who the bloody hell is he?' Ethan Brady said. 'And why is he a suspect?'

'I'm afraid I'm not at liberty to go into details,' Anna said.

Ethan grimaced. 'But surely we have a right to know who this man is if you think he might have our children. And why he's in the frame.'

'He's one of a number of people whose names have cropped up during the investigation,' Anna said. 'And I'm sorry but we can't share that information with you.'

'Does he live around here?' Kenneth Tenant asked. 'At least tell us that.'

Anna shrugged. 'We don't know where he lives at present. And I need to ask you to refrain from revealing this name to the media at this stage. If he is somehow involved then we have to be concerned about how he might react. We want to make further enquiries before we go public.'

They weren't happy but all agreed to keep the information to themselves – at least for now.

As she walked into reception, Anna spotted Ruth Brady at a table in the café. She was staring into the middle distance, seemingly unaware of what was going on around her. Anna was tempted to go over and talk to her, to see if she was OK, but Walker appeared at that moment and said, 'I've just come off the phone to the detective who's been looking for Palmer. He spoke to the parents and he reckons they know where he is but are refusing to say. He's given me their address.'

'Do we need to call to make sure they're in?'

'He says they almost certainly will be. The mother suffered a severe stroke a couple of years ago and is confined to a wheelchair. Her husband gave up his job to care for her and they rarely go out apparently.'

Anna decided to leave Ruth to her own tortured thoughts since there was nothing she could say to help ease her suffering.

Seconds later she was in the passenger seat of the pool car and her mind was dialling back over the events of the morning, starting with her online search for James and Alice Miller. She thought briefly about checking in with her private investigator but decided that he hadn't had enough time to come up with anything.

She went back over the interviews with Ruth and Ethan Brady and Sarah Ramsay, and the revelation about the affair and the baby that Sarah was expecting.

And then she thought about how the DNA trace on the cigarette butt had opened up a whole new line of enquiry.

Anna tried to pull all her thoughts into focus, to look for clues that weren't obvious.

They were half way to Woolwich when she hit on something. She took out her notebook and flipped through the pages.

'What is it, guv?' Walker said.

Anna didn't respond until she found what she was looking for.

'Here it is,' she said. 'I thought so. Jonas Platt spent fifteen months in prison for assaulting a man. That was seven years ago. We know that Ross Palmer also got banged up at roughly the same time.'

'Were they in the same prison?' Walker asked.

'Let's find out.'

She took out her phone and called DC Sweeny.

'I need to know where Ross Palmer and Jonas Platt served their prison sentences,' Anna said. 'And were they inside at the same time?'

Seconds later Sweeny provided the answer.

After hanging up the phone, Anna said, 'They were both in Winchester at the same time. And that means there's a good chance they knew each other.'

'So perhaps they even stayed in touch,' Walker said.

CHAPTER FORTY-SIX

Michael and Ingrid Palmer lived in a pre-war semi on the outskirts of Woolwich. It had pebbledash walls and a wheelchair access ramp at the front door.

The man who answered the door was in his late fifties with iron-grey hair that was receding at the front and long at the back. He wore an open-neck blue shirt, denim shorts and brown carpet slippers.

'Are you Mr Michael Palmer?' Anna asked.

He gave a stiff nod.

'I'm Detective Chief Inspector Tate.' Anna showed him her warrant card. 'This is Detective Inspector Walker. We're with the Met's Major Investigation Team and we would like to have a word with you and your wife.'

'Is this about Ross?' he asked.

Anna nodded. 'We need to ask you some questions about him as a matter of extreme urgency.'

'Has he turned up?'

'No, he hasn't.'

'Well then, I'm not sure how we can help you. I told that other detective who came here on two occasions that we don't know where he is.'

'I'm aware of that, Mr Palmer, but since then your son has been linked to another crime, one that is far more serious than the assault he carried out in the pub at London Bridge.'

A deep frown entrenched itself on his brow.

'What's he supposed to have done now then?' he said.

'We'd rather come inside and discuss it with you. Hopefully we won't take up too much of your time.'

There was a moment's hesitation before he stepped back and invited them in.

'My wife is in the back garden,' he said. 'I'll have to go and fetch her. She had a bad stroke a while ago and is no longer able to walk unaided. Thankfully she didn't suffer any mental impairments, but she does get upset very easily, especially where our son is concerned. So would you please take that into consideration when you ask your questions?'

'Of course, Mr Palmer,' Anna said. 'We fully understand.'

'And please do call us both by our first names. We don't do formalities in this house.'

There was a musty smell inside the property, and Anna's first impression was that the place needed a makeover. Everything seemed outdated, from the peeling paint on the hall ceiling to the threadbare carpet.

Michael led them into the small living room where the sun streamed in through the open patio door, spreading a white beam in which dust swirled.

His wife was in a wheelchair on the patio, facing a large lawn that needed mowing and weeding.

'We can do this outside,' Anna said. 'There's no point making your wife come in when she's enjoying the sunshine.'

'Well, if that's OK,' Michael said. As they stepped outside he gestured towards a rattan dining table with four chairs around it.

'Make yourselves comfortable.'

His wife spun her wheelchair round when she heard his voice and alarm flashed on her face at the sight of their visitors.

'They're police officers, Ingrid,' Michael said. 'They want to talk to us about Ross.'

She was a plump woman and looked about the same age as her husband. She had a distinguished face with finely chiselled features and a proud, aquiline nose. Her hair was hidden beneath a wide pink sun hat.

'Has he been arrested?' she said.

'No, he hasn't,' Anna told her. 'But as I just explained to your husband, he is now a suspect in a crime that was committed on Monday.'

'We haven't seen him,' she said. 'He left here two months ago and hasn't been back.'

Anna sat at the table where she could feel the full force of the afternoon sun on her face. Michael sat opposite her and placed a hand on his wife's shoulder. Walker remained standing next to the back wall so he was in the shade.

'You probably know from the news about the nine children who were abducted from the nursery school in Rotherhithe,' Anna said, getting straight to the point. 'They're being held hostage and the kidnappers are threatening to kill them unless a six-million-pound ransom is paid.'

The couple looked at each other and Michael said, 'Of

course we've heard about it. And we've seen that horrible video with the man wearing the balaclava. But are you suggesting that our son has got something to do with it?'

Anna nodded. 'We believe it's possible. You see, we've uncovered evidence that puts him at the layby in Kent where the minibus used to take the children away was abandoned.'

'But that's insane,' Ingrid said. 'My boy wouldn't do something like that. Granted, he has a short fuse and has misbehaved in the past, but he's not a big-time criminal.'

'I think that many people would disagree with you there,' Anna said. 'His record speaks for itself. He was done for shoplifting, jailed for robbing a jewellers and had his sentence extended for stabbing another prisoner. Plus while on probation he attacked someone in a pub and tried to trash the place. And then there's his conviction for possessing indecent images of children.'

'That was years ago,' Michael said. 'He got involved with the wrong people and they led him astray. He's not a paedophile.'

'That may be so,' Anna said. 'But the discovery that Ross might be one of the kidnappers has made us all the more concerned about the safety of those nine children. So I'm sure you can understand why we're desperate to find him.'

'We've told your people that we don't know where he is,' Ingrid said. 'He said he was going abroad so I expect he's already gone by now.'

'Well then, let's talk about the incident in the pub,' Anna said. 'We understand that he was with a woman when he kicked off. Do you know who she is?'

Michael cleared his throat. 'We've been asked that question and the answer is still no.'

Anna pursed her lips. 'Are you sure about that, Michael? The police officer who spoke to you before is under the impression that you lied to him to protect your son.'

Michael shook his head. 'That's not true.'

'Really? Because it's one thing to help your son evade arrest for a relatively minor assault in a pub. But it's quite another to aid him if he's part of the gang that is holding nine innocent children hostage. And if even one of those children is killed then you'll have that on your conscience for the rest of your lives.'

The couple looked at each other and something unsaid passed between them. Anna could tell from the look in their eyes, and in that moment she knew for certain that they were holding something back.

'I've just been with the parents of those children,' Anna said. 'They're devastated and terrified. And they fear they will never see their sons and daughters again. So if you do know where Ross has gone then you have to tell us.'

Neither of them spoke for about thirty seconds, but Ingrid started shaking her head as soft tears rolled down her cheeks.

Michael lifted his hand from her shoulder and ran it gently through her hair.

'You have to tell them what we know,' Ingrid said to him. 'If Ross is involved then he can't expect us to help him.'

Michael nodded and turned back to Anna.

'It's actually true that we don't know where Ross is,' he said. 'He wouldn't tell us where he was going for the very reason that he feared we would tell you. He got a new phone when he left here and he wouldn't give us the number. But he has called us a few times to say he's OK and that he'll soon be leaving the country and won't be seeing us for a long time.'

276

'So what else haven't you told us?' Anna said.

'We know who he was with in the pub at London Bridge,' Michael said after a long pause.

'So why didn't you tell the other detectives when they came looking for him?'

'Because he begged us not to. He wanted to carry on seeing her and he knew that wouldn't be possible if you had her name.'

'So who is she?' Walker asked, stepping out of the shade, notebook in hand.

'Her name is Lucy Knight. She and Ross were together before he went to prison all those years ago and he started seeing her again when he got out.'

'So they're close?' Walker said.

'They used to be. In fact, shortly after his arrest she told him that she was pregnant with his child. Unfortunately the baby, a little boy, died of meningitis at the age of three months.'

'Is Ross staying with her now?'

'No, he isn't. She lives with her father in Clapham and he knows it would be too risky to move in with them while he's trying to stay one step ahead of the police. But he told us that he's staying in a flat fairly close by there until he can get the money together to move abroad.'

'So do you think that Lucy Knight knows where the flat is?' Anna asked.

He shrugged. 'I can't be certain, but it's possible.'

'Where does this woman work?'

'From home,' Michael said. 'Well, kind of. Her dad runs a greasy spoon café on Clapham High Street. She lives with him in a flat above it. She's got two brothers but I don't know if either of them is also living there.'

Ingrid looked up, sniffed back tears and said, 'I told Ross not to get involved with her again, but he wouldn't listen. She's not a nice person and they're not a nice family, especially her younger brother Kevin who's heavily into drugs. He was the bastard who got Ross into trouble in the first place. He has no interest in children but Kevin told him he could make money by hosting photos and videos on his site. That was why he started downloading all that filth. It wasn't because he's sick.'

'So how did your son get involved with this girl and her family in the first place?' Anna asked.

Ingrid was too upset to carry on speaking so Michael answered. 'They knew each other back when we all lived on the same council estate before it was pulled down. Ross, Lucy and her brothers Kevin and Craig were part of the same gang. Their dad Frank was a loud-mouthed bully who was always getting into fights and trouble. He got worse after his wife Eileen died of cancer and he had to take care of them by himself.'

'Were either of the brothers the accomplice who managed to get away after the jewellery shop robbery?'

'We think so, but we can't be sure,' Michael said. 'They both denied it when the police questioned them and Ross would never say. He's kept schtum to this day.'

'We'll need Lucy Knight's phone number and address,' Anna said.

'I don't have her phone number but her address is easy to find. It's Knight's Café on Clapham High Street.'

'Do you know if she has a criminal record?'

Michael shook his head. 'Not a clue, although it wouldn't surprise me. You must understand that we haven't heard anything about that lot since Ross went inside. As far as we were concerned they were consigned to history. We were gutted when Ross told us he'd started seeing her again.'

Anna made up her mind that what she'd been told was the truth. She believed Mr and Mrs Palmer to be a decent enough couple who had unfortunately given birth to someone who had caused them problems throughout his life.

'Before we go, there are two more quick questions I need to ask you,' she said. 'Has your son ever mentioned the Peabody Nursery School or a woman named Sarah Ramsay?'

They both shook their heads.

'What about a man named Jonas Platt? Does that ring a bell with either of you?'

She got the same response.

Anna took out one of her cards and placed it on the table.

'If there's anything else you can think of that will help us then please phone me. We're in a desperate race against time because the kidnappers have set a deadline of eleven o'clock tomorrow morning for the ransom to be paid.'

She got up then and told them that she and Walker would see themselves out. As they stepped back inside the house they heard Michael start to sob along with his wife.

CHAPTER FORTY-SEVEN

As they set off on the ten-mile journey across South London to Clapham and the home of Lucy Knight, Anna was fired up. Adrenalin was fuelling every part of her body; they were getting somewhere at last.

'Ross Palmer is part of this,' she said to Walker, who was driving. 'I can feel it in my blood. He was waiting at the layby for the minibus when he dropped the dog-end. I'm sure of it.'

'But fuck knows how he's going to react when he gets wind that we're on to him.'

'I admit that's a worry,' Anna said. 'But let's take it one step at a time. We need more info on his girlfriend and her family. They sound like a right bunch of reprobates.'

She called DC Sweeny and gave her a list of tasks.

'Find out all you can about a woman named Lucy Knight,' she said. 'See if she has a criminal record. She was the one with Ross Palmer when he ran riot in the pub at London Bridge. According to Palmer's parents he's been seeing her.

So we're on our way to her place now. She works in her father's café in Clapham High Street. His name's Frank. Also, obtain a copy of the CCTV footage from the pub.'

'I'll get on to it right away, ma'am,' Sweeny said. 'Meanwhile, I've talked to the prison governor at Winchester. He remembers both Palmer and Jonas Platt. He can't recall if they hung out together but he knows for certain that they didn't share a cell.'

'OK. Then get DI Bellingham to go and see Platt. I want to know if the pair stayed in touch. And find out if we've searched Platt's home yet and accessed his phone records.'

'Is there anything else, ma'am?'

'Not right now. But keep me informed of any developments at your end.'

As hard as she tried to concentrate on the task in hand, Anna couldn't help but think of the nine abducted children. Time was running out, and some disturbing questions got her heart pumping furiously.

How were the kidnappers treating them? Was Liam Brady still alive? Where were they being held? Would they be released as soon as the ransom is paid?

'It might help to share your thoughts, guv,' Walker said. 'I can tell from the sound of your breathing that you're working yourself up into a frenzy.'

'Nonsense. My breathing is perfectly normal.'

He grinned. 'You're forgetting how long we've worked together. I know when the pressure is getting to you. Just like you know when it's getting to me. It's why we make such a good team.'

She sighed heavily and looked out of the side window. London was still basking under the warm summer sun and

281

the traffic was building up ahead of the early evening rush hour.

'I'm just worried about those kids,' she said. 'What if I'm wrong about Ross Palmer? If I am then we're wasting precious time.'

'We can only do our best, guv, and work with what we have,' Walker said.

'But if our best isn't good enough then the consequences for those kids and their parents could be horrific.'

Walker shook his head. 'You need to be more positive, guv. If I was one of those parents then there's no one I would rather be working the case than you. It's no secret that you're one of the best DCIs in the Met.'

She turned back to him. 'I really don't think so, Max. If I was that good I wouldn't still be searching for my own daughter ten years after she was abducted. And it's not as if I don't know who snatched her. In my mind that makes me a big fucking failure.'

'You shouldn't be so hard on yourself. You've done everything you can to find Chloe. You couldn't possibly have known where her father would take her or what name he'd give her. And don't forget, it's so easy to disappear these days and to stay below the radar no matter how many people are looking for you.'

Anna had told herself the same thing many times over the years but it hadn't made her feel any less of a failure.

'And besides,' Walker added. 'The end could be in sight as far as the hunt for Chloe is concerned. I've got a feeling that this new information you've got is going to lead you right to her and her shit-bag father.'

*

They found Knight's Café easily enough. It was about fifty yards from the railway station, just off Clapham High Street, and sandwiched between a charity shop and an estate agents.

Walker parked the pool car at the kerb with two wheels on the pavement. But as soon as Anna got out she noticed that the café wasn't open, which struck her as odd considering the time of day. She walked up to the door which had a closed sign on the inside of the glass.

She peered in and decided that it wasn't the sort of place she'd go to eat a cooked breakfast or relax over a cup of coffee. She counted ten Formica-topped tables with plastic chairs fixed to the tiled floor. Chalk-board menus almost covered one wall and the other walls were bare.

Anna couldn't see anyone inside, but she could see a pile of unwashed dishes on the counter.

'It seems they've shut up shop for the day.'

The voice came from Anna's left. She turned to see a middle-aged woman standing outside the charity shop with her arms crossed and a cigarette between her fingers.

'Oh, hello,' Anna said. 'Do they always close this early?'

The woman shook her head. 'It's because Lucy is on her own. Her dad and brother are away and she doesn't see why she should work herself into the ground by doing everything by herself. She went out about half an hour ago.'

'Any idea where she's gone?'

'She said she needed to get a few things from Sainsbury's up the road. Then she's got some tidying up to do in the café. I doubt she'll be much longer, though. If it's just a drink you want there's a nice little coffee bar up there on the left.'

Anna reached for her ID and held it up for the woman to see.

'We're actually here to talk to Miss Knight,' she said, as Walker stepped up and stood by her side. 'Do you know her well, Miss . . .?'

The woman took a final puff on her fag and dropped the butt on the ground.

'It's Mrs actually,' she said. 'Radcliffe. Fiona Radcliffe. And I know Lucy well enough to be on first-name terms with her. But that's because I'm always popping in for teas and snacks.'

'I understand that she and her father live above the café.'

'That's right. They were here before we opened up and that was three years ago.'

'Does Lucy have a boyfriend that you know of?'

Mrs Radcliffe looked a bit uncertain so Anna said, 'Whatever you tell us will be treated with the utmost confidence. Miss Knight's name came up during the course of a serious investigation and we need to find out as much about her as possible.'

Mrs Radcliffe looked from Anna to Walker and back again.

'Well, actually, I have seen her with one youngish-looking man,' she said. 'I know she's not married so I assumed he was her boyfriend.'

Anna took out the photo of Ross Palmer, unfolded it, and showed it to her.

'Would this be him by any chance?' Anna said.

Mrs Radcliffe studied the picture for a few seconds, her eyebrows coming together.

'Yes, I'm pretty sure that's him. But I've never spoken to the man. I've only seen him in the café a couple of times when he came to pick Lucy up.'

'So you don't know where he's living?'

'I'm afraid not.'

'And when was the last time you saw him?'

'That would be about three weeks ago. But I only got back from holiday on Sunday so I haven't been here for a fortnight.'

Anna was about to say thank you when Mrs Radcliffe lifted her head and pointed up the high street.

'Now would you believe it? There's Lucy now.'

The street was fairly busy but there was only one young woman heading towards them.

'That's her with the bags,' Mrs Radcliffe said.

The woman was walking fast with her head lowered, and she seemed to be struggling with two heavy Sainsbury's carrier bags.

She was whippet-thin and wearing skin-tight black leggings and a leopard-print top. Her long blonde hair hung loose and looked limp and lifeless.

She was almost at the café before she looked up and spotted them. She stopped dead and stared, and Anna guessed she'd tumbled they were police officers and was trying to decide what to do.

Anna solved the problem for her by stepping forward, warrant card in hand.

'I gather you are Lucy Knight,' she said. 'I'm DCI Tate and this is DI Walker. We'd like to ask you a few questions about your boyfriend, Ross Palmer.'

Close up, Anna saw that her face was awash with freckles and she had large piercing brown eyes.

'He's not my boyfriend,' she snapped. 'And for your information I don't know where the fuck he is.'

'That's not what we've heard, Miss Knight.'

'Well, you've been misinformed then.'

'Look, we'd rather not talk about it out here on the street,'

Anna said. 'But we are going to talk about it, so why don't you let us help carry your bags up to your flat.'

Lucy looked at Mrs Radcliffe, who said, 'I haven't said anything to them, Luce. They only just got here and I told them you were out.'

Walker stepped up to Lucy and reached for the carrier bags, but she jerked them away from him.

'I don't have to talk to you and I don't have to let you upstairs,' she said. 'So just leave me alone.'

'If you don't talk to us here then we will need to take you to the station to be formally questioned,' Anna said.

'What about? I haven't done anything.'

'Well, for one thing, you were an accessory to the crime Ross Palmer committed in the pub at London Bridge,' Anna said. 'And I suspect you know that he's now involved in the Peabody Nursery investigation, where nine small children have been taken hostage.'

Mrs Radcliffe gasped and put her hand over her mouth.

Anna nodded towards her. 'That's what happens if we have this sort of discussion in a public place, Miss Knight. People get to hear what we're saying. Now I'm sure you don't want that.'

That shook Lucy up and her features stiffened. This time when Walker reached for her bags she let him take them. Anna then gently grasped her elbow and led her up to the door next to the café.

Lucy unclipped her key chain from her belt and let them into the flat. As they mounted the stairs Anna asked her where her father was.

'He's away with my brothers on one of their fishing trips,' she said. 'But don't ask me where because they never tell me.'

'Do your brothers live here as well?' Anna asked.

'No. They've got their own places. Kevin lives in Balham with his girlfriend and Craig has a flat in Streatham. But Kevin does work here part-time.'

There was a door at the top of the stairs which gave access to a wide hallway. To the left was an open-plan kitchen and dining room. To the right there were more doors, all closed.

Anna and Walker followed Lucy into the kitchen where Walker placed her shopping bags on a worktop.

'You can ask your questions in the living room,' she said and walked back out of the kitchen into the hall. 'It's through that door on the left. I need to use the loo first.'

Lucy entered the toilet, closing the door behind her, and Anna and Walker let themselves into the living room, which was large but basic. There was a three-piece suite that had seen better days, a side cabinet, coffee table and huge plasma TV.

Lucy didn't take long and when she reappeared she walked straight into the living room. She removed her mobile phone from the back pocket of her leggings and sat on the sofa.

'I want to know who told you I've been seeing Ross,' she said.

Anna sat opposite her on one of the armchairs.

'It was his parents,' she said.

Lucy nodded. 'Well, it's true. I did see him for a while after he got out of prison because there's history between us. But about a week ago he called to say that he wouldn't be seeing me any more because he was moving away.'

'So you know where he's been living since he moved out of his parents' house.'

'He refused to tell me. He said it was best I didn't know.'

'You need to do better than that, Miss Knight,' Anna said.

Lucy shrugged. 'I can only tell you what I know. I've admitted we've been seeing each other. But it's over and he's gone. End of story.'

'So why weren't you surprised when I told you downstairs that Ross is involved in the kidnapping of those children from the nursery school in Rotherhithe? I'm sure you've heard about it.'

'I was surprised. I just thought you were making it up to get a reaction.'

'Going away on holiday, are you, Miss Knight?' Walker said, and Anna looked up to see that he'd picked up a couple of travel brochures from the side cabinet.

'That's none of your bloody business,' Lucy replied.

Walker held them up so that Anna could see the covers.

'These are expensive packages,' he said. 'Barbados, Mauritius, Dubai. I'm surprised you can afford to go to these exotic destinations. I know I can't.'

She started to respond, but just then her mobile beeped to signal an incoming text and it seemed to throw her. She covered the phone with both hands.

'Aren't you going to see who's sent you a message?' Anna said. 'It might be Ross?'

'It won't be,' she said, but then she read it anyway and shook her head. 'It's a friend, asking me if I'm up for having a drink tonight.'

Anna stuck out her hand. 'Mind if I see for myself?'

'Of course I mind. You've got no right.'

Anna left her hand where it was, said, 'Just give me the phone, Miss Knight. Otherwise I intend to take it from you. And that's because it just occurred to me that you probably used it to send a text when you went into the toilet. And what you've just received is a response.'

'You're wrong about that.'

'Then prove it.'

Lucy gave a loud grunt of exasperation and stood up.

'See for yourself then,' she said and dropped the phone onto the coffee table. 'While you do that I'm going to get myself a drink.'

She stormed out of the room and Anna signalled to Walker to go with her. She then reached out to pick up Lucy's phone, but before she had a chance to look at it she heard Walker cry out.

Still clutching the phone, she leapt to her feet and dashed into the hallway.

At first she didn't see Walker or realise what had happened. But then as she moved along the hall she saw him sprawled on his back near the bottom of the stairs.

'I didn't see it coming,' he said. 'The bitch suddenly turned around and kicked me, then ran into the kitchen.'

Anna went after her. The kitchen door was closed and when she grabbed the handle and started to turn it Lucy yelled from inside.

'Open that door, copper, and I'll stab you. I'm holding two knives and I swear I'll use them.'

Anna stopped turning but left her hand where it was.

'You need to put the knives down, Lucy. This is ridiculous. Take this any further and you'll be in serious trouble.'

There was no response and Anna was in two minds about what to do.

'Don't chance it, guv,' Walker said as he came up behind her. 'I think she's crazy enough to attack you.'

Anna knocked on the door with her free hand. 'What is it you want, Lucy? Tell me.'

No response.

And then a thought occurred to Anna. 'Oh fuck,' she said. 'I'm sure I noticed a back door when we arrived.'

Walker moved her to one side and pushed the door open so that he would be the one to face down a knife-wielding Lucy.

But the kitchen was empty and Anna was right. There was a door on the other side of the adjoining dining room and it was open. Together they rushed over to it and saw that it led to a metal fire escape. They stepped onto it. Below them was a parking area for residents with extra space for delivery vehicles. But there was no sign of Lucy Knight.

'She can't have gone far,' Anna said.

They hurried down the stairs, looked around the parking area and then ran along an alley that took them back onto the high street. But Lucy had vanished.

'Shit,' Anna said, as they hurried back up the fire escape to the flat.

Walker didn't speak until they were back at the top.

'I'm sorry, guv. When she kicked me I just lost my balance and went flying.'

'Are you hurt?'

'I'll have some bruises, I'm sure. But my pride has taken a huge fucking hit.'

Anna then looked at Lucy's phone again and was relieved that she hadn't been locked out of it. She tapped on the message icon and a list of incoming and outgoing texts appeared. At the top was the name Ross and when she opened it up there was his phone number along with an exchange of messages.

The latest read:

Cops here looking for you. Don't come. Meet later.

'She must have sent that one when she went to the loo,' Anna said.

The response had arrived when they were in the living room.

Say nothing and don't let them take you anywhere. I'll be gone from here soon.

'You could ring the number,' Walker said. 'Or send him a message and he'll think it's from her.'

'I've got a better idea,' Anna said.

She pulled out her own phone and called DC Sweeny.

'I need an urgent trace on the phone number I'm about to give you, Megan. It's a mobile and I suspect it's still switched on and therefore transmitting a signal.'

Six minutes later Sweeny came back.

'We've got it, ma'am,' she said. 'Not the exact address but the signal has been triangulated to a street. It's not moving and believe it or not it's less than a mile from your own location.'

She gave Anna the name of the street and she and Walker sprinted out of the flat and across the road to the pool car.

CHAPTER FORTY-EIGHT

The phone signal was coming from Wigmore Road, between Clapham and Stockwell. As they raced towards it, Anna contacted central control and requested back-up. She also gave a description of Lucy Knight and said she was wanted in connection with the Peabody Street kidnappings.

'She was last seen in the vicinity of Clapham High Street,' she said. 'And send units to Knight's Café in the high street. I want the café and the flat above it sealed off and a forensic team sent there.'

'I feel a right twat,' Walker said when Anna had finished dishing out instructions. 'I shouldn't have let her get the jump on me like that.'

'Maybe you're getting too old for front-line police work,' Anna said with a smile. 'If you want me to give you a desk job then just say the word.'

'Very funny. But seriously, she caught me unawares.'

'What exactly happened?'

'I was walking behind her towards the kitchen. Then she

turned around as though to retrace her steps. It meant I was suddenly standing between her and the stairs and she gave me an almighty kick.'

'And down you went.'

'Exactly.'

'Well, it was a desperate move on her part. She knew that once I'd looked at her phone she'd be in trouble.'

'And she clearly wasn't prepared to disappoint Palmer. Remind me what he put in that message.'

'He said say nothing and don't let them take you anywhere. He also said he'd be gone soon from wherever he is.'

'What I don't understand is, if he's one of the kidnappers, then why is he here? You would expect him to be with the kids.'

'Well, maybe that's where the children are,' Anna said. 'In Wigmore Road.'

They got to Wigmore Road in minutes. It was lined with a mix of terraced and detached houses along both sides, many of which had been converted into flats.

It was a short road, maybe a hundred yards in length, and there were double yellow lines to prevent on-street parking.

There was only one car in breach of the restrictions – a red Audi saloon that seized Anna's attention straight away.

The car's boot was open, and as they approached it they saw a man walking out of the large detached house it was parked in front of. He was carrying a rucksack in one hand and a coat in the other.

'Holy fuck, that's him,' Walker shouted.

The man stepped onto the pavement and looked their way,

and Anna recognised him at once from Ross Palmer's photograph. Almost six foot tall, cropped hair, square face. He was wearing a white T-shirt and jeans.

He clocked them at the same time, and as Walker floored the accelerator, Palmer panicked and dashed back towards the house. He was trying frantically to open the front door as Walker brought the car to a screeching halt right behind the Audi.

Anna was out of the car in a flash, but at the same time Palmer pushed the front door open and disappeared inside, slamming it shut behind him. In his haste he dropped the coat and rucksack on the ground and didn't pause to pick them up.

When Anna reached the front door she tried to open it but it was locked. There was a panel on the wall next to it with five buttons labelled Flats 1–5.

'You try to get someone to open up,' Anna yelled to Walker as he ran up behind her. 'I'll see if I can get around the back.'

'Be careful, guv. The bastard might be armed.'

But being careful wasn't an option. Ross Palmer had to be stopped. As far as she was concerned, his desperate bid to escape was clear evidence that he was involved in the kidnappings.

There was a wooden door between the side of the house and the perimeter fence that looked fairly old. Anna braced herself to kick it open, but after pressing down on the rusty thumb latch she discovered that it wasn't locked. She went through shoulder first and as she did so she heard a cacophony of police sirens approaching.

A narrow pathway along the side of the house led to the back garden, and her heart revved into full throttle as she hurtled along it.

She reached a paved patio, beyond which lay a sprawling lawn surrounded by well-tended flower beds.

She got there just in time to see Ross Palmer scrambling over the rear fence.

She broke into a sprint across the grass, dragging in ragged gulps of air as she went.

She couldn't remember the last time she'd had to climb over a fence, and she wasn't sure she'd be able to make it in one go, but she was determined to try.

So she ran as fast as she could and simply jumped up onto it. She felt the pain in her knees and chest, but despite that she managed to throw her arms over the top and pull herself up.

There was a wide alleyway on the other side running between two rows of back gardens. Anna caught sight of Palmer as he fled to the left.

But by the time she'd dropped onto the alleyway he had disappeared from sight. She went after him and reached the end of the alley seconds later. It opened out onto another residential road, this one full of parked cars.

She stood on the pavement gulping air into her heaving chest. She looked up and down the street, scrunching up her brow against the sun's glare. But she couldn't see Palmer, and she realised to her frustration that she had lost him.

She grabbed her phone from her pocket and called it in. She was told that the area would be swarming with police within minutes.

But Anna wasn't at all reassured. Palmer had a head start and she'd be surprised if he didn't manage to make good his escape.

CHAPTER FORTY-NINE

Anna felt sick to her stomach as she walked back round to the front of the house in Wigmore Road.

On the way she fumbled a cigarette into her mouth and had a much needed smoke.

She was absolutely gutted. They'd been so close to nabbing Ross Palmer. If only they'd arrived a few minutes earlier they might have caught him before he left the house. Or a few seconds later and he might not have made it back inside.

What made it doubly galling was that his girlfriend had also managed to give them the slip.

Would they be spotted by any of the patrols that were now searching for them? Anna very much doubted it. South London was an easy place to lose yourself in, especially if you were familiar with the streets, housing estates and large industrial complexes.

Two patrol cars had already arrived in Wigmore Road and uniformed officers had taken up position to keep nosey neighbours at bay.

Walker was standing on the pavement in front of the house talking to a grey-haired man and he was clearly relieved to see her.

'You had me worried,' he said. 'By the time I got through to the back of the house you were—'

Anna waved an arm to stop him talking. 'Forget that. Just tell me if you've had a look around inside.'

'I have,' he said. 'And no – the children aren't here. But then we didn't really expect them to be.'

He was right, but nonetheless Anna felt her heart drop and her stomach muscles contract.

Walker gestured towards the grey-haired man, who was somewhere in his late sixties or early seventies and wearing a sweat-stained shirt over baggy shorts.

'Mr Dunne here opened the front door so I was able to check Palmer's flat.'

'How did you get in?'

'Mr Dunne's the landlord and has a key. He opened all five flats for me. None of the tenants are in. He was just going to tell me what he knows about Ross Palmer.'

Anna introduced herself and said, 'First of all, how long has he been living here, Mr Dunne?'

'Two months. The flat was empty and I got a call from a friend of mine who reminded me I owed him a favour. He said his mate needed somewhere to kip for a few months and was willing to pay over the odds. So I let him move in and I've had no trouble until today.'

'Who was the mate?'

'Frank Knight. He runs a café over in Clapham. We used to hang out together years ago and we sometimes meet up for a drink.'

'Do you know where Ross Palmer has gone?'

'No, I don't. He hasn't been around for a few days. Then he suddenly turned up about forty-five minutes ago and I only saw him by chance because I was out the front. He said he needed to pack a few things because he was going away on a trip. But that was all he said. I went back indoors and the next thing I know the police are ringing the bell.'

'We'll need to talk to you again, Mr Dunne,' Anna said. 'So please don't go anywhere.'

'I don't intend to. But what's all this about?'

'You'll know in due course. Meanwhile, nobody is to leave or enter this house without our permission. And my officers will need to carry out a thorough search.'

She told Mr Dunne he could go back to his flat and then pointed to the rucksack and leather jacket that Palmer had dropped to the right of the front door.

'I'll check his stuff and the car while you go and have a look around his flat,' she said to Walker. 'And get a forensics team out here pronto.'

Anna slipped on a pair of latex gloves and picked up the rucksack. It was lighter than she'd expected but that was because there was very little inside. Just two shirts, a pair of jeans, three pairs of pants and four unopened packs of Marlboro cigarettes.

'This can't be right,' she said aloud to herself. 'Would he really have risked coming back just for this stuff?'

She got her answer a moment later when she unzipped one of the pockets and found a large padded envelope. Inside was a brochure for the Peabody Nursery in Rotherhithe, a printed floorplan showing all the rooms, nine hundred pounds in new twenty-pound notes, a passport in the name of Gerald Tyler but with Palmer's picture inside, and a small photo album containing mostly photos of his parents.

Anna then picked up the leather jacket. In the right-hand pocket was a key fob for the Audi and in the inside pocket was a Samsung mobile phone. She quickly discovered that it was password-protected and would have to be unlocked by a technician.

Next she checked the interior of the Audi, hoping to find a clue as to where he'd been going. But there wasn't a sat nav and there were no maps with markings on.

She got one of the uniforms to radio in the car's number plate and was told that it was registered to a Frank Knight, Lucy's father.

'There's nothing in the flat of interest,' Walker said when he came back outside. 'He's left some clothes and books and a pair of shoes. But that's all.'

She showed him what she'd found in Palmer's rucksack and jacket.

'We need to unlock the phone,' she said. 'I'd like you to take it back to the office and get that sorted, Max.' She took out Lucy's phone from her pocket and handed it to him. 'Get that checked as well. I'd like a printout of the call log and most recent messages.'

'And what about you, guv?'

'I'll get one of the squad cars to take me back to Clapham. I want to have a poke around in the flat above the café. Afterwards we'll get the team together and brief them. Meanwhile, it's time we went public with Palmer's name and picture. Let's get it out there. We now know the bastard is involved in the kidnappings and I'm guessing he's been staying at the house where the children are being kept. He must have come back here for the passport and cash after he learned that we were on to him.'

'So who the fuck tipped him off then?' Walker said.

Anna shrugged. 'That's what troubles me, Max. The only people we told were the parents, the teachers and Palmer's mum and dad.'

Anna continued to berate herself as she sat in the back of the squad car. She just couldn't believe that Ross Palmer and his girlfriend had got away.

At some point she would go back over everything that she and Walker had done. Had they made mistakes or just been unlucky? Either way, there were lessons to be learned, but it would have to wait because now wasn't the time to focus on anything other than finding those children.

At least they were making progress. The brochure in Palmer's rucksack provided an irrefutable link between him and the Peabody Nursery. And they now knew that there was no innocent explanation for the cigarette butt with his DNA on it that was found close to the abandoned minibus. He must have been there waiting for the children to turn up.

It was also beginning to look as though he was in cohorts with the Knight family. Was it possible that Lucy's father and her two brothers were the men who had carried out the kidnappings? And was Lucy the young woman on the minibus handing out sweets to the children as they stepped on board?

Knowing the identities of the gang was one thing but it didn't necessarily mean they were any closer to finding the children. However, it did mean that the whole situation had become far more precarious.

The kidnappers would have counted on remaining anonymous. Their intention would have been to take delivery of the ransom money and then divvy it up in their own good time. But if, as now seemed likely, the Knight family were involved, then they would no longer be able to return to their homes unless they were prepared to hand themselves in. And if they weren't then they'd have no choice but to see the plan through in order to raise enough money to start new lives.

Anna wondered if they had already made arrangements to leave the country. Was that why Lucy had a collection of travel brochures?

It was four p.m. when the squad car pulled up outside Knight's café. Two marked cars were already parked on the pavement and three officers in high-vis jackets were standing guard outside the café and the door to the upstairs flat.

Inside, both premises were already being searched. Anna went up to the flat first. There were two bedrooms and it was obvious which was Lucy's. The wardrobe and chest of drawers were packed with her clothes. On the dressing table there were perfumes and hair brushes and a leather box containing cheap-looking jewellery.

There were more travel brochures on the bed and these too featured exotic destinations such as Hawaii, the Seychelles and Goa. But Anna found nothing else of interest.

It was a different story in the father's bedroom. One wall was half-covered with what appeared to be family photographs. They were all framed and of various sizes. Many showed a woman who was presumably Frank's wife. In some she was by herself and in others she was with her husband. And there were plenty of pictures of the couple's two sons and daughter taken at different stages in their lives. There was a montage of baby pictures and some of them in their teens.

But the photo that Anna was particularly interested in appeared to be the most recent and it showed Frank Knight standing in between his two sons. They were each holding a fishing rod and there was a lake in the background.

Frank was a tall, thin man in his sixties with rugged features and a wide smile. His sons were in their thirties or forties. One was just as tall as his dad and looked very much like him. The other was shorter and quite plump. They all had dark receding hair.

Anna took a photo of the picture with her mobile and then a couple of Lucy that showed her looking only slightly younger than she did now. She then forwarded them to Walker before calling him.

He was already in the office and told her that he'd just brought DCS Nash up to speed.

'Well, the pictures you're about to receive are on the wall in Lucy Knight's flat,' Anna said. 'I'm assuming the three men are her father and brothers. Get someone to show it to Sarah Ramsay or the teachers. I've got a feeling they might be our kidnappers. And show the picture of Lucy to Felicity Bradshaw. Ask her if she's the woman she saw on the minibus.'

As she hung up one of the uniforms appeared in the bedroom and said, 'We've found something that you need to see, ma'am.'

She followed him into the kitchen where the contents of Lucy's two Sainsbury's shopping bags had been laid out across one of the worktops.

'Blimey,' she blurted before a hard lump formed in her throat.

Among the items on the worktop were about two dozen bags of Smarties, half a dozen bags of Skittles, five packets of chocolate biscuits, two large bags of assorted crisps, two boxes of Cheerios and three cartons of child-friendly fruit juice.

Anna sucked in a slow, deep breath and said, 'There's no prize for guessing where this lot was supposed to end up.'

CHAPTER FIFTY

'I'm so sorry, sweetheart. It wasn't meant to happen, but when she said she knew I was seeing someone it all came out. I couldn't stop myself talking about you and the baby. We're both in such a terrible state over Liam and I suddenly felt the need to get it off my chest . . . And yes, I regret it . . . It was stupid of me and poor Ruth is now in a worse state because of it. I feel so bad.'

Each word was like a dagger being plunged into Ruth's heart. Ethan thought she was upstairs asleep on their bed, which was why he didn't see the need to keep his voice down.

He'd come up to check on her a few minutes ago and she had kept her eyes shut, not responding when he asked if she was awake.

She had followed him down the stairs shortly after, not with the intention of eavesdropping, but because she wanted to ask him questions about the child that was growing in his bitch's body.

Had they decided on a name? Was he going to get involved

in bringing it up? Was there a risk that it would have cystic fibrosis?

These were questions that she'd been too messed up to ask him after he'd broken the news to her the night before. And after returning from the community centre today all she had wanted to think about and talk about was her own son. But while lying awake upstairs she had suddenly felt the need to know more.

So she'd come down to confront Ethan. She had been about to open the kitchen door when she'd heard his voice and known immediately that he was on the phone. Talking to his bitch. Calling her sweetheart. Telling her how sorry he was for letting the cat out of the bag.

Bastard.

It's me he should be apologising to, she told herself. Me who deserves his sympathy. Not that stuck-up tart who failed miserably to protect the children in her care. To protect *our son*.

As she listened to his voice the rage built up inside her to a point where she could no longer control it. Heat burned in her chest, her throat, and a flash of adrenalin swept through her.

She pulled down the door handle and burst into the kitchen. Ethan was sitting on one of the stools at the breakfast bar, his white mobile phone to his ear, his eyes wide with shock.

'I've heard every bloody word, you piece of shit,' she screamed at him. 'Tell that whore that the next time I see her I'll give her more than a fucking slap.'

She ran at him and tried to grab the phone, but he was too quick for her and managed to shove it into the front pocket of his jeans.

But he wasn't quick enough to stop her slamming into him, and he was knocked backwards off the stool onto the floor.

She stood over him, fuming, her heart drumming in her chest like cannon fire.

'I can't believe you're worried about Sarah fucking Ramsay when you should be thinking about Liam,' she bellowed. 'Why can't you see that? Why do I have to tell you? It's not right.'

He rolled across the floor and scrambled to his feet.

'Leave it out, Ruth,' he said, holding his arms up in a gesture of appeasement. 'I just thought she deserved an explanation. That's all. Nothing more.'

Ruth swallowed down the urge to cry and stared at him, her breath wheezing loudly in her chest.

'It's correct what you just told her,' she said. 'I am in a terrible state. But that doesn't mean I don't care that you're still talking to that woman. It's as though you've ripped my heart out of my body and now you're stamping on it to cause me as much pain as you can.'

'Ruth, I'm really sorry. I shouldn't have called her. I accept that. It was a mistake.'

She gave a derisive snort. 'Do you ever listen to yourself, Ethan? According to you every bad decision you make is just a mistake. You refuse to take responsibility for your actions. And you only care about yourself.'

He shook his head. 'You can't really believe that. I've only ever wanted what's best for this family, for Liam. It's been hard these past three years and I want us to have a future.'

'Is that why you started screwing Sarah Ramsay?'

'I've told you why it happened and I deeply regret it. But we need to move on. And we can if only you'll let us.'

'And do you seriously believe it will be as easy as that?'

Ruth shot back. 'She's having your baby, for God's sake, and I know about it. How do you think that makes me feel?'

He started to reply but then thought better of it and took a deep breath instead.

'That's it, Ethan. Just avoid the question. Well, I've got other questions that you will have to answer sooner or later. Like, do you want it to be a boy or a girl? Have you and her decided on names? Are you going to love it as much as you love Liam? Or will you love it more if it's healthy because he or she will be less of a burden. And how much—'

She halted in the middle of the sentence when she heard his phone ring. Ethan instinctively reached into his jeans pocket.

'Let me talk to the bitch,' Ruth yelled. 'She's got a bloody nerve calling back.'

She lurched forward just as he pulled the phone from his pocket and before he had even had a chance to look at it. She grabbed the device from him with one hand and pushed him away with the other.

'Please, Ruth. No. Let me have it back.'

Ruth turned her back on him and swiped the *accept call* icon with her thumb.

'Now listen to me, you bitch. I'm not . . .'

'Who are you?' said the caller, and Ruth froze because it was a man's voice and one she didn't recognise.

'I'm Ruth,' she muttered after a moment. 'Ethan's wife.'

'Then where is he? It's him I want to speak to.'

Ethan tried to take the phone from her but again she pushed him away and held him at arm's length with her hand against his chest.

'Tell me who you are,' she said into the phone.

'Don't dick me around, lady,' the man replied, his voice louder. 'Is your husband even there?'

'Yes he's here, but I'm not . . .'

'Then put him on the fucking phone because I need him to do something for me. And if he doesn't do it then I'll go and take it out on that sick little son of yours.'

Ruth felt her heart explode in her chest and she had to lean against the worktop because she feared her legs were about to give way under her.

'P-please don't hurt him,' was all she managed to get out.

Ethan, seeing how shocked she was, seized the opportunity to try again to grab the phone and this time he succeeded. He quickly retreated to the other side of the room, leaving Ruth standing there, unable to move, her head spinning.

As she watched Ethan whisper into the phone a chill raced over her skin. She couldn't hear what he was saying, but the look on his face was one of abject terror.

He listened and spoke for just a matter of seconds before ending the call. Then he made a point of switching off the phone and putting it back into his pocket.

'I have to go out,' he said to Ruth, and she felt the bile rise up in her throat. 'While I'm gone I want you to stay here. Keep calm and don't do anything stupid.'

CHAPTER FIFTY-ONE

Anna was being chauffeured back to MIT headquarters in the squad car when she received an unexpected call from Jack Keen. The private investigator wanted her to know that he had spent the day searching for James and Alice Miller.

'I know you must be working your socks off,' he said. 'But you did ask me to keep checking in.'

'It's not a problem, Jack,' she said as she felt sweat pricking her palms. 'What have you got?'

'Not much so far, I'm afraid. You were right about there being an awful lot of people out there with those names. So it's just a question of plodding on and hoping I'll get lucky. But I have found out a bit about both Paul Russell and the pub landlord who referred Matthew to him.'

Anna took out her notebook and pen.

'So let's hear it,' she said.

'Well, to start with, Russell told you the truth about his illustrious career as a master forger,' Keen said. 'I've spoken to a couple of my contacts in the underworld who knew him. He had a solid reputation and did a lot of work for one of the most well-connected London gangs. In return they provided him with protection. A couple of senior officers within the Met were on their payroll and they saw to it that he was never collared.'

That came as no surprise to Anna. It was not a secret that until recently corruption in the Met had been widespread and problematic. Now, at last, the bad apples in the force were being rooted out as part of a well-resourced crackdown on organised crime in the capital.

'According to my sources, Russell retired from the business a few years ago and it was generally assumed he had moved away from London,' Keen said. 'They weren't aware that he's dying of cancer.'

'And what about this pub landlord who put Matthew in touch with him?'

'Chris Foreman used to run a boozer in the City, close to where Matthew worked. I spoke to one of Matthew's former colleagues and he confirmed that Matthew often drank there. Foreman was involved in all kinds of shady dealings before he died after a heart attack two years ago. It's believed he used to allow drugs to be sold on the premises and he was also known for fencing stolen goods. So I'm assuming that your ex sounded him out about obtaining fake passports and Foreman told him about Russell.'

'That all sounds plausible,' Anna said. 'Have you found any records of the passports being used?'

'No, and I'm not sure I will. The whole system of passport records and border controls has been a total mess for years. That's how so many people have been able to enter the country illegally and work here under the radar. It's only recently that the government has been getting to grips with it.'

Keen had nothing more to offer but said he would keep looking and phone with another update tomorrow.

Anna was naturally disappointed, but she forced herself not to dwell on it. She couldn't afford to, not now that the pace of her investigation into the kidnappings had accelerated so dramatically.

There was a heavy buzz of excitement in the office when Anna got there. The room was filled with detectives, uniforms and auxiliary civilian staff who had gathered for the briefing.

The first thing Anna noticed was that a second whiteboard had been put up and on it were pinned photos of Ross Palmer and the Knight family.

Then she noticed the tired eyes and stained armpits of most of her team. It had been a long time since they'd had a case that required the team to work around the clock. Anna felt grateful for their dedication, with no complaints from anyone. They were all entirely committed to bringing those children back safely.

DCS Nash was present and he told her that he would be attending a meeting with the Commissioner and the Home Secretary after the briefing.

'I've been keeping them up to date with developments,' he said. 'And the Commissioner has just informed me that the ransom will be paid if we don't get to the kids before tomorrow's deadline. Taxpayers will foot the bill, but the powers-that-be think it will be the right thing to do politically. Sure it will set a very bad precedent, but that'll be a problem for another time.'

Anna wasn't at all surprised. The government had been forced into a corner. No way could it take a principled stand against paying ransoms when the lives of so many children were at stake.

Before she convened the briefing, Anna went to the vending machine in the hall and helped herself to a coffee and a bar of chocolate. She then got Walker to tell her where they were with Ross Palmer and the Knight family.

'You'll be glad to know that your instincts were spot on, guv,' he said. 'DS Crawford showed the photo of Frank Knight and his sons to Paige Quinlan. She identified them as the three men who turned up at the nursery.'

'She's absolutely sure?'

'One hundred per cent.'

'Has Sarah Ramsay seen the photo?'

'Not yet. Crawford didn't bother to call on her after Paige confirmed it was them, which seemed fair enough.'

'What about Felicity Bradshaw? Has she seen the photo of Lucy Knight?'

'She has indeed, but she doesn't think it was Lucy who she saw on the minibus. She says that woman appeared to be much younger. And she had dark reddish hair, not blonde.'

'So is that everything?'

'Well, Palmer's phone has just been unlocked and DC Shepherd is checking through it now. DS Willis is going through Lucy's phone. Sweeny, meanwhile, has been digging into various databases and she's got a report for us.'

'Sounds good,' Anna said. 'So let's get on with it.'

The excitement had reached fever pitch by the time the briefing got started because most of what Anna was going to say the team already knew.

She began with how the discarded cigarette butt had led them to Ross Palmer. She gave them a breakdown of his convictions for shoplifting, possessing indecent pictures of children and robbery. And she told them all to view the CCTV footage that showed him kicking off in the pub at London Bridge.

She then explained that Palmer's parents had revealed that their son had rekindled his relationship with Lucy Knight and her family after he was released from prison.

'This afternoon we interviewed Lucy but she attacked DI Walker and managed to slip away from us,' Anna said. 'We then turned up at the flat where Palmer has been staying these past two months, but he had it away on his toes before we could arrest him. It's worth noting that Frank Knight arranged for Palmer to stay in the flat.'

She went into detail about the messages that Palmer and Lucy had exchanged.

'We believe that Palmer somehow found out that we were on to him and so he returned to the flat to collect some of his things. But as he was running away from us he dropped his rucksack. Inside was a fake passport with a different name but his picture inside. There was also a wad of cash totalling nine hundred pounds and one of the Peabody Nursery brochures.'

She told the team about the sweets and other stuff that Lucy had just been to buy at Sainsbury's on Clapham High Street.

'The most obvious explanation is that she got them for the children,' Anna said. 'And I'm guessing that Palmer was going to pick them up before heading back to the house where the kids are being held.'

She threw to Walker then and he said that Paige Quinlan, one of the nursery teachers, had identified the Knight brothers and their father as the kidnappers.

'We've already given their names and the picture we've got to the media, along with photos of Palmer and Lucy,' he said. 'But they're not the only people involved. Mrs Felicity Bradshaw, the neighbour who witnessed the kids being herded onto the minibus, says that Lucy wasn't the woman she saw waiting on board.'

Walker then mentioned the connection between Ross Palmer and Jonas Platt, the man who harboured the grudge against Sarah Ramsay over the death of his daughter who choked on a grape in the Peabody Nursery at Lewisham.

'The pair were in Winchester prison at the same time,' he said. 'DI Bellingham has just phoned in after talking to Platt. He says Platt remembers meeting Palmer inside but says they did not stay in touch. And there's nothing in the man's phone records or online history to suggest he's lying, but of course that doesn't mean he isn't.'

It was then DC Sweeny's turn to report on what progress she'd made with seeking out background information on the Knight family.

'Well, we know that the Palmers and the Knights go back a long way to when they all lived on the same council estate,' she said. 'Ross Palmer and the two Knight brothers, Kevin and Craig, were part of a young gang that caused a lot of problems there.

'Both brothers have form. Craig was done nine years ago for burglary and did a short stint at a young offenders' institution. Kevin has a few minor offences against his name but has never served time. Their father Frank was banged up for three years when he was in his early thirties for a knife attack on one of his neighbours.

'I haven't found out much more about him yet except that

his wife Eileen died five years ago from cancer. The family have run the café in Clapham for nine years.'

'Do we have addresses for the brothers?' Anna asked.

Sweeny nodded. 'Armed response teams are on their way as we speak. From what I can gather Craig lives by himself in a flat in Streatham and Kevin is shacked up with his girl-friend in Balham.'

'That tallies with what Lucy told us,' Anna said. 'I don't suppose we know anything about the girlfriend?'

'Not as yet, ma'am.'

'Well, the sooner we do the better because I'm wondering if she's the girl Mrs Bradshaw saw on the minibus.'

Anna then started to outline the steps that now needed to be taken. And she spoke of her concern that they couldn't be sure how the gang would react now that their identities were known.

But she was interrupted before she had finished by DC Shepherd, who stood up from the desk where he'd been checking through Ross Palmer's mobile phone.

'I've got something for you, guv,' he said, and the excitement was evident in his voice.

He held up Palmer's phone and looked around the room.

'Well, don't keep us in suspense, detective. What is it?'

He picked up his notes from his desk and glanced at them before continuing.

'As instructed, I've started going through the call log and messages,' he said. 'Over the last two weeks Palmer's called and received calls from four other phones. Two of them are unregistered and are probably untraceable pay-as-you-gos. They're both currently switched off and aren't transmitting signals.

'The third belongs to Lucy Knight and that's in our possession. But the fourth is registered to none other than the owner of the Peabody Nursery, Sarah Ramsay.'

Anna inhaled a sharp breath.

'Are you positive about that?' she said.

He nodded. 'I've just had it confirmed by the service provider.'

'So how many calls have there been between them?'

'He called her twice and she called him twice. The last call was ten days ago when she phoned him.'

Anna turned to Walker and said, 'I want her picked up straight away and brought here. That woman has got some fucking explaining to do.'

CHAPTER FIFTY-TWO

There were a number of officers still at the Peabody community centre, including uniforms and detectives, so a unit was sent from there to Sarah Ramsay's house, which was only a short distance away.

Luckily she was at home, and forty-five minutes after being picked up she was facing Anna and Walker across the table in an interview room at MIT headquarters.

She hadn't been told why she was there and her eyes looked bleary and confused. She was wearing a bright red T-shirt over jeans and her face was without make-up.

Anna had the impression she'd got ready in a hurry. Even her long black hair was unruly, and stray strands kept flopping across her face.

'I hope we didn't drag you away from anything important,' Anna said.

Sarah's eyes darted nervously between the two of them.

'I was reading a book and trying to take my mind off everything that's happening, just for a few minutes at least,' she replied, her voice thin and high. 'So no, it was nothing important. But I'm assuming that this is, otherwise I'm sure you wouldn't have sent a car to pick me up.'

There was a large envelope on the table between them. Anna extracted three photographs. She placed one face up in front of Sarah.

'Do you recognise that woman?' she asked.

As Sarah looked at the photo, a frown wrinkled her brow.

'I've never seen her before,' she said. 'Who is she and what has she got to do with me?'

'Her name is Lucy Knight.'

Sarah curled her lip. 'And am I supposed to know her?'

Anna ignored the question and placed the second photo on top of the first.

'What about these three men?' she said. 'Have you seen them before?'

This time Sarah's eyes bulged as she picked up the photo.

'My God, it's them,' she blurted. 'These are the three men who took the children. They're the kidnappers.'

Anna nodded. 'Your colleague Paige confirmed that for us earlier.'

'Well of course she would. She was there with me.'

'So do you still maintain that you don't know who they are?'

Sarah's frown deepened. 'Of course I do. Are you suggesting I'm lying? Is that what this is about?'

'I'm merely asking you some questions, Miss Ramsay,' Anna said.

'Then let me ask you something,' Sarah responded indignantly. 'Who are these men and have they been arrested?'

Anna pointed to the photo. 'The man in the middle is a

café owner named Frank Knight. The other two are his sons Kevin and Craig. Lucy Knight is his daughter. And they haven't been arrested because we don't know where they are.'

'But you think I do. That's it, isn't it? Jesus Christ, you're still convinced I'm involved in this. How many times do I have to tell you that it has got nothing to do with me?'

Anna flipped over the third picture and dropped it on top of the others.

'Now tell me if you've ever seen this man before.'

Sarah peered at it and a look of disbelief poured into her face.

'That's Callum Chambers,' she said without hesitation. 'I've met him but only once, and that was well over a week ago.'

Anna felt a jolt of unease.

'His name is Ross Palmer,' she said. 'Why do you call him Callum Chambers?'

Sarah raised her shoulders. 'Because that's what he told me his name was.'

Anna threw a glance at Walker, who was as surprised as she was.

He said, 'So how did you make this man's acquaintance, Miss Ramsay?'

Sarah leaned on the table, her fingers intertwined, and she struggled to keep her voice steady.

'He contacted me by phone,' she said. 'He told me he'd heard that my business was for sale and that he was interested in buying it. He asked if he could come and see the Peabody Street Nursery and I arranged it.'

'And so you let him look around.'

'Of course, but only when there were no children on the premises. He seemed genuinely interested. He gave me his phone number and his card and claimed he was a cash buyer. But after his visit he didn't get back to me so I phoned him, twice as I remember. He said he needed more time to think about it.'

'Do you still have his card?'

'I think so.'

She picked up her handbag from the floor, dug out her purse, and produced an unimpressive card that simply said: *Callum Chambers Investments*. There was a mobile number but no email address, which in itself should have rung alarm bells.

'The only other person in the nursery when he came was Tasha,' Sarah said. 'It was at the end of the day and we were clearing up. We both showed him around and he asked lots of questions.'

And that was when he familiarised himself with the layout, Anna thought. It was how he was able to produce the floor-plan and tell his accomplices what to expect when they arrived.

'So I gather that you're telling me I was conned,' Sarah said. 'Callum Chambers is really Ross Palmer, whoever he is.'

Anna nodded. 'That's right. And Palmer is part of the kidnap gang. We believe he was driving the minibus the kids were transferred to. But what I don't understand, Miss Ramsay, is why you didn't think it necessary to have the man checked out. Surely it's something you should do with all prospective buyers to avoid being misled and having your time wasted.'

'But I did do that,' she answered. 'After the visit Ethan came to the nursery on his way home from work to spend some time with me. Tasha had left by then and I told Ethan about Callum Chambers. He said he would find out what he could about the man and I was happy with that because he's a computer geek and knows where to look for information. I even showed him the security footage of the man entering the building.'

'Well, that's really odd,' Anna said. 'You see, when we showed Ethan Brady that photograph of Ross Palmer, he told us he had never seen him before.'

Sarah Ramsay refused to accept that the man she loved could possibly be involved in the abduction of nine children, including his own son.

'It's an absurd conclusion to draw,' she said. 'He probably just didn't realise from this picture that it was the same man.'

'You told us he offered to find out what he could about Callum Chambers,' Anna said. 'Did he provide you with any information?'

Sarah bit into her top lip and Anna saw the first flicker of uncertainty in her eyes.

'He didn't actually,' she said. 'But perhaps he forgot. And I didn't bother to remind him after Chambers, or whatever the man's real name is, said he needed to give more thought to buying the business.'

'So you simply took Ethan's word for it that he would do some digging on your behalf.'

'Correct. But then I had no reason at all to think he wouldn't.'

The two women stared at each other for several seconds and Anna could tell that Sarah still did not believe that her lover might be implicated. But the more Anna thought about it, the more convinced she became that he was. There was one thing in particular that clinched it for her, and she mentally cursed herself for not having attributed significance to it before now.

'Were you aware that Liam Brady wasn't meant to be at the nursery on Monday morning?' she said. 'Ethan had arranged for his wife to take the boy to the Shrek Adventure on the South Bank. He even went and bought the tickets. He was therefore shocked when he discovered that Ruth hadn't taken him, and I got the impression that he was pretty angry with her.'

'So you're suggesting that he didn't want him to be there because—'

'Because he knew exactly what was going to happen. Yes,' Anna said. 'Did you know before Monday that Liam wouldn't be there?'

Sarah's face turned as white as foam, and when she spoke her voice was smaller, fearful.

'He came to my house on Sunday morning, which was pretty unusual,' she said. 'He'd apparently told Ruth that he had to go into the office. I have no idea if she believed him or not. Anyway, he told me then that Liam wouldn't be there on Monday, which was why I was surprised when Ruth suddenly turned up with the boy. But I remember now that he asked me a couple of questions that didn't strike me as odd at the time but do now.'

'So what were they?'

'He asked which teachers would be in on Monday morning and how many kids had been booked in. I told him and shortly after he said he had to make a phone call. He went into the garden to do it while I poured us each a glass of lemonade.'

'So the clear implication there is that he phoned someone

to pass on what you'd told him,' Anna said. 'And if we assume that it was one of the kidnappers then that's how the gang knew what to expect when they arrived.'

Sarah started to shake her head and bite her knuckles at the same time. Beads of perspiration appeared across her forehead.

'Tell me what Ethan has been like these past few weeks,' Anna said. 'Has he been behaving differently?'

Sarah nodded. 'He's definitely been more distant and moody. He hasn't really come to terms with my pregnancy and I suspect that he's been struggling with the guilt. And then there's Liam's condition. It's always playing on his mind, and he feels bad that he can't do more for him.'

It was all Anna needed to hear. She told Sarah that an officer would come in and take down a statement from her.

'So what do you intend to do about Ethan?' Sarah asked.

'We'll pay him a visit,' Anna said. 'And I must ask you not to contact him before we've spoken to him. At this point he doesn't know he's a suspect and we want it to stay that way.'

Anna and Walker rushed out of the interview room before Sarah could ask any more questions. Anna gave the gist of what Sarah had said to one of the detectives and asked him to take her statement.

'And I don't want her to leave this building unless I've cleared it,' she said.

She then had a quick word with DS Shepherd about the call log on Ross Palmer's phone. There was something she wanted to check before getting the team together again. She then told her detectives that Ethan Brady, the father of one of the children, was now thought to be a key figure in the kidnappings.

She gave them a summary of the interview with Sarah Ramsay and then said, 'I've just checked the log on Palmer's mobile and he received a call from an unregistered number this afternoon, just five minutes after I showed Ethan Brady and several of the other parents the photo of Palmer. I now believe that the call came from Brady and he was alerting Palmer to the fact that we were on to him. DI Walker and I will now go to his house in Bermondsey to find out what the hell is going on.'

She asked if the armed response teams had been to the homes of the Knight brothers. They had, but both properties were empty and according to neighbours they had been for several days.

'I think it's fair to say that we know the identities of most of the kidnap gang, along with the person who provided them with inside information,' Anna said. 'Now we just have to find the bastards.'

She intended to end the meeting there so that she could rush off to Bermondsey, but DCS Nash chose then to drop a bombshell.

'It seems the kidnappers have already gone into panic mode,' he said. 'The Commissioner has just informed me that they've been in touch with him. They've increased the ransom demand from six to ten million and brought the deadline forward to midnight tonight. They say they'll text details of the payment method to the Commissioner just before then. And they've repeated their threat that if the transaction doesn't take place instantly then four-year-old Grace Tenant will be the first to die and the murder will be recorded on video and uploaded to the internet.'

CHAPTER FIFTY-THREE

Ruth had once again turned to the bottle to escape the ever worsening nightmare that had consumed her.

She was on her third glass of straight vodka but so far nothing had changed. She was still feeling hollow inside, and sucking air into her lungs like a drowning woman waiting to be rescued.

Ethan had been gone for a couple of hours and she didn't know when she would see him again. A small part of her hoped he would never come back into her life. He had caused so much damage and so much pain. There was no forgiving what he'd done.

It was bad enough that he'd had a sordid affair and got his mistress pregnant. But even that paled in comparison to the outrageous plan he cooked up, a plan that had placed their own son in mortal danger.

Ruth had known nothing about it until it came out as part of his tearful and pathetic confession the previous evening.

And he'd had the frigging cheek to make her feel bad because she hadn't taken Liam to the Shrek Adventure.

'He wasn't supposed to be there on Monday morning,' he told her. 'I didn't want him to be among those taken. It was all worked out. He was meant to be with you. But you took him to the nursery instead.'

So it was her fault! She was to blame for the fact that Liam had been kidnapped along with eight of his nursery school friends.

And by telling her what he had done he had placed her in an impossible position. He warned her that if she told the police the men who had Liam would hurt him, perhaps even kill him. The bastard appeared not to accept responsibility for what had happened. Or even acknowledge that he was in way above his head.

'All you have to do is keep quiet and hold your nerve, Ruth,' he had said. 'When the ransom is paid all the kids will be released and no one will be any the wiser.'

He then sought to put her mind at ease in respect of Liam's medication.

'When I heard he'd been taken I panicked. I called the guys straight away and told them what had happened. One of them met me and I gave him a bag filled with Liam's medication and instructions on how to administer it. And I told them to play safe and keep him away from the other kids, which was why he wasn't in the photo and video posted online.'

He tried to make it sound like it wasn't really a big deal, that all the kids, including Liam, were perfectly OK at the house in the country where they'd been taken.

'Everything was in place to make them comfortable,' he told her. 'Toys, television, food, sleeping bags. Having the guy in the balaclava make those threats on the video was just a scare tactic. The kids won't be harmed.'

'But what if the ransom isn't paid?' she asked him.

'It will be. Trust me. The government will come under so much pressure it will have no choice. And as the parents we're among those applying that pressure.'

Recounting that conversation was like chewing on a razor blade. Ruth felt a sense of dread rising inside her, and salty tears started streaking down her cheeks.

She poured another vodka, then rolled the drink around in her mouth. Her mind was in disarray and she couldn't think straight. She wanted to call Ethan to find out what was happening but she couldn't because both his phones were switched off.

She had asked him to send her a picture of Liam to show that he was alive and well. He had promised to do so but she was still waiting.

She closed her eyes and tried to empty her mind. The silence in the house drummed in her ears and she could feel the panic gushing through her veins.

Then suddenly the doorbell rang, and it came as such a shock that it caused her to drop her glass and spill vodka all over the sofa.

CHAPTER FIFTY-FOUR

It was Ruth who opened the door and it looked to Anna as though she'd been crying again. She was pale and glassy-eyed, and her nose was red.

'Hello, Ruth,' Anna said. 'We're here to talk to you and your husband.'

Ruth looked from Anna to Walker and then at the five uniformed officers who were standing behind them on the path.

'Ethan's not in,' she said, clearly flustered. 'He's gone out and I don't know when he'll be back.'

'Then can you please tell us where we can find him?'

'I don't know. He didn't say where he was going. Look, is this about Liam? Has he been found?'

'No, he hasn't been found yet,' Anna said. 'But we're hoping he soon will be with your husband's help.'

Ruth's eyes narrowed. 'What's that supposed to mean?'

'We'll explain inside. And you need to know that the officers who are with me are armed and they're going to search your house.'

Anna didn't have a warrant but she pushed that to the back of her mind. She wasn't going to let that stop her; she'd deal with the consequences later. She waited for Ruth to object, but instead the woman appeared to have fallen into a state of shock. Her lips were parted as though she wanted to say something but couldn't get it out.

Anna took her gently by the arm and directed her back into the house and along the hall to the living room. Inside, Anna saw an empty glass on the carpet and a half-empty bottle of vodka on the coffee table.

Ruth stood in the middle of the room, filling the air with her boozy breath. Her eyes stretched wide as she watched the uniforms rush past the living room door into the kitchen and up the stairs.

'We need to make sure that your husband isn't here,' Anna told her.

Ruth suddenly came out of her shock-induced trance. She glanced at Anna and found her voice.

'So what is this about?' she said. 'Why do you want my husband?'

Anna looked at her. She was wearing the same loose-fitting top and trousers she'd had on earlier at the community centre. But it struck the detective that she appeared different and seemed somehow . . . diminished.

Anna had come here not knowing if this woman, Liam's mother, was aware of her husband's involvement in the abductions. But now she believed that she was. It was there in her expression. The guilt. The worry. The fear. The panic.

'We have reason to believe that your husband helped plan the abduction of his own son along with the other children from the Peabody Nursery,' Anna said. 'And it's obvious to me from the look on your face that I'm not telling you anything you don't already know, which makes you as guilty as he is.'

Ruth dragged in a sharp breath and moved her head from side to side.

'You're wrong,' she muttered. 'I didn't . . .'

She was distracted by one of the uniforms entering the room to tell Anna that the house had been searched and Ethan Brady wasn't here.

'So where is he, Ruth?' Anna said. 'And where are the children? You might as well tell us because we now know the identities of all those involved. So even if you receive the ransom money none of you will get to spend any of it.'

Ruth just stood there, motionless, and Anna knew that her mind was working, battling with indecision. She could see that the woman was emotionally distraught and conflicted, and sensed it wouldn't take much to get her to open up.

'You may or may not know that in the last half hour the ransom demand has been increased from six to ten million pounds,' Anna said. 'And the deadline has been brought forward to midnight. If it's not paid or there's a delay in paying it then one of the children will be murdered. Would you really want that on your conscience?'

Ruth started moving her head from side to side again and tears filled her eyes.

The pressure finally got to her and she started to sob, holding her head in her hands and rocking back and forth.

'I only found out last night,' she blurted out through the tears, and it sounded like there was gravel in her throat. 'He told me what he'd done and why he'd done it. And he swore me to secrecy. He said if I went to the police Liam would be harmed so I didn't tell you. I didn't dare. Can you blame me?'

CHAPTER FIFTY-FIVE

Ruth sat on the sofa and gulped down another shot of vodka before she began to offload the burden she'd been carrying.

'All I know is that Liam and the other children are being held at a house in Kent,' she said. 'But I promise you I don't know where it is.'

It wasn't what Anna wanted to hear, but she encouraged Ruth to keep talking in the hope that she would offer up a clue to the location of the house.

'A couple of hours ago a man named Ross Palmer called Ethan on his secret phone, the one he's been using to talk to that Ramsay woman,' Ruth said. 'I grabbed it from him because I thought it was her. But it wasn't. It was Palmer and he said he needed Ethan to do something for him. He warned that Liam would be harmed if Ethan didn't do it.'

'What was it he wanted Ethan to do?'

'He told Ethan he had to pick him up in his car. He said the police were after him and he'd had to leave his own car. So Ethan went out to get him to take him to the house.'

'This secret phone of Ethan's – what's the number?'

'I have no idea, but I do know that his regular phone is switched off. That's why I haven't been able to reach him.'

'Do you know Ross Palmer?'

'No, and I didn't even know he existed until last night.'

Anna took out Palmer's photograph and asked Ruth if she recognised him. She shook her head. Anna got the same response when she showed her the photos of the Knight family.

'I only know that Ethan has got mixed up with a group of people he used to hang around with years ago,' Ruth said. 'It started after that man Palmer was released from prison. He contacted Ethan and asked for money. He said that Ethan owed him so my husband dipped into our savings and gave him several thousand pounds. I knew nothing about it. After that Ethan didn't hear from him for a while, but then a couple of months ago Palmer got back in touch demanding more money because he'd got into trouble again and was on the run from the law.

'This time he really scared Ethan and when Ethan said he couldn't help him he threatened to hurt me and Liam. And that was how it all started: Ethan needed to find a way to raise a large sum of money.'

'Can we backtrack for a moment,' Anna said. 'Why did your husband feel obliged to give Palmer money?'

Ruth sipped at her vodka and pulled a face as she swallowed it.

'Palmer said Ethan owed him for the years he spent in prison. You see, Palmer was jailed for robbing a jewellery store, but he had an accomplice who got away and he never revealed that person's name to the police.'

'And let me guess,' Anna said. 'Your husband was that accomplice.'

Ruth nodded again. 'He told me when I first met him that he'd been involved with a gang on the estate where he lived. He said they sometimes broke the law but I thought it was all minor stuff and he never mentioned robbery. I suppose he was ashamed.'

'But it still doesn't make sense to me,' Anna said. 'Surely Ethan could have raised money some other way to get Ross Palmer off his back. Kidnapping a bunch of children and demanding a whopping six-million-pound ransom is a bit bloody extreme, not to mention dangerous.'

'And that's why this is not just about Ross Palmer,' Ruth said. 'If it was he could have taken out a loan.'

'So what is it about?'

Ruth pinched the bridge of her nose. 'It's about timing as much as anything else, or at least that's how Ethan sees it. The thing is, when Palmer appeared on the scene Ethan was already desperately looking for ways to raise cash. He did ask me about remortgaging the house but I talked him out of it.

'He wanted to take Liam to America and pay for several pioneering treatments for cystic fibrosis. One even claims it can lead to a cure. But they're very expensive and we would have had to move there.

'What I didn't know was that he also wanted to give Sarah Ramsay a pot of money. He knew her business was suffering and she was trying to sell it. He didn't want her to be swamped by money worries when she was pregnant with their baby, let alone once it was born. So he decided to view the situation he was in with Palmer as an opportunity to solve all his problems in one go. That was when he put his mind to it and came up with the plan to kidnap the children.

'He told Palmer about it and Palmer jumped at the idea. He in turn approached those other men who were all keen to make what they considered to be easy money.

'It was Palmer and the others who arranged to rent the house and to steal the minibuses. Ethan provided them with information about the nursery and the children. And he was the one who was going to arrange for the transfer of the ransom money so it wouldn't leave a trail. According to Ethan, Sarah Ramsay knew nothing about it.'

'And am I right in saying that on the day they struck your son wasn't supposed to be there?' Anna said.

'You are. That was why Ethan bought us tickets for the Shrek Adventure. Only I decided to do something else instead.'

She went on to explain how this caused Ethan to panic and he had to arrange for Liam's medication to be sent to the house.

'That was the reason our son did not appear in the video and photograph with the other kids,' she said.

Ruth lost it then and burst into tears, and Anna realised how hard it had been for her to let it all out. But keeping it bottled up had proved too difficult – especially when it was no longer necessary since her husband had already been exposed.

'Are you sure you don't know where in Kent the house is?' Anna asked her.

Ruth fought back the tears and wiped her eyes on the back of her hand.

'I honestly don't,' she said.

'OK then, what's your husband's mobile number?'

Ruth told her and Anna tapped it into her phone and rang it. But the call failed to connect.

'We have to find that house,' Anna said. 'Do you think your husband may have written the address down somewhere?'

Ruth shrugged. 'I don't even know if he was aware of the address. He told me he didn't get involved in renting the place.'

'We'll look around anyway,' Anna said, and stood up.

She started to leave the room in order to instigate a search when Ruth called her back.

'I do know how to find out where Ethan is,' she said. 'I should have thought about it before now but my mind is in such a muddle. About nine months ago there was a spate of vehicle thefts around here. So we had a GPS tracking device fitted to the car. If you check the app on my phone you should be able to pinpoint its exact location.'

CHAPTER FIFTY-SIX

The GPS tracker on Ethan Brady's car was giving out a clear signal. The location of the vehicle appeared on his wife's mobile phone app. It was three miles from the layby in Kent where the minibus had been dumped.

Anna switched from the map to the satellite view and saw that the blue dot was parked right on top of a large secluded house just off the road between Farningham and the village of Shoreham.

'That has to be where they are,' Anna said.

'Then we need to turn up mob-handed,' Walker replied, looking over her shoulder.

Anna nodded. 'But we're going to have to be careful. We've got to assume there are guns in that house as well as children.'

Minutes later they were on their way there, not in the pool car, but as passengers in one of the squad cars.

Ruth remained in the house with two PCs, and before leaving there Anna had told Met control to alert Kent police in Maidstone. It would be up to them to dispatch an armed response unit and coordinate the approach to the house. But Anna made it clear that she didn't want anything to happen until she got there.

It was half eight already and would soon be dark. The police radio airways crackled with constant news of progress from various officers.

Anna took a call from Nash, who told her to keep him updated. He also said he'd ordered a news blackout.

It wasn't long before the property in question was identified and the address known. The house was owned by a couple who now lived abroad and rented it out through an agency as a holiday home.

The agency had been contacted and confirmed that the property was currently occupied by a Mr Frank Knight who had booked it for a period of three weeks. It was a large place with five bedrooms, a conservatory, garden and separate garage. It was also surrounded on three sides by woods which could be clearly seen on the satellite image.

Anna spoke directly to a DCI Bancroft in Maidstone who had been assigned to liaise with her. She told him she thought there would be at least seven people in the house in addition to the nine children. These would be Ross Palmer, Frank Knight, his sons Kevin and Craig and daughter Lucy, plus Kevin's girlfriend and Ethan Brady.

'There could be others,' Anna said. 'I'm pretty sure they don't know that we've sussed out where they are and that we're coming for them. But that doesn't mean they won't be ready for us.'

They agreed to rendezvous in a pub car park on the edge of Shoreham village. From there they would descend on the house while praying that the children were there.

*

DCI Bancroft and two armed response teams were waiting in the pub car park when Anna and Walker arrived. Bancroft was a rakishly handsome man in his forties with dark hair and smoky eyes.

He shook their hands and said, 'We've put things in motion and we're ready to move in on the house right away.'

A large map of the area around the house had been spread out on the bonnet of one of the vehicles.

The officer in charge of leading the assault explained how they would go about it. He said that a small team with binoculars had already taken up position in the woods around the house. They had instructions to watch it but not move in.

'They just reported in to say that there are people in the house,' the officer said. 'It's a two-storey property with entrance points at the front and back. There's a glass conservatory at the rear and they can see a couple of men inside. They've also spotted someone in the kitchen and one small child has been seen looking out of an upstairs window. Plus, there's a minibus parked around the side of the building and three cars are blocking the driveway so vehicles can't enter.'

Anna was impressed and also encouraged. These guys knew what they were doing and she was glad of that because they were about to embark on a mission that had the potential to end in a terrible bloodbath.

The officer said that three separate teams would approach the property from different directions using the woods as cover until they reached the garden and the driveway. Then they would storm the house, hoping that the element of surprise would work in their favour.

Anna, Walker and Bancroft would go in once the property was secure so they were all kitted out in bullet-proof vests.

By the time they were ready to roll, darkness had fallen over the Kent countryside.

CHAPTER FIFTY-SEVEN

Anna had been on numerous armed raids during her time on the force, but none as terrifying as this one. The lives of nine small children were at stake, and as ever, one small error at any point could have the most disastrous consequences.

They followed the convoy of ARVs and marked police cars along the country roads.

As they neared the house the vehicles pulled over to the side and armed officers ran into the woods like Special Forces soldiers.

Fortunately the trees were fairly spread out and the moon was full so Anna, Walker and Bancroft were able to follow them as far as the perimeter of the property.

When Anna saw the back of the house her heart flipped. The conservatory was all lit up and she saw figures moving around inside. But she was too far away to be sure if they were men or women.

Her eyes were moving from window to window when she

heard the crackle of a radio and then a muted voice saying, 'Go, go, go.'

Black-helmeted officers who had been standing to Anna's left rushed out of the woods, vaulted the low perimeter fence and dashed across the lawn carrying their standard issue semi-automatic rifles.

Those people in the conservatory got a nasty shock when two of the windows were smashed in and the door was kicked open.

Anna watched the commotion that ensued with bated breath. She heard a voice yelling repeatedly, 'Get on the floor . . . get on the floor.' And this was followed by more shouting.

Anna walked out of the woods and the others followed. She was just climbing over the fence when two shots rang out and a second later she heard what sounded like a child screaming.

Protocol dictated that they should wait for the 'all clear' signal before entering the house, but it suddenly occurred to Anna that if Chloe was one of the nine children then she would not hold back for any reason. So she decided to ignore protocol and hurried across the lawn to the shattered conservatory.

Inside, armed officers were standing over two figures on the floor with their hands secured behind their backs. She recognised them at once as Kevin and Craig Knight. They were dressed casually in T-shirts and shorts and they were both very much alive.

'We've got a stand-off upstairs, ma'am,' one of the officers said. 'There's a man in the bedroom with the children. He's got a gun and he's demanding that he speaks to the detective in charge.'

The door from the conservatory into the living room was wide open and Anna stepped through it. The living room was filled with more armed officers, and she was in time to see a hysterical Lucy Knight being dragged out through another door. The woman caught sight of Anna before she disappeared and yelled 'Murderers' at the top of her voice.

Anna then saw a body on the floor in the centre of the room. It took her a moment to realise it was Lucy's father Frank. He was lying on his back having been shot in the chest. His shirt was covered in blood and there was a revolver lying on the carpet next to him.

'We had no choice,' one of the officers said. 'He fired the first shot.'

Anna was furious that the situation had escalated so quickly, that they had a death on their hands – and that the man lying on the floor in front of her in a pool of his own blood would now never be tried for Tasha Norris's murder.

She became aware of the sounds from upstairs. Raised voices and children sobbing. Dread balled like a fist inside her and she hurried up there.

There were more officers on the landing and they were gathered either side of a door to one of the bedrooms.

'It seems he's got all nine children in there,' an officer told her as she moved forward. 'He's threatening to shoot them unless we let him talk to you.'

Another officer was standing in the doorway, his rifle aimed into the room.

Without hesitation, Anna stepped up beside him. As the room came into view her breath caught and her heart leapt.

Ross Palmer was standing on the far side of the room behind a king-size bed. Eight distraught children and a red-headed woman in her twenties were sitting on the floor behind him, packed together like sardines in a tin.

Anna would discover later that the woman was Kate McLean, Kevin's girlfriend, and she'd been overseeing the children when the police arrived. She was also the woman who'd been seen on the minibus in Peabody Street.

Palmer was using the ninth child, a small boy in a Superman T-shirt, as a shield. Anna realised at once that it was Liam Brady and he was being made to stand on the bed in front of Palmer, who had one arm wrapped tightly around his tiny body.

In his other hand Palmer held a revolver that was pointed at Liam's head, making it too risky for the officer to take a shot at the man. Liam was looking straight into Anna's eyes, scared into silence by what was happening, his bottom lip visibly trembling as he did his best to hold in his tears and not make a sound.

The room was huge, and there were toys and sweet packets scattered across the floor. A large wall-mounted TV was showing a children's programme, the light, musical soundtrack completely at odds with what was going on in the room.

'I'm Detective Chief Inspector Tate,' Anna said. 'I'm the officer in charge and I understand that you want to speak to me.'

Palmer seemed remarkably calm and Anna wasn't sure if that was a good or bad sign.

'You're the one who came to the flat,' he said.

Anna nodded. 'I am.'

'Well, I've got a question and I'm guessing you're the only one who can answer it for me,' he said, his voice seamless, flat, devoid of any emotion.

343

'I'm happy to answer any question if I can,' she said. 'But you have to let these children go first. You must realise that the game is up, Mr Palmer. And if you hurt any of these kids you'll make it a hundred times worse for yourself.'

He smiled then, and Anna noticed that he had small sharp teeth, just like the man in the video wearing the balaclava.

'I guarantee that if the blood of any child is shed then you'll regret it far more than I will, detective,' he said.

One of the children, a little girl, stood up and started wailing.

'I want to go home,' she sobbed. 'I'm scared and I want my mummy.'

Palmer's smile vanished and he snapped his head towards her.

'Sit the fuck down,' he snarled, and it was so loud and sudden that even Anna flinched.

The little girl, who she now recognised as Grace Tenant, did as she was told but carried on crying.

Palmer tightened his grip on Liam and the poor boy's eyes pleaded with Anna to save him.

'So where were we?' Palmer said. 'Oh, that's right. You were going to answer my question.'

'So what do you want to know?' Anna said.

He licked his lips, swallowed, said, 'I want to know how the fuck you found out about me and the rest of 'em. We were all so careful. Was it Ethan Brady? Did that scumbag tell someone?'

'Where is Ethan?' Anna asked him.

'He's in the basement. The bastard turned chicken and tried to get us to throw in the towel, which was a bit much seeing as it was his idea in the first place.'

'What have you done to him?'

'You'll find out soon enough. But let's get back to my question. Were we grassed up or did we fuck up?'

'It was you who fucked up,' Anna said. 'We found a cigarette butt at the layby where you abandoned the grey minibus. It had your DNA on it, which led us to your parents and, from there, to Lucy Knight. And then you made a second mistake by returning to your flat to pick up your passport and stuff. As you know you dropped your coat with your phone in it. So we discovered from the calls that you'd been in touch with Sarah Ramsay and had visited the nursery, presumably to recce it.

'Sarah then told us that she'd shown Ethan CCTV footage of you posing as Callum Chambers. And yet when we asked him if he recognised you from the photograph he said he didn't. So we knew he was lying.

'And finally you made a third mistake by getting him to pick you up in his car, which has a GPS tracker fitted.'

It took Palmer a few moments to absorb what he'd been told and as he thought about it he shook his head and muttered something under his breath that Anna couldn't make out.

'So now you know,' she said. 'That's why the plot failed and it's why we're here to arrest you.'

Palmer gave a sarcastic laugh. 'I can't believe I was so stupid,' he said. 'My mum always told me I'd regret it if I didn't stop smoking.'

Behind him the children were becoming ever more restless and noisy.

He turned to look at them, but this time, instead of an angry outburst, he said, 'Get them out of here, Kate. No point dragging this out.'

The young woman jumped up and without a word herded the children out of the bedroom between Anna and the armed officer.

Then Palmer said to Anna, 'So you've answered my question, Detective Tate. Now you need to carry out my instruction or else little Liam here will have his head splattered all over the room.'

Liam's eyes were squeezed shut, his shoulders bobbing up and down as he hiccupped through the sobs that were wracking his little body.

'I want you to tell all those trigger-happy coppers to exit the house with the other kids and go into the back garden,' Palmer said. 'Then you're going to walk downstairs with Liam and me. On the table next to the front door you'll find the keys to Craig's car. You'll pick them up and the three of us will go outside and go for a ride with you driving.'

'It's not going to happen,' Anna said.

Palmer lifted his brow. 'If it doesn't then you'll be responsible for this boy's death. And no matter how you try to justify your actions you will know it to be true. And I'm sure you won't want that on your conscience.'

Anna didn't think for a minute that he was bluffing. For a second she pictured Chloe in Liam's place and it made her heart beat that much faster.

'You should know, detective, that I would have been prepared to carry out our threat if the ransom hadn't been paid,' Palmer said. 'So I have no qualms about killing this kid. After all, I've got nothing to lose and this is the only play I've got left because no way am I going back to prison.'

It was a quick and easy decision for Anna to make. She

didn't think for a minute that this man would put the gun down, no matter how long she spent trying to persuade him to. And the more angry and anxious he became, the more risk there was that he'd squeeze the trigger.

So she told the armed officer to back away from the doorway and shouted out an instruction for all those on the landing to retreat downstairs and out of the house and into the back garden. She knew they wouldn't be happy but they would also know that it was the most sensible option in the circumstances.

'Just make sure that they know I'm not stupid,' Palmer called out. 'I'll be twisting and turning all the way out to the car. So if they're crazy enough to take a pot shot there's a good chance they'll hit the boy instead of me.'

A minute later Anna told him the house was clear and he stepped out from behind the bed carrying Liam, who had gone limp in his arms but was still sobbing.

'I'll follow you down,' Palmer said.

Anna walked slowly about five yards ahead of him, her limbs stiff and numb.

She knew that once they stepped outside the marksmen would have him in their sights through their night-vision technology, but she felt confident they wouldn't fire unless they had a clear shot.

She also knew that if they managed to reach the car and drive away from the house the team would follow. Palmer would also know that but he'd be thinking that he'd at least have a chance to get away.

The keys to Craig Knight's car were on the table next to the front door. Anna picked them up and walked outside. Palmer followed.

There were no shooters in sight but Anna knew they were there, watching and waiting with their fingers poised on the triggers.

Palmer lifted Liam high so the boy's face was against his own and moved across the driveway, twisting constantly from side to side to make it impossible for the shooters to risk firing.

Anna got to the car and turned to face him.

'Leave the boy here,' she said. 'I'll be your hostage and I promise to get you as far away as possible.'

Palmer started to reply, but suddenly Liam let out a loud scream and tried to shake himself free. In doing so he thrust his head back into Palmer's face. It caught Palmer by surprise and clearly hurt him from the sound he made.

And as Liam continued to struggle the back of his head struck Palmer's face again, and this time the man lost his balance and fell backwards onto the ground.

What followed took place in the blink of an eye.

Liam managed to break free of Palmer's loosened grip and stay on his feet long enough to run towards Anna.

She scooped him up in her arms.

At the same time Palmer pushed himself up to a sitting position and yelled for Anna not to move.

'If you do I'll . . .'

He didn't get to finish the sentence thanks to a bullet that tore into him from somewhere out in the darkness. The trouble was it struck his left shoulder and Anna saw that the gun was still firmly gripped in his right hand.

She also saw him smile crookedly as he took aim at Liam.

Anna spun around instinctively to shield the boy. The gun exploded behind her and smashed into the middle of her back. The pain was excruciating, and the impact drove her forward into the side of Craig's car where she clung on desperately to Liam fearing that Palmer would fire again.

But he never got the chance because bullets came out of nowhere and two of them hit him: one in the head and one in the chest.

Only then did Anna allow herself to slide to the ground with Liam still in her arms.

CHAPTER FIFTY-EIGHT

Anna survived for two reasons: the low-calibre bullet had failed to penetrate the protective vest she was wearing, and Ross Palmer had shot her in the back instead of the head.

It still hurt like hell but she didn't lose consciousness and after a couple of dizzy minutes she was back on her feet. By then Liam had been taken from her. He was distressed but thankfully unhurt.

A paramedic appeared and eased off the bullet-proof vest in order to examine her back.

'You've got a bad bruise but you are one lucky lady,' he said.

He gave her an injection for the pain and she declined to go and sit in one of the ambulances.

'I've got more work to do,' she said.

Minutes later they found Ethan Brady in the basement. He was tied to a chair and covered in blood, having been beaten about the face.

But he was awake and able to ask Anna if his son was all right.

'He seems to be,' Anna said. 'But that's no thanks to you. And for your information Ross Palmer and Frank Knight are dead. So you could say they've escaped justice. But you won't be so lucky, Mr Brady. I expect that by the time you see freedom again that boy of yours will be an old man.'

She told the uniforms to untie him and asked Walker to go with him to the hospital so his wounds could be treated before he was formally charged.

But he didn't look seriously hurt and it would turn out that the hiding he'd taken had resulted in a broken nose, cut lip and cracked rib.

Anna was far more concerned about the children. Back upstairs she found they'd been gathered in the back garden and were being well looked after by uniforms and paramedics who had arrived on the scene in rapid response ambulances.

The kids were all upset, of course, but it appeared that none had been physically harmed in any way.

Anna insisted on speaking to the four who'd been arrested before they were driven away. But Lucy and her brothers refused to answer her questions. However, Kevin Knight's girlfriend, Kate, was keen to point out that she had been the one charged with keeping the kids occupied during their stay in the house.

'Nobody touched them,' she said. 'Honestly, they were well looked after.'

She went on to shed some light on what had happened inside the house. The children had apparently been given regular doses of a mild sedative to keep them docile and she personally had made sure that Liam was given his medication.

Anna asked her why Ethan had been beaten and she replied, 'When he brought Ross back here this afternoon the pair got into a big argument because Ethan wanted us to call a halt to what we were doing. He said everything had changed because you knew who we were. But Ross and Kevin's dad were having none of it. They said it was more important than ever that we got the ransom money because we couldn't go home. So when Ethan threatened to phone the police Ross laid into him and then they locked him in the basement.'

Anna doubted that Ethan's last-minute change of heart would be viewed sympathetically when he eventually came before a jury. As the main architect of the kidnap plan he was looking at a long, long stretch.

It was decided that the children did not need to go to hospital. The sooner they were reunited with their parents, the better.

But they were briefly examined by the paramedics at the scene, and while this was being done the parents were contacted and given the good news.

More squad cars were summoned to take the children home, and Anna decided to go with Liam so that she could tell his mother what had happened.

She left DCI Bancroft and his team in charge and on the way back to South London she sat in the back of the squad car with Liam. She felt tears burn her eyes when he snuggled up to her and held her hand.

'I'm taking you back to see your mummy,' she told him.

'I missed her,' he said. 'And daddy.'

'I know you did, Liam. How do you feel?'

'I'm hungry. I didn't like what they gave me for dinner so I didn't eat it. I wanted ice cream instead.'

'Was it horrible in that house?'

He shook his head. 'Not all the time. They had some nice toys. But the men were mean sometimes and shouted at us. And the girls moaned a lot.'

She phoned Nash, partly to stop herself crying. She had already filled him in on events in the house and now she wanted to talk about Ruth Brady.

'You're aware that she's known since last night what was going on,' she said. 'But I really don't think she deserves to be charged with anything because she was warned that her son would be harmed if she talked.'

Nash agreed with her and said he would talk to the CPS.

'Meanwhile, let her have her son back and make sure she gets all the support she needs,' he said.

Ruth broke down when she saw her son and it started Liam crying again. She swept him up in her arms and squeezed him so tight Anna thought he might break.

It was an emotional reunion, and the joy and relief on the mother's face was a sight to behold.

Ruth stopped smiling only when Anna told her what had happened to Ethan.

'He'll be charged with conspiracy to kidnap,' Anna said. 'And I've warned him to prepare himself for a long stay in prison.'

Anna remained with her for almost an hour because she sensed that Ruth wanted her to. By then a family liaison officer had arrived and the two uniforms who had been with her in the house departed.

'We'll need to talk again,' Anna said before leaving. 'And can I suggest that you don't speak to the media. We can handle that on your behalf. And avoid the other parents because they'll be gunning for you.'

'I can't really blame them,' Ruth said, and Anna wondered if she knew quite how tough her life was going to be in the weeks and months ahead.

CHAPTER FIFTY-NINE

Day four

Anna didn't get to go home that night. After leaving Ruth Brady's house she went to MIT headquarters to start processing the mountain of paperwork the case had thrown up.

Plus, there were interviews to be conducted with Ethan Brady, Lucy Knight and her brothers, and Kate McLean. And Nash was insisting that she take part in a press conference at which they could tell the world that the children had been rescued safely without the ransom having been paid.

She took time out to phone Tom, who was delighted with the news, but she didn't tell him how close she'd come to being shot dead. He said he would come to the house later and bring a bottle of champagne to celebrate. Although that was the last thing that Anna wanted right now, she was looking forward to just getting home and seeing him.

And so the new day dawned, and even though she hadn't slept and was suffering back pain, Anna managed to see it through to the end – the formal interviews, the briefings, the paperwork, the press conference. What kept her spirits up throughout was seeing some of the parents on the news bulletins with their children.

The feedback from the family liaison officers was that most of the kids were largely unaffected by the experience. They'd slept through much of it and had spent most of their waking hours watching the television and playing with their friends. There was apparently no evidence that they had been physically punished or abused in any way.

During the interviews the Knight brothers claimed that their dead father had pressured them into taking part, which Anna found hard to believe. It was revealed that the entire family had racked up substantial debts, partly because the café in Clapham was no longer making money, but mainly because they spent more than they could afford on drink, drugs and gambling.

The brothers cleared up one loose end by confirming that Jonas Platt had not been involved in the kidnappings. They said they hadn't heard of him until his name cropped up in one of the news reports they saw.

As for Ethan Brady, he confirmed everything his wife had said about what had motivated him to embark on such a despicable venture. He also said that he was the one who'd suggested having the ransom paid using a virtual currency.

'It's become the tried and tested method among kidnappers,' he said. 'So long as the right security software is utilised it's relatively easy to ensure that the transfer is seamless and untraceable.'

When Anna asked him if he felt guilty for putting the other parents through such torment his answer was, 'Those smug bastards with their healthy kids and cash in the bank deserved it after the hard time they gave us over Ethan's condition.'

He was unrepentant about what he'd done, but he cried when told that his wife was refusing to see him.

Anna finally left for home at seven that evening after being on the job for a straight thirty-six hours. She was looking forward to her bed and a good night's sleep.

Just as she walked through the front door, throwing her keys onto the sideboard and shouting hello to Tom, her phone rang.

Jack Keen's name flashed up on the screen and she held her breath for a moment, wishing for good news when she answered. But after congratulating her on the successful resolution to the case, he ensured that sleep would be the furthest thing from her mind.

'I finally traced your ex-husband, Anna,' he said. 'But you need to brace yourself because it's not good news, I'm afraid.'

'Just tell me, Jack.'

'Well Matthew, or James as he then called himself, died just under three years ago, only weeks after returning to the UK from abroad and setting up home in Southampton. I found out by checking the Register Office. There's a death certificate in the name James Miller.'

'Are you sure it's him?'

'Positive, and I'll tell you why in a moment. But first you need to know that he didn't die of natural causes, Anna. Matthew was murdered.'

EPILOGUE

It had been two days since Jack Keen had told Anna that her ex-husband had been murdered. Anna was still reeling from the shock of it as she sat in the cramped office of the detective who had been in charge of the investigation.

His name was Frank Hunter and he was in his fifties, with a square jaw and even features. He was sitting facing her across his desk. She had come to see him because she had to be sure that there was no mistake – and because there were questions she needed to ask him.

After a brief introduction he took three photographs from a large brown envelope. The first photo he showed her was of a man with no hair lying face down on grass. He was wearing a pale blue shirt and black trousers, and the shirt had a large round bloodstain on it.

For the second photo the man had been turned onto his back and his face was visible. While there was a striking resemblance, Anna held onto a small bit of doubt, a small bit of *hope* that perhaps it wasn't Matthew, after all. The photo had been taken almost three years ago, seven years after he had disappeared with Chloe. This man's face was thinner, and the nose seemed different somehow, as though it had been damaged at some point and not repaired properly.

But then she was handed the third photo of a man lying on his back on a mortuary slab and her heart turned cold when she saw the familiar tattoo on his chest.

'That's him,' she said. She pushed the photograph back towards the detective, her hand trembling as she did so. 'That's Matthew. So now you need to tell me what's happened to my baby. Where is Chloe?'

ACKNOWLEDGEMENTS

I'd like to say a special thank you to my editor Katie Loughnane. It's been an absolute pleasure to work with her on this book and her input has been invaluable. I'd also like to express my appreciation for the early involvement of Victoria Oundjian who encouraged me to develop the story from the initial idea. My thanks also go to the rest of the team at Avon/Harper Collins who, as well as being true professionals, know how to throw a great party.

AT YOUR DOOR

There's a killer on the loose . . .

DCI Anna Tate is back – and
there's danger ahead . . .

Coming August 2019

Pre-order your copy now